SOMEWHERE WARM — NO PLACE SAFE

David Kellough

ISBN: 1514307685
ISBN 13: 9781514307687
Library of Congress Control Number: 2015912498
CreateSpace Independent Publishing Platform
North Charleston, South Carolina

*Ye shall know the truth
And the truth shall make you free.*
                    —John 8:32

CHAPTER ONE

It had been bone-chilling cold all morning. Gray Chicago skies. No wind. In this quiet suburb south of the city, three inches of fresh snow blanketed the ground and lay softly on lawns and park benches—and on top of the gravestones in Oakwood Cemetery, where a funeral procession of more than twenty dark cars arrived and slowly ground to an uneasy stop. Drug Enforcement Administration special agent Tom Morgan, thirty-five years old and just under six feet tall, stepped out of the limousine that had brought him to this miserable place, and, accompanied by his uncle Jim, aunt Joan, and cousins Matt and Mark and their wives, he walked to the hearse immediately ahead. Their frosty breath filled the air.

Morgan had lifted weights routinely since he was fourteen. He had played football throughout high school, and as a marine who had survived two tours in Iraq following graduation from Purdue—making captain before he was twenty-seven—he was 195 pounds of rock-hard muscle, as fit as any man alive. During all those years, he had met many challenges. But this was one for which he had not been prepared, and his well-muscled body, barely camouflaged beneath his overcoat, slumped as he trudged forward. Now, he and his uncle and cousins would be the first of the eight pallbearers who would carry the mortal remains of his sister, Elaine, to her final resting place, where she would lie for eternity beside their mother and father.

When one of the attendants from the funeral home opened the rear door of the hearse, Morgan's knees nearly gave way beneath him, and tears again filled his eyes. He gritted his teeth. With his left hand, he grasped a front handle of his sister's casket, and with his right he pushed a mass of brown hair off his forehead and then wiped away his tears. God damn it, he thought. God *damn* it! Will this never end?

Morgan had already seen more than his share of death, beginning with two of his closest friends in high school, who died from drug overdoses. It was those incidents, which for years had haunted him, that eventually propelled him to join the Agency. He'd also lost both of his parents, more than one friend in Iraq—including his all-time best friend, Adam Wells, who had served alongside him—and now it was his only sister. He'd seen her alive for the last time just four days earlier, and her death was yet another bitter, bitter pill. He had gone over the details repeatedly, and despite all the arguments he might have made to the contrary, he could not escape feeling that her death was, in the final analysis, his fault. He had chosen this damned profession with the DEA. He had allowed her to be seen with him in broad daylight, on a downtown city street, and this was the result. Now, his uncle, cousins Matt and Mark, and four of Elaine's closest friends joined him, to carry her body the awful distance to the gravesite Morgan knew all too well.

The Chicago Regional Office of the DEA was downtown, not far from where he and Elaine had eaten lunch those few days earlier. She had been home for Christmas vacation from grad school at Purdue, staying with him in his condo, as she always did when she was on break. She'd been planning a New Year's Eve party. She was going shopping and had called, wanting to meet for lunch. And, she'd made it clear. She didn't want any excuses. It was the holidays. He could certainly take off for an hour or so to meet with her, his "favorite sister," as she always called herself.

Of course he wanted to meet with her. After all, it was the holidays, as she'd said. And, since she was his "favorite sister", he was always inclined to bend to her wishes. He wanted her to be happy. So he had given in. He had suggested they meet at O'Mally's, a little more than a block from his office. They'd each had some Irish stew, to fight off the winter cold, and a beer. It was going to be another few days before she had to return to school, and then, in just another few months, she would be graduating and getting her doctorate. He'd offered a toast to the holidays and to her forthcoming degree, and she had insisted that he swear, as her only brother, he would be there to watch her walk.

Of course he would be there. "Absolutely!" he had said. After all, he had attended her other graduation ceremonies, hadn't he? They lifted their glasses and clinked them together in another toast. He would be there—for certain. Meantime, the New Year's Eve party would be fun. The New Year was going to bring great things. She was "finally, *finally*," she had said, "going to get out into the real world."

What a horrible irony, Morgan thought afterward. As they left O'Mally's and waited at the intersection to cross Michigan Avenue, a quick burst of five, six, seven shots—maybe more, Morgan wasn't sure—rang out from a black sedan that raced past them, amid blaring horns from other cars and screams and shouts from nearby pedestrians. Then, in scarcely more than a second, it was over. Elaine lay beside him on the concrete, her chest and abdomen ripped apart by the bullets he knew had been meant for him. Her wonderful, warm smile that he had viewed only moments earlier had been blasted into cold, pale oblivion, and she lay ashen in a pool of blood. There had been no time for him to respond. No time to pull his .45. No time to get the license number of the sedan as it disappeared beyond on-coming traffic. On his knees, he lifted her head and shoulders into his arms and pulled her to his chest. God damn it! a voice deep within him cried out as his face contorted uncontrollably and tears fell down his cheeks. He pushed her dark hair back from the blank stare of her face, her mouth open as if to cry out as well, but there were no words. No sound at all. Only silence and the pounding, pounding, pounding of his heart, which ached like a knotted rope pulled hard and tight in his chest. She had always been so dedicated to doing the right things—to working hard, to always, *always* making near-perfect grades. She was absolutely driven to be the best she could possibly be. She had wanted to make a difference in the world, and now she was gone even before she had a chance to begin.

As he and the other pallbearers lumbered forward with the weight of her casket—the soles of their shoes crunching and creaking in the fresh snow—they approached the tan-colored burial tent, intended to provide at least some protection from the morning freeze. And as they entered and placed her casket over top of the open grave, feelings of disgust swept over him. She had given so much, and her life had been taken by some unknown sons-of-bitches who couldn't have cared less. He slowly stepped back, and as he and the other pall-bearers joined his aunt Joan and the wives of Matt and Mark to form the front line of mourners, others gathered behind them.

Nearly everyone wept. Tears and coughs and anguished sighs came not only from those in the front row but from those behind as well. Morgan's best friends from the Agency, Dan Weber and Scott Sullivan, moved in close and—first one and then the other—reached out and placed a hand on his shoulder, which made more tears well up in his eyes, and he bowed his head. This time, with nearly-numb fingers, he reached into a side pocket of his topcoat for the handkerchief he had placed there hours earlier and wiped at his tears, which, before he could get to them, felt like ice on his cheeks.

Some of Elaine's girlfriends wept audibly behind him, as did his aunt Joan beside him. She placed a gloved hand into the crook of his right arm, sobbed, and leaned against him. He would have tried to comfort her and the other women too, if he could have. But he could not comfort himself.

Father Reilly, who had conducted the funeral mass at St. Gregory's, stepped forward, Bible in hand. He turned to face Morgan and the others, then blessed the gravesite. Morgan couldn't imagine what more the man might say in an effort to bring solace to any of them.

"We don't know why God didn't prevent Elaine's death and allow her more time with us here on Earth," he began. "But let me assure you, He has a purpose and a plan for each of us. And His plans are not subject to accidents, to circumstances, to illness—or to the actions of evil-doers."

Morgan listened. God has a plan? What sort of plan could possibly include the death of someone like Elaine? If He had a plan, why didn't He simply do away with the evil-doers? Or why even permit them to exist in the first place? Morgan didn't believe any of it. In fact, even with his Catholic upbringing, he wasn't sure he believed in much of anything anymore. All he knew for certain was that he hated his life, his job, and everything that had brought him—and Elaine—to this. Even more, however, he hated the no-good sons-of-bitches who had killed her. And somehow he had to find a way to get them.

Yet even if he could string them up by their thumbs, castrate them, and strip off their skin before blowing their brains out, he knew it wouldn't provide sufficient vengeance for them taking her life. And in the penetrating chill of this tent in Oakwood Cemetery, he was left with nothing but his sorrow, his disgust, his hatred, and that awful, gut-wrenching despair that continued to cry out, Why? Why her? Why her and not me? But there was no answer. No answer from God. No answer from heaven. No answer from anywhere.

Finally, Father Reilly completed his message, led the assemblage in the Lord's Prayer, and then raised a crucifix and gave the final benediction. Afterward, very gradually, friends and family members said their last tearful good-byes. But in the end, Morgan could not say good-bye. In fact, he would not. This was not over. He would not rest until every last one of the sons-of-bitches responsible for her death was brought to justice, or shot. And maybe he'd be the one to pull the trigger.

CHAPTER TWO

After the graveside service, Morgan returned to the funeral home with his aunt and uncle, and then rode with them to his condo near downtown, followed closely by cousins Matt and Mark and their wives, a number of Elaine's friends, and a few of his as well, including Dan and Scott from the Agency. In a modern, twenty-story building with guards and buzzers, the condo was, apart from his office, the one place in which he—and Elaine too, when she was with him—typically felt reasonably safe.

Morgan had purchased it seven years earlier, not long after he had left the corps and joined the DEA. He had used his half of the million dollars in insurance money left to them by their father to pay for it. The money had also permitted him to furnish it, at least somewhat handsomely, and since it was relatively spacious, especially for a place near downtown, it would adequately accommodate those coming from the cemetery. Also, while food for the afternoon was limited to the pizza, chips, veggies, and dips he had purchased the evening before at a nearby grocery, there was plenty of beer and wine in the refrigerator and liquor in the cabinet. He put the bottles of bourbon, vodka, scotch, and rum out on the kitchen counter, along with some mixers and ice, and invited everyone to help themselves. And although he didn't often have more than two or three drinks on any one occasion, he knew today would definitely be different.

He poured his first and second drinks from the bottle of Dewar's on the counter, each time adding some ice and soda; and, as the afternoon wore on, he poured a third, a fourth, and even a fifth drink, until he very nearly staggered. He hadn't thought ahead or planned how many drinks he might have; but the truth was, he didn't give a damn if he got drunk, or if anyone noticed. Elaine had lost her life because of his fucking job, and it had made a mess of his life as well.

Among other things, his love life had certainly suffered. In his years with the Agency, he'd not found it possible to have even one lasting relationship. While there'd been a woman here and there, for a few weeks or a few months at a time, invariably the job brought every relationship to an end. As a special agent, he was sometimes assigned to work undercover; and if a woman could not know where he was or what he was doing for long or strange hours, that invariably took its toll. And if he revealed what his job was and what he was doing, ultimately none of them could take the days and nights of waiting, not knowing what might have happened to him—if he had been shot, or worse.

So, sooner or later, each relationship failed. Each time, his work and sacrifice resulted only in heartache, and now he was more alone than ever. Not only did he not have a woman in his life, he didn't have Elaine either. And the money left to them by their parents—once a form of at least some comfort to him—now meant nothing. It couldn't bring Elaine back, and it couldn't bring relief from his pain. The emptiness made him feel sick, and angry.

As everyone talked with him and reminisced, it was clear they were trying to recall good and fond memories of him with Elaine. Dan and Scott reminded him of the really raucous party they'd had on his thirtieth birthday. Elaine had been present, and it had taken them the remainder of that weekend to clean up his condo and heal from all the revelry. Another story, told by his aunt Joan, made him remember a special time when he was thirteen and Elaine was six, and their families had traveled to Orlando and Disney World. He and Matt and Mark were going to ride Space Mountain, and Elaine had fought and kicked and screamed, wanting to ride it with them. Eventually their parents had relented and permitted her to ride in the car with Morgan. However, once inside, where there was so little light, the loops and jerks and turns of their car had really scared her, and she'd screamed even more than before. But Morgan had held her close and comforted her, and when they exited the ride, she told everyone what he had done and called him her hero. Morgan knew Joan had told the story in order to recall a pleasant memory, but it had all happened more than two decades earlier. They weren't thirteen and six anymore, and now he couldn't feel himself any kind of hero at all.

He did appreciate these and other efforts to recall happier times, and he likewise appreciated the words of encouragement offered by some for the future. Gradually, though, the stories and reminisces and kind words drew to a close, and one by one guests and friends departed. At length, even his uncle Jim, aunt Joan, and Matt and Mark and their wives prepared to leave as well. As they did, his uncle—a stout man almost Morgan's height—grasped him by his upper arms and looked into his eyes.

"Thomas," he said, "you've been through a hell of a lot, losing your schoolmates, your mom and dad, your friends in the marines, and now Elaine—which affects us all. But you're a strong man, Thomas, and Joan and I and Matt and Mark have every confidence in you. Somehow, we know, you'll get the bastards who've done this terrible thing and see that they're brought to justice. With God's help, we know you won't fail."

Morgan nodded his head affirmatively, although at this moment he hadn't any idea how he might get anybody, even with God's help—again, if there was a God. Finally, with hugs and kisses and a few more tears, even they said their good-byes, and after they departed Morgan was, like all the days before, once again alone.

With the door closed, he returned to the kitchen, poured another drink, and carried it along with the now nearly-empty bottle of Dewar's into the living room. There, amid the quiet, he slumped onto the couch and sat motionless except for his breathing. He had hours earlier removed his jacket and loosened his tie. Now he took the thin, black silk garment from around his neck, leaving the knot still in it, and tossed it onto one of the overstuffed chairs beside the couch. He breathed deeply, and then drank even deeper from the scotch in his glass. There was just no reason why this should have happened to Elaine and not him. No reason at all. He poured the last few ounces of Dewar's into his glass, and as he sipped his way toward the bottom he ran the events of that fateful day with his sister over and over in his mind. Why would God—if in fact there was such a being somewhere in the universe—allow something like this happen to someone like Elaine? There was just no understanding it. No understanding it at all. And though he continued in his efforts at conscious thought, gradually his thinking slowed. Leaning back on the couch, he turned his head slightly to one side and allowed his eyes to close. He felt his now-empty glass slip from his hand and heard it land on the carpet. But he didn't care. He didn't move. He only wanted sleep and the peace he hoped it might bring.

CHAPTER THREE

The following morning Morgan awoke still on the couch, his head pounding as if a sledgehammer were beating a huge, tin drum inside his brain. With his eyes still closed, he smoothed his right hand over his forehead, using his thumb and fingers to massage his aching temples and swollen eyelids. Then he slowly sat upright and looked around. He saw the glass he had dropped the previous evening, still on the carpet between the couch and coffee table. However, he had absolutely no intention of trying to pick it up, since he knew if he leaned forward, his head would surely explode.

With some effort he stood and walked into the bathroom, turned on the faucet, and applied hands full of cold water to his aching face and head. Then he looked in the mirror, seeing a somewhat abused replica of himself. He checked his watch, wondering what he would do—what he *could* do—now. But as it was not yet noon on Saturday, the answer was not much—at least not today. He returned to the living room and the kitchen, poured himself a Coke from the fridge, and popped two of the remaining pieces of cold pizza into the microwave. In thirty seconds they were ready. He sat on one of the stools at the counter, ate the pizza, and then poured the remainder of the Coke into his glass, this time adding some rum. He liked the taste of it. The rum and Coke went well together, and he hoped the drink and the pizza might quiet the still-constant pounding in his head.

When he finished the pizza, he returned to the living room, found his cell phone in the pocket of his suit coat, and plugged the phone into its charger cord. He turned on the television. DEA rules concerning bereavement provided two weeks off in the event of the death of a member of the immediate family. Problem was, he couldn't imagine what he might do with himself for another entire week. He thought of calling his boss, George Blackburn, but even if he reached him on his cell, George would almost certainly be unable to tell him anything more than they already knew—which was almost nothing. He flipped through the channels on the TV, from news to paid programming to movies to sports. He thought he might watch a few movies, or perhaps a Bears game, during the remainder of the weekend—although he had no real interest in doing either. The truth was, he could do little more than think of Elaine and the pain he felt from her loss. He poured another glass of rum and Coke and decided that, as soon as the weekend was over, he would definitely return to work and start trying to find the sons-of-bitches who had killed her. Whoever the hell they were, they would pay. By God, they *would* pay!

CHAPTER FOUR

Arriving at the DEA office building on Monday morning, Morgan walked across the polished marble floor of the lobby, checked in with the guards, and, after inserting his plastic admittance card in the slot near the elevator, he stepped aboard for his usual ride to the third floor. There he said a brief hello to the receptionist and then walked along a broad, open walkway between the windowed, perimeter offices to his left and multiple cubicles on his right. When he reached his own cubicle, he sat at his desk and for a moment scanned the few framed photos sitting there—the first with him and some fellow agents, including Dan and Scott, out drinking and celebrating after a successful bust, and another with them on a boat, fishing on Lake Michigan. And, of course, there were his two favorite pictures of himself with Elaine—the first with him beside her in her cap and gown, when he'd gone back to Purdue to see her receive her undergraduate degree, and the second, two years later, when he'd returned again to see her receive her master's. He picked up the second photo and slowly smoothed his fingers over the glass. He had been so proud of her and so pleased to be there to take part in her life.

Suddenly, his boss appeared at the entrance of his cubicle and walked in. Blackburn was a big, bear of a man in his mid-fifties, with graying hair at his temples and meaty, paw-like hands. He was often gruff with others—or, at a minimum, perfunctory. At the same time, he invariably showed considerable respect for Morgan. He had attended Elaine's funeral service at St. Gregory's, and there he spoke especially thoughtfully—not only to Morgan but to his relatives as well—when he expressed his condolences. This morning he also seemed particularly thoughtful in the words he chose.

"Morning, Tom," he said as he sat down on the chair beside Morgan's desk. "What are you doing back here already? You know you've still got another week off."

Morgan replied that he knew, but he couldn't stay home and just sit around his condo. He had to get back to work—or go crazy. And anyway, he wanted to know if they had found out anything yet that might lead to Elaine's killers.

"No, nothing yet," Blackburn said. "But the police are working on it of course, and we're helping any way we can."

"Yeah, I know, George. I do. But you know how many killings there are in this city every month. The cops have got their hands full, and I want to be here to help."

"Well, I understand," Blackburn said as he stood and shook Morgan's hand. "Good to have you back." He paused. "But if you change your mind, remember you've still got the time coming—just like all the vacation time you never seem to take."

After Blackburn departed, others began gathering in and around Morgan's cubicle. First to arrive—from their own cubicles nearby—were closest friends Weber and Sullivan. Weber's black hair was neatly parted and combed like always, as if he had some special oil or tonic on it, and it shone under the fluorescent lights. He was two or three inches shorter than Sullivan and Morgan and had a wiry build. But he was well-muscled, and, though he typically wore black-framed glasses for paperwork in the office, he was absolutely a dead-on, expert marksman—better than anyone in the department, even Morgan. Sullivan was, by contrast, just under six-feet tall, like Morgan, and hand-some. His sandy hair, his medium-blue eyes, and even his Irish surname all testified to his Gaelic heritage. Morgan was happy to see them both, and he stood and hugged them when they walked in.

Gradually, others from throughout the department filtered in as well. Virtually every one of them had at-tended Elaine's funeral, and a few, like Weber and

Sullivan, had been present for her graveside service. They all wanted to express their condolences again. Unfortunately, no one had heard anything—from the police or otherwise—about who might have been responsible for her murder. When Morgan asked, the answer from each of them was the same.

"No. Sorry. Nothing so far."

In fact, they indicated they thought Morgan himself would likely be the best source of information, since this was clearly an attempt on his life—no doubt carried out by members of one of the gangs he had infiltrated when working undercover. But, out of respect, they had wanted to give him some time before discussing the subject with him.

Whether or not agents worked undercover, it was typically not that difficult to locate, arrest, and convict the occasional street-peddler for selling marijuana, coke, heroin or some other narcotic or controlled substance. The problem was, it was often virtually impossible to get any of the street-peddlers to identify their suppliers— either the middlemen who provided drugs to them or their bosses on up the line, who the peddlers might not even know. And if they did know them, the code of conduct observed on the street dictated that nobody ratted on anybody, even with the promise of shorter jail time. Prison was never a particularly safe place, and it was especially not safe for anyone who was known to have ratted-out a higher-up.

As a result, when Morgan was assigned to work along with other agents in an undercover operation, he and the others would first get to know some of the street-peddlers in their respective parts of town. Then they would try to get introduced to some of their suppliers or middlemen, and perhaps eventually even meet their bosses. With that kind of information, the Agency always hoped to disrupt the local market—or at least a significant portion of it.

In preparation for those assignments, Morgan would typically let his hair grow and perhaps wear it in some unusual way. He'd also grow a moustache or a goatee or beard. In his most recent assignment, he had let his hair grow quite long—down to his shoulders in fact—and he had grown a full beard, which he trimmed only moderately. With those changes in his appearance, some fake IDs, and a little running-around money provided by the Agency, he had also rented a dump of an apartment in a not-so-nice part of town, using the name Tommy Morro. He also used that name to get another cell phone, in which he recorded the names and numbers of those he'd met in and around the drug trade. He received calls from drug contacts on that phone, and he kept his old phone plugged in and charged back in his cubicle. If Elaine or anyone from the office needed to get in touch with him, they called that phone, which he too called several times each day to retrieve any messages. But he was careful to always, *always* remove from this new phone's call list every call made to his regular cell—or anybody else outside his circle of drug contacts. If anybody ever got hold of his new phone, there would be no way to tie him back to the Agency, Elaine, or anybody else he knew personally.

Every phase of these operations was always carefully planned, and each was considered by everyone in the Agency to be an extremely important effort. At the same time, it was always an unnerving goddamned job—even for an ex-marine. Day to day, Morgan was, like the other special agents, entirely on his own, and one mistake or indication that he might be connected to the DEA or some other area of law enforcement and he could wind up very dead, very fast.

For a time, his last assignment had gone exactly as planned. He started by hanging out on the street and in some seedy bars in the part of town assigned to him, and gradually he began meeting and getting to know a few of the peddlers in the area. Of course he didn't really get to know them. They typically used only first names or some creative handle like "Double Dose" or "Bonito" or "Freddie the Line." But he did get those names and others. And sometimes he got their cell numbers too. Over time he managed to befriend some of them, especially Freddie the Line, a scrawny, haggard-looking little weasel of a black man who always seemed a bit jumpy. Freddie was a chain smoker, and he blew a fair amount of coke as well. Morgan had often scored a line or two from him, and after several such purchases, as they sat together one evening in a neighborhood bar called The Inferno, Morgan thought he might persuade Freddie to introduce him to a supplier.

"Hey, Freddie," he said quietly as he leaned closer to him, "I been meanin' to ask you about you hookin' me up, so I can start sellin' some stuff, like you."

Freddie looked at him as if he had invaded some sacred territory. "You crazy, man? I'm doin' my own thing here. I don't need no competition." He puffed on his cigarette.

"No, it's not like that," Morgan said. "I'd find my own area. You know. Someplace away from here, where you don't work."

"I don't know, man. I work different places."

"Well, think about it, will ya? I mean, I'd like to get back into business."

"What you mean, *back* into business?" he said.

"Well, I was dealin' in Colorado—in Denver. But things got a little bad for me there. That's why I came over here."

Freddie didn't respond either way. And Morgan didn't want to press him on the issue, at least not for the time being. But a week or so later, he brought the subject up again, while the two of them were playing pool in another bar called the Big Break.

"You know that thing I was askin' you about?" Morgan said. "You know, about you maybe hookin' me up to somebody? Well, I was wonderin' if you'd thought about it."

"I don't know, man," Freddie said, continuing to sound reluctant. "I'll have to talk to my man and see what he says."

Eventually, after another conversation or two, Freddie finally relented and introduced Morgan to his supplier, Carlos Monterra—a middleman who, in the few times Morgan met with him, never smiled. He usually had several people around him, and he was one serious son-of-a-bitch. As it turned out, he also proved to be a genuine badass.

Morgan had made good progress. He had been seen routinely around his neighborhood. He'd gotten to know more and more people in the trade in his area, and he had been accepted into the circle of buyers and sellers. But one night, while sitting at the bar in one of his hangouts, he recognized a peddler he had known years earlier by the name of Jimmy O. Morgan had arrested Jimmy in a bust, and as soon as he saw him, he looked away.

However, despite the elapsed time and Morgan's now long hair and beard, he would later discover that Jimmy had apparently recognized him as well—*and* Jimmy knew Freddie the Line. Morgan hadn't known that either of them was in the bar. It was crowded and full of smoke and conversation. But he would learn only a short time later that they had been—and that Jimmy had told

Freddie, and Freddie had wasted no time in informing Monterra. Later that same night, before Morgan left the bar, some of Monterra's men grabbed him, dragged him into the alley out back, took him to a crack house somewhere off a street he did not know, and tied him to a chair in the basement. Morgan would later recount that the experience of that night and the next day was a nightmare—only a living, breathing nightmare! It was like being thrown by an earthquake into a dark chasm from which there was no escape, and he had thought he would almost certainly meet his end in that basement—especially when Jimmy O repeated his accusation directly to Monterra, who stood by as stone-faced as ever.

"Yeah, it's him all right," Jimmy said nervously. "He's the same son-of-a-bitch who busted me a few years back."

Morgan thought they would kill him for sure, but instead, after rifling through his wallet and cell phone and finding nothing of consequence, Monterra had his men beat him with rubber hoses filled with sand.

"Where the hell you come from, man?" one of Monterra's men yelled at him, and Morgan began repeating the same lies he had told Freddie. He was from Colorado. He had left there because he was wanted. And a few months ago he'd come to Chicago, where he didn't know anybody.

Another of Monterra's men yelled, "Yeah, nobody 'round here seems to know you that good. You from the DEA? Are you, fucker?"

Blows to Morgan's head, shoulders, arms, and legs burned like hell itself, and the beatings were repeated intermittently, not only that first night, but the next day and even into the next night, leaving him bleeding, with welts and bruises and lumps and the worst headaches he had ever known. Sometimes they also yanked his hair back and put a gun to his head, and though he thought each of those times might well be his last, he kept denying, denying, denying *any* involvement with the DEA.

"I never seen this guy before in my life," Morgan kept saying again and again about Jimmy O. "I don't know who in the hell he thinks I am, but I sure as hell ain't with the DEA. I'm from Denver!" He cried out with each of the blows, but no matter where or how hard they were delivered, he would not confess.

Fortunately, he was sometimes left alone—sometimes for hours—and especially at night. At one point in the early-morning hours of the second night, he managed to untie himself, climb out of one of the basement windows, and slip away down the alley behind the place. Afterward he spent several days in the hospital, and it took several weeks for him to recover completely. When he finally did recover, he was transferred to the St. Louis office for six months.

Meantime, he identified Freddie, Monterra, and several of his henchmen. They were rounded up and arrested on charges of drug trafficking, kidnapping, and assault on a federal officer. Several months later

Morgan came back to Chicago, still with long hair and a beard, in order to provide testimony in court. Freddie, Monterra, and the others were eventually found guilty and sentenced, and Morgan spent six more months in St. Louis. He had only returned to Chicago and to work there—once again clean shaven and with shorter hair—this past fall. Yet despite his year-long absence and his changed appearance when he eventually did return full-time, someone had obviously recognized him. Whoever it was, he felt it had to be somebody connected to Freddie or Monterra. But with both of them and several of Monterra's men in prison, who exactly was it?

From the little evidence the police had so far, it had not been possible to identify anyone. Neither Morgan nor any of the passersby on the day of the shooting had actually seen anybody—only the black sedan speeding away. And while the cops had been quick to arrive on the scene—and they had recovered a few empty shell casings that matched the caliber of the bullets that killed Elaine—there was nothing else. No fingerprints on the shell casings. Nothing. Busy as the sidewalks had been, when the burst of shots rang out, most pedestrians had ducked for cover.

Elaine's murder had been reported extensively on TV and in the *Tribune* and other papers. There had even been a reward offered for information leading to the arrest and conviction of her killers. But no one had come forward with anything that led anywhere. There was virtually nothing to go on. Even so, Morgan was determined to find something. He had been assigned to work in the office on other, developing cases, and as he did so he took every available opportunity to continue his search for clues that would lead him—and the police—to those responsible for Elaine's death.

Day after day he left his condo and took a cab to the office, always looking over his shoulder for anyone who might still be hunting him. In his cubicle, whenever possible, he pored over old files on his computer, looked at old names, reviewed photographs, courtroom recordings, and more, hoping to uncover some clue—anything—that he might pass on to the cops. He urged agents still working undercover to listen for any talk on the street, and while a few leads did emerge, each one eventually led to a dead end. Weeks went by. Nothing that anybody heard tied anyone to the shooting. They had no gun; and even if they had one, it would almost certainly have been stolen, and there would be no records linking it to any of the individuals involved. The weeks turned into months.

Still, Morgan would not give up. He continued to trace and retrace every possible detail he could think of. He searched through more computer files on known peddlers, middlemen, and others. He talked with still more agents in the field, but in the end he could find nothing. Day after fruitless day he went from his condo to his desk and back again, continuing to look over his shoulder and often drinking at night—in part due to the sadness he continued to feel about losing Elaine but also in part due to his frustration at being unable to find any leads to her killers. Occasionally, Dan or Scott stopped by, or they went out somewhere, away from downtown. But he was spinning his wheels and getting nowhere. It was like walking in mud, and still more weeks passed. He was lost in a series of dark, dead-end corridors, one after another.

Late one morning in mid-April, as he sat in his cubicle drumming his fingers on his desktop, he looked up to see Blackburn approaching in his raincoat. The weather had been miserable. Most days were still cold, and if there was no snow, there was wind-blown rain. Blackburn looked as if he were on a mission, and since Morgan knew he'd been less than productive in recent months, he thought the old man might be about to give him some kind of pep talk. Blackburn stepped into his cubicle and sat in the side chair.

"Tom," he began, "I know you've been preoccupied these past months, trying to find clues about who might've killed your sister, and believe me, I understand. But I think we should talk. What do you say we go have some lunch?"

Morgan paused, and then pushed his chair back from his desk. "OK, George," he said. A pep talk would be OK. No problem. But he hoped the old man wasn't about to give him another undercover assignment. He was exhausted. He picked up his raincoat, and they headed for the elevator.

Outside, the sun was shining for the first time in days, although it was still cold. A strong breeze whipped their coattails as they walked, and some large clouds moved above, driven by the wind. They walked briskly, and then turned into a restaurant a couple of blocks from the office. Inside, they were shown to a corner booth. They took off their coats, settled in, and began studying the menus. After the waitress took their order, Blackburn began.

"Look, Tom," he said as he placed his napkin in his lap, "this is awful, what happened to your sister—and to you. I think I know what you've been going through. You haven't been able to come up with anything for the cops in all these months, and I know you're frustrated and discouraged. But something will break loose. I know it. Meantime, I think you should take some time off—go somewhere, get away from all this for a while."

Morgan was surprised at Blackburn's suggestion. "Well, I know I haven't been my old self," he said. "But I don't know about going anywhere. I still want to get these sons-of-bitches, George."

"I understand," Blackburn responded. "Believe me, I do. But I feel sure that a little time away could make a big difference. And look," he went on, "I've already talked with some of the people upstairs. You've got several weeks of vacation time built up, plus your unused bereavement. You could take some real time off—a kind of sabbatical if you will—for at least a few weeks, maybe even a couple of months, with full pay. Meantime, the police will probably crack this thing."

Morgan paused. "Well, I have to admit some time off sounds good. Maybe a trip is what I need. Got any suggestions as to where?"

"Hell, anywhere," Blackburn said. "You could try Florida. It's great down there this time of year. Or maybe the Bahamas or Puerto Rico. Years ago my wife and I went to the Virgin Islands on our honeymoon, and it was fantastic! Feels like a whole new world down there. Tell you what," he continued, "don't worry about that just now. I'll file the paperwork to get this thing started. You'll figure out the rest. All I know is, based on the kind of winter we've had—and this cold-ass spring—if it was me, I'd go somewhere warm. You'll probably be a hell of a lot safer if you get away from here for a while, anyway."

When they finished their lunch, Blackburn picked up the check; and as they headed back to the office, Morgan continued to roll the old man's suggestions over in his mind. Yeah, maybe a trip was what he needed. He'd have to think about where, though.

CHAPTER FIVE

When Morgan stepped from American Airlines flight 2142 at Cyril E. King Airport, a mile or two outside the small city of Charlotte Amalie on the island of St. Thomas, United States Virgin Islands, the pupils of his eyes winced sharply in the glare of the Caribbean sun; and before he took his first step down the gangway, he reached instinctively for the aviator-style sunglasses tucked in his shirt pocket. It was early May, and the humidity and heat of the midafternoon sun immediately encircled him, melting onto his skin like a hot, wet blanket. He had seen on his phone before leaving Chicago that he could expect temperatures in the low- to mid-eighties, and he judged it to be at least that, perhaps more. Yeah, this was somewhere warm all right.

"Watch your step, please," the female flight attendant cautioned as Morgan and the other departing passengers began their descent toward the tarmac.

On the stairs he leaned slightly to his right to compensate for the weight of the leather carry-on that hung from his left shoulder, and by the time he reached the last step on the gangway he could feel sweat already forming on his back and under his arms. With his free right hand, he pushed his hair back off his forehead, where a glaze of perspiration now felt almost cool in the gentle breeze that drifted across the airport grounds.

So this is the Virgin Islands, he thought, as his eyes swept over the soft, green hillsides in the distance. Blackburn had said it was a whole new world down here. Well, maybe it would be. He could use a whole new world about now.

Crossing the tarmac, he headed for the entrance to the terminal, walking with other passengers beneath a broad, outdoor concourse bordered on one side by a high wire fence, where some renovation was taking place. Here the shade provided at least some relief from the intensity of the sun, but the low, tree-covered hills in the distance still seemed to shimmer in the heat. A few hundred yards in the other direction, bulldozers and graders raised clouds of dust where it appeared they were working to extend one of the runways or perhaps add another one.

Now that he was here, he wasn't 100 percent sure he had made the right decision in leaving Chicago. As much as he hoped getting away for a while might help his state of mind, he didn't want to think he was abandoning efforts to help track down Elaine's killers. He had never shrunk from any responsibly, not as a student and athlete in high school, not as a member of the ROTC at Purdue, not as a marine—including his two battlefield deployments—and certainly not during his years with the Agency. Still, it probably wasn't a bad idea to get away for a while. Maybe the cops would crack this thing while he was gone, like Blackburn had said. And if they didn't, maybe he'd do a better job when he got back.

In the baggage-claim area, the air-conditioning felt pleasantly cool, and he watched his fellow passengers as they gathered around the luggage conveyor. Some talked. Among the men from the flight, the few who had worn suits or sport coats on the plane had long since removed their jackets, which were now carried over their forearms or tossed over damp shoulders, and the women—even those in shorts or skirts—likewise seemed to be affected by the heat. Morgan took a handkerchief from his hip pocket, wiped the remaining perspiration from his forehead, and gradually the suitcases, large and small, began to appear on the conveyor, from which their owners, one by one, whisked them away. Finally, Morgan's single, brown leather bag, which matched his carry-on, appeared as well, and he pulled it from the conveyor.

These two pieces of luggage had been among the gifts he'd received from his parents more than a decade earlier, when he had graduated from college; and though neither had wheels—and as a result both were somewhat more cumbersome than they otherwise might have been—he had not found it possible to discard them in favor of something more practical. They were a reminder of the love and support his parents had always, *always* given him. Now, he carried both pieces and made his way outside the terminal to the taxi stand.

When he arrived there, a woman in her early-forties, with peroxide-blond hair and a still-youthful figure, left the man Morgan thought to be her husband and walked slowly in his direction. She wore an emerald-green skirt with a matching, tropical-print blouse, and as she approached he could not help but notice how her thighs pushed gently at the interior of the skirt and her well-proportioned calves tapered smoothly onto slender ankles. He thought he had seen her looking at him more than once while in the baggage-claim area. Now, as she came toward him, looking directly at him as she approached, he was sure of it. She held a cigarette between the index and middle fingers of her left hand, where there was a white-gold wedding band and matching engagement ring with a sizable diamond.

"Do you happen to have a light?" she asked, smiling and parting her lips just slightly.

Morgan recognized the obvious flirt. He didn't smoke. He had never liked the smell or taste. And beyond that, he had always been interested in staying in shape—ever since high school. If she wanted a light, he knew she could have approached a porter or someone else who was already smoking.

"Sorry," he said. "I don't smoke."

"And I don't suppose you'll be staying at Frenchman's Reef either?" she responded, smiling again. There was something absolutely resolute about her gaze at him. She did not look away, not even for an instant, as she asked the question.

"No, unfortunately not," he said.

"Oh, too bad," she added. "I had hoped to find a match—either here or there." She smiled again at Morgan, but without a return smile from him, she turned and walked back toward her husband, who was now watching their bags being loaded into a cab.

If there was one thing Morgan regarded highly, it was fidelity. He knew it was not possible to have a lasting marriage, family, true friends—or much of anything—without it. His parents had it. Their marriage had lasted nearly twenty-five years, and he knew it would have continued considerably longer had their time together not been cut short—first by his mother's breast cancer and only a year later by his father's fatal car crash. Now, as the woman rejoined her husband, Morgan felt a certain disdain for her. She obviously had precious little fidelity or concern for her husband.

After they entered the cab and departed, Morgan stepped toward the curb and placed his bags on the concrete walkway. Another taxi—a dusty brown Toyota that showed not only some age but a significant amount of wear—pulled up to the taxi stand. The driver, a thin, balding black man in his late-fifties or early-sixties, exited the automobile and approached.

"Dem yoh bags, man?" he asked in what Morgan recognized as a type of island creole.

"Yep, they are," he responded with a slight smile, taking some delight in the lilt of the driver's English.

The driver lifted the bags into the trunk of the Toyota, secured the closure of the trunk lid with a piece of green, plastic-coated wire and then politely opened the rear door of the sedan for Morgan, closed it behind him, and entered the driver's seat.

"Charlotte Amalie?" he asked, as he eyed Morgan in the taxi's rearview mirror.

"Yes," Morgan replied. And as the cab jostled forward over the innumerable ruts in the airport exit road, he added, "The Harborview Hotel."

"Oh, you gon ta like te Harborview," the driver responded in his creole, smiling and showing a partially-gold crown on one front tooth as he looked around briefly at Morgan. "A fine hotel she," he added. "From tere you can see te whole harbor out in front of te city. Beautiful!"

As the cab pulled out onto the main road and headed east, Morgan couldn't help but comment on what he initially took to be the driver's carelessness.

"Drive on the left here, do ya?" he asked, almost imitating the driver's creole English.

"Oh, yes, sir," he said. "We drive on te left here in te Virgin Islands." Then he resumed talking about the Harborview, and for a few minutes Morgan listened to his descriptions, which made him see the hotel all over again, just as it had appeared when he had previewed it online. Situated on a hillside, but down somewhat near the water and only a short distance from the center of Charlotte Amalie, the hotel commanded a sweeping view of the entire harbor with its brilliant blue waters, its boats, and cruise ships. Morgan settled back in his seat and thought about the peace he hoped to find there. After a time he didn't hear the driver anymore. His senses were absorbed by the beauty of what he saw through the cab's windows.

To his right the blue-green Caribbean swept toward shore, gradually changing from a deep blue at depths beyond the coral reefs to a beautiful, pale aqua in the shallows near land. To his left the green hillsides, dotted here and there with homes, rolled gently, smoothly, in their descent toward the sea. And everywhere they were covered with the lush foliage that permitted his mind to drift effortlessly. He thought how beautiful it was, and there was a kind of peace to it all.

The cab continued briefly along the rough coastal road, first in, then out, as it followed the jagged contour of the shoreline. Then, as if they had entered another land, the highway suddenly became smooth, and the driver's voice interrupted Morgan's thoughts.

"Tere be she," the driver announced. "Charlotte Amalie!"

Morgan immediately noted that the passing hills were now dotted with more and more white and pastel-colored homes and other buildings, most with reddish tile or metal roofs. And as he looked forward through the Toyota's dusty windshield, he could see almost the entire town, draped like a multi-colored garland on the hillsides surrounding the harbor. White, ivory, and pale-yellow homes and commercial buildings were joined by others of soft pink and goldish-tan. Across the harbor, two cruise ships sat motionless at their docks, pristine white against the blue water. To Morgan, the colors were absolutely brilliant—and in stark contrast to the dull hues of black and gray he had left in Chicago.

Gradually the cab moved inside the city limits along Waterfront Drive, where he gained an even better view of the ships at their docks. To his right, sea gulls hovered, seeming to hang almost motionless in the air near the water's edge, and to his left, shops, restaurants, and cafés blinked past the cab's windows.

Suddenly Morgan felt the cab jerk, just slightly. It was only the smallest of movements at first—hardly more than a shudder. But then immediately he heard the unmistakable thump and bang of metal against metal as the right side of the cab collapsed against a mass of white that streaked and screamed past the passenger-side windows, shattering them and sending the cab careening to its left, jumping the curb and slamming hard into the wall of nearby shops. At the point of impact, Morgan's left cheekbone and forehead smashed hard against the Toyota's doorpost behind the driver, and as he recoiled against the backseat, he pulled his bent sunglasses from his face, which now felt numb. As if in slow motion, the window of the storefront where they had landed collapsed to the sidewalk. Morgan felt for the handle to open the back door, and he and the driver stepped out of the cab almost simultaneously.

"Jesus Christ!" yelled the cab's driver as he raised his fist, shaking it at a departing van, its white side scraped its full length with the brown paint of the Toyota. "Dat man, him sideswipes us!" he shouted. He slammed the cab's driver-side front door, which rebounded from the car's bent frame.

A young white woman, tanned, with dark-brown hair and beautiful brown eyes, probably in her late twenties, Morgan thought, rushed from the store where the window had collapsed. Her hair hung to her shoulders, and she pushed it back on one side as she approached.

"Are you two all right?" she asked, looking first at the driver and then at Morgan, who had already retrieved the handkerchief from his pocket and was dabbing at the cut on his forehead above his left eye. Some blood oozed from the cut.

"I think so," Morgan responded, with the hint of a smile that was intended not so much for her as it was in recognition of the sheer irony of coming all the way to this place of seeming beauty and peace only to get into a stupid accident. "But I'm not so sure about this cab," he added with a note of sarcasm.

"Sheet, man!" exclaimed the driver. "I got ta call te cops!" He fumbled in his pockets for a moment, seemingly unable to locate his cell phone.

"Here, use mine," Morgan said as he handed his phone to the driver, who took it and began dialing.

"I'm really sorry about your store," Morgan said, "or, I mean, your *gallery*," he continued as he surveyed the paintings and sculpture now clearly visible through the open window.

"Yes, well, thank you," the young woman replied. "At least I have insurance. Fortunately no one out here was hit. Did you just arrive on the island?"

"Yeah," Morgan said. "Not more than half an hour ago."

"I'm afraid the driving around here is pretty crazy sometimes," she continued. "Can I get you something for your eye?"

"Oh, I think I'll be all right." He dabbed again at the cut with his handkerchief.

"Well, at least let me introduce myself," the brunette continued, extending her hand and smiling. "My name's Vivian. Vivian Petersen."

Morgan took her hand and, smiling back, said "Hi, I'm Tom. Tom Morgan. And again, I'm sorry about the mess we've made of your place."

"Well, don't worry about it," she said. "As long as the two of you are all right."

"I'm afraid I wouldn't take it so lightly," Morgan responded. "Are all you Virgin Islanders so easygoing?"

"Probably," she said, smiling again, catching Morgan's attention with her candor. He noticed now more than before the whiteness of her teeth, which seemed all the brighter in contrast to her dark tan and deep-red lipstick. He also realized that her dark hair showed traces of auburn in the sun.

By now the traffic moving past hardly seemed to pay more than casual notice of the cab's mishap, as did the sidewalk passersby, who simply made their way around the vehicle, glanced almost incidentally, and then moved on. When the police arrived, they had questions not only for the cab's driver but for Morgan and for the gallery's owner, Miss Petersen. Morgan noticed the clean, pressed condition of their uniforms as well as the cleanliness of their blue-and-gold police cars, giving him the overall impression that they were indeed professional and that they might actually catch the driver of the white van. In any case, his real interest was in putting the incident behind him and getting to his hotel. When the questions ended, he said good-bye to the driver, who by this time had called for another cab and had Morgan's luggage transferred. He also returned Morgan's phone, and for the man's trouble Morgan gave him a sizeable tip—at least one the man would not easily forget. Then he said good-bye to the brunette as well, again taking her hand. But this time he said her name when he spoke.

"Good-bye, Vivian. Nice to meet you," he said with considerable sincerity. "Just sorry it was under such circumstances."

"Nice meeting you too, Tom," she answered. "Perhaps we'll run into each other again sometime before you leave the island." She smiled. Morgan smiled too, recognizing the double meaning of the words she had chosen, and he gave a modest wave back to her as he entered his replacement cab. Damn, she was good looking, he thought. Too bad he would be on the island for only a short time.

"Where to?" asked his new driver, whose creole closely matched that of his former cabby.

"The Harborview," he said.

"Oh, you gon ta like te Harborview!"

Morgan smiled, visibly and inside, recognizing that his previous driver had used precisely the same words. He wondered if the hotel—or perhaps all the hotels on the island for that matter—might prompt or even pay the locals to use those words.

After driving only three or four short blocks, the driver made a slight turn off Waterfront Drive, briefly ascended a portion of an adjoining hill and then turned into the entrance of the Harborview. Large, regal-looking palms lined the short, circular driveway, and other trees with bright-orange blossoms stood majestically in front of the hotel. The white stucco exterior of the four-story building, with its red tile roof, looked simultaneously sturdy and cool, even in the heat of the day. The lawn beneath the trees was clipped short and edged neatly along the drive, walkways, and flower beds. The entire property looked extremely well-kept; and it was absolutely no less beautiful than the pictures he had seen on the hotel's website.

The driver pulled the cab under the front portico, and after taking Morgan's bags from the trunk he placed them off to one side, where a bellman retrieved them and took them into the lobby. Morgan pulled out his wallet and paid and tipped the driver, who wished him a pleasant stay then assisted some departing hotel guests into his cab and drove off.

Before walking inside, Morgan paused to scan the flowers of some hibiscus amassed near the hotel's double-door entrance. He took a long, deep breath, filling his lungs with the delicate fragrance. Maybe he really would find some peace in this place.

Inside, the walnut-stained hardwood floors of the lobby were punctuated here and there with thick rugs and handsome furniture, also trimmed with dark wood. Near the windows rested large, clay pots, with palms six to eight feet tall, and above, paddle fans worked slowly, suspended from the equally-dark, wood beams of the ceiling. The air felt cool and comfortable, and after passing a number of other hotel guests, Morgan approached the front desk. When he greeted the clerk and gave his name, he raised his eyebrows, causing him to grimace just slightly.

"Um. Nasty looking cut there, sir," observed the clerk, who was a young, black man, somewhat shorter and considerably younger than Morgan.

"Oh, this'll be OK," he said, "if I can get to my room and get some ice." Morgan again pulled the handkerchief from his pocket and dabbed at the wound, which was no longer producing any blood or lymph.

"Certainly, sir. We have your room ready for you. Number 311. Are you still planning to be with us the full two weeks?"

"Yes, that's the plan," Morgan responded. He had booked his plane ticket only one way, in case he decided to cut his visit short or extend it. He knew he could stay on longer if he decided to. Blackburn had made it clear he had as much as a couple of months if he wanted. He'd just have to see how he felt about the place.

"Well, here you are," the clerk said, handing Morgan a key. He summoned the bellman, and when he arrived with Morgan's bags on a metal cart, he led the way to the elevator, the third floor, and then down the hallway to number 311. As he departed to retrieve a bucket of ice, Morgan surveyed the room. The floor was the same, dark walnut he had seen in the lobby. Likewise, the bed's headboard, the nightstands, the desk, and even the coffee table and trim on the sofa in the seating area were of a similar dark wood. It all looked comfortable indeed. He walked briefly out onto the balcony, noting he had an unobstructed view of the swimming pool below, and then beyond, the harbor and the cruise ships. The view was magnificent.

When the bellman returned, Morgan tipped him, not only for his assistance with the bags but also for his politeness in offering to get the ice.

"If you needs anyting else, sir," the bellman said, "jus' let te bell desk know."

"Thanks," Morgan said, feeling somewhat tired from the long day. "I'll do that."

After the bellman departed, he soaked a washcloth in the bathroom sink, wrung it out, and grabbed a handful of ice cubes, making a cool compress for his cheek and the cut above his eye, which by now was swollen to a plump bluish-black. He applied the compress and again walked out onto the balcony and scanned the harbor, with its blue-green waters, boats moving here and there, and the two passenger ships still moored at their docks, as before. Several small islands, a short distance away, helped to form the outer perimeter of the harbor, and off toward the western horizon, a few scattered clouds shone orange, pink, and purple in the rays of the late-afternoon sun. It was altogether beautiful. And while he had arrived a bit battered, he was nevertheless at least somewhat pleased to be here. Maybe, in time, he'd even be able to straighten out this mess that was now his life.

CHAPTER SIX

During Morgan's first few days on the island, he fell into a kind of routine. Each morning following breakfast in the hotel's coffee shop, he would go to the fitness club for a workout. He had abandoned his weight training months earlier, when he'd started concentrating on finding Elaine's killers, and it felt good to get back to his old exercise routine. By mid-morning he would leave the hotel grounds and walk through some of the nearby downtown streets, some of which still bore the names given them by the island's original Danish settlers, such as Tolbod Gada, Raadets Gada, and Dronningens Gada. Occasionally he would also look into some of the area shops and purchase items that he did not have or had failed to bring with him—flip-flops, some comfortable deck shoes for walking around, and especially sunglasses to replace the pair bent and twisted in the wreck of the cab.

Gradually he became acquainted with most of his closest surroundings, including many of the town's historic landmarks—Fort Christian, built by the early Danes; the ninety-nine steps that led to Bluebeard's Castle; Emancipation Park, which commemorated the freeing of the island's slaves; and others. Then, by mid-day, he would invariably return to the hotel and in the afternoon lie on one of the chaise lounges at the Harborview's pool, soak up some much-needed sun, and read about other features of the island beyond Charlotte Amalie. Yet despite these efforts to occupy his thoughts with things other than Elaine and her killers, he somehow could not help but—at least occasionally— think of that last day with her. So early each evening, in a further attempt to escape the memories that continued to torment him, he would join other hotel guests— and, he presumed, some locals as well—in the hotel's Sundowner Bar.

Located on the lobby level on the western end of the hotel, the Sundowner was an open-air, combination bar and restaurant, situated in such a way that it provided an ideal vantage point from which to view each day's setting sun. Morgan discovered it could be reached either directly up a flight of stairs from the pool deck, or from his third-floor room, down the elevator and through the lobby.

The restaurant portion of the Sundowner was filled with dining tables, each with blue napkins and topped with a matching blue umbrella. A three-foot-high stucco wall—punctuated at intervals with pillars topped by hurricane lamps—formed the perimeter on three sides, and adjacent to the restaurant area, a sizeable, rectangular bar, surrounded by comfortable bar stools, stood prominently beneath a low, thatched roof of dried palm fronds. The floor of the entire area was tiled with large, flat terra cotta tiles, which Morgan thought handsome—and certainly practical in the event of rain. In short order the bar became his favorite place to spend early-evening hours and try to relax as he watched the setting sun. He also discovered that, most evenings, a steel band played a steady stream of island music, beginning at Happy Hour and lasting well into the evening.

Following his afternoons at the pool, he would typically go first to his room to shower and freshen up, and then take a seat at the Sundowner's bar, listen to the band, and have a drink or two, sometimes three. Rum was a component of many of the most popular drinks served there, and after trying a number of them—some with a variety of fruits and others with small, paper umbrellas—he ultimately settled on rum and Diet Coke as his drink of choice. In the waning hours of each day, he would see the trade winds scatter thin wisps of clouds off toward the west, where the last rays of sun would catch them, bathing them in orange and pink and purple, just as he had seen them on the day of his arrival. Most evenings he would have dinner at the bar as well, often engaging the bartender, Jerry, or one of the bar's patrons in some idle conversation. If he was not preoccupied with thoughts of Elaine and finding her killers, he would sometimes linger there for perhaps another hour or two or even three and listen to the band before returning to his room and bed.

After those initial few days, however, he grew restless with his routine, and one morning, instead of browsing through the nearby streets, he walked to a car-rental agency and rented a red, four-passenger Jeep with a tan canvas top. With that and the road map they provided, he determined to broaden his explorations beyond Charlotte Amalie.

He had already noted from the less-detailed maps he had studied during his afternoons at the Harborview's pool that there were only a few principal roads traversing the island east to west and north to south. Route 30 traveled east and west, more or less following the southern shore, from a point well west of the airport where he had landed, eastward through Charlotte Amalie and then to the eastern-most end of the island and the small village of Red Hook. Route 35 was the main road traveling north and south, from its southern-most point in Charlotte Amalie through the island's center to the northern shore and Magens Bay. And finally, Routes 38, 40, and 42 wound their way more or less east and west, but through the mid-section of the island and its Central Highlands.

There appeared to be no particular points of interest on the western-most end of the island. Nevertheless, on his first day out, to satisfy his curiosity, he decided to drive to this area known simply as West End. It didn't take long for him to gain a reasonable familiarity with driving on the left. What initially presented the biggest challenge was driving in the city, negotiating through intersections, simultaneously avoiding cars—and pedestrians in two crosswalks—and winding up in the proper lane at the completion of the turn. However, after a few near incidents with oncoming traffic, even this became almost routine.

As he was already familiar with Route 30 west to the airport, he took Route 35 north out of Charlotte Amalie and followed it for a mile or two until he entered the Central Highlands. There he headed west on Route 38, where the road became quite steep, with twists and turns that kept him tugging at the steering wheel, first in one direction, then in the other. After a time it was almost as if the Jeep weren't moving at all, but that it was stationary, with the roadway coming at him in a kind of unrolling stream of blacktop he was obliged to negotiate.

As he climbed the Jeep over more and more of the highway, the density of the vegetation increased until, at the center of the island, it grew unobstructed right to the sides of the road, making it difficult—and often impossible—to see around one curve to the next. Then, as he began to gradually push his way out of this heavily wooded section, he saw lower areas where the hills rolled more gently toward the blue-green waters of the sea, and here and there the land was almost flat, with open fields. He stopped the Jeep for a moment and, from his location still relatively high up, he could see there was little human activity on this end of the island—certainly no towns or resorts and only occasionally a rather rustic-looking home or other building. It appeared to him that there was a kind of perpetual sameness to life here. He felt the area had undoubtedly looked like this not only the day he had arrived on the island, but almost certainly the week and month before, and perhaps even the year and decade before that.

His eyes traced the shape of the land, which at some places dropped off in abrupt cliffs that plunged to narrow, rocky beaches below. Everywhere the sea looked massive and powerful as it hurled itself, blue and white, onto the land. He watched it all for a time, and then, at length, he turned the Jeep and headed back to the hotel and the Sundowner.

CHAPTER SEVEN

The following day was Sunday, and Morgan decided to visit the north shore of the island and in particular Magens Bay, which was reportedly exceptionally beautiful and excellent for swimming. At mid-morning, he put the top down on the Jeep and left the hotel in the flip-flops, short-sleeved shirt, and ball cap he had worn the day before; however, today he replaced his cargo shorts with his bathing suit in anticipation of a day at the beach.

Leaving Charlotte Amalie, he again picked up Route 35 and wound his way north into the Central Highlands, where once again the vegetation became increasingly dense; and, just as the day before, as the road looped back and forth toward higher and higher ground, the trees and underbrush grew thick, right to the edges of the roadway. Finally, when he emerged from the last of the hills, he looked north toward the sea. There, in the distance, was Magens Bay—a large expanse of brilliant, blue water perhaps a mile wide, protected on both sides by large, tree-covered hills, which, at least on this day, kept the surface of the bay an absolute, even calm. He drove the Jeep down the winding road as it continued to loop back and forth until, after some distance, he neared the water's edge. He parked the Jeep beneath some sea grape and coconut trees that grew nearby, tucked the keys into a front pocket of his bathing suit, and walked, towel in hand, toward the water.

The sun above was intense, and the white sand of the beach stretched in a smooth, near-perfect crescent in between the vibrant green of the hillsides. He dropped his towel, ball cap, sunglasses, and flip-flops, walked to the water's edge, and waded in to his waist. The clear, salty liquid surrounded him, cool and refreshing on his skin. Then he plunged forward, head first, letting the water wash around and over him.

As he swam briefly beneath the surface, his eyes closed, he suddenly found himself thinking again of Elaine, and once more he saw those images of her lying lifeless on the sidewalk, with the blood from her chest and abdomen flowing out onto the pavement and the black sedan speeding away into traffic. This time, the images also made him think of his best friend, Adam Wells, who had died in a similar way in Iraq, sprayed from his right thigh to his throat with machine-gun fire, right in front of him. Morgan swam to the surface, almost gasping for air. He tore at the water with his arms and reached out, pulling hard with each stroke, propelling himself farther and farther out into the bay. Finally, nearing exhaustion, he turned and swam back toward shallower water, where he stood, his heart pounding. He walked onto the beach, collapsed on the sand, and rolled over on his back, his chest heaving with each breath. Crazy, goddamned imperfect world, he thought. The good get killed. And the evil go unpunished. He didn't know how he would ever be able to find Elaine's killers. Adam's death had been one thing. At least he had died on the field of battle, with a weapon in his hand and with honor. But Elaine had been defenseless. Murdered. He had hoped, months earlier, that perhaps God, if there was one, might somehow help him discover the clues to bring her killers to justice. But the months of work and effort and endless hours of searching had produced absolutely nothing.

He continued to lie in the sand, still on his back, his arms outstretched. The pain of not knowing how or when or if he might ever find her killers was almost more than he could bear. He continued to lie there for a time, until he finally caught his breath. Then he gathered his things and walked back to the Jeep for his return to the Harborview.

By the time he finished his shower and arrived at his favorite barstool at the Sundowner, it was late afternoon. Jerry poured his first drink of rum and Diet Coke—and then a second and then a third. Morgan watched as members of the band set up their instruments and began playing, and he tried to focus on their music. He ate dinner, and as night began to fall, he also talked with one and then another of his fellow patrons at the bar. But no matter what he tried, he could not escape the images of Elaine and her murder. They pursued him relentlessly, lurking on the fringes of his consciousness, seeming to stalk him; and when he thought he might have eluded them or they had perhaps drifted off like the evening clouds, they returned again, and then again, consuming every other conscious thought. He had two more drinks before he decided to end the evening. It was well past dark, and members of the band were packing up their instruments when he finally left the bar. He was definitely going to call Blackburn tomorrow, to see if the Agency or the police had uncovered anything. He hoped like hell that they had.

CHAPTER EIGHT

The following morning Morgan awoke early and went downstairs to the coffee shop for breakfast. After his workout, and allowing for the two-hour time difference between Charlotte Amalie and Chicago, he unhooked his cell from the charger cord and punched up Blackburn's number. The old man's phone rang once, twice and then a third time. Finally he answered.

"Blackburn," he said in his typical gruff manner.

"Hey, George. It's Tom."

"Hey, Tom," Blackburn returned, sounding somewhat warmer, with a hint of cordial surprise in his voice. "Are you starting to enjoy yourself down there yet?"

"Yeah, the weather's good," Morgan said. "And I've seen a little of the island."

"Nice there, isn't it? So what's up?"

"Well, not much really," Morgan continued. "I was just calling to see if anything has turned up about Elaine's shooters." There was a pause.

"No, Tom, sorry to say, nothing yet. But I talked with some people over at the station yesterday. They're still working on it."

"Damn!" Morgan said, somewhat under his breath but still audibly. "I was hoping you might have something to tell me." There was another pause.

"Look, Tom, you know how this stuff goes. It's likely to take some time yet before anything breaks loose. But like I said, it *will* happen. I want you to try to put this thing out of your mind for a while. Let us and the police handle things; and you try to enjoy yourself some, OK? I assure you, as soon as we find out anything, I'll call you."

"OK, George," he said, sounding agreeable, but still wishing they had discovered *something*. "I'll try to be patient."

"Good," he said. "And by the way, if you want to get in touch with me about anything, just call me on my cell. In the meantime, like I said, go out and try to have some fun while you're there."

"All right," he answered. But even as he did so, he was not certain what he could or would do to "have some fun," as the old man said. At the same time, he supposed he'd have to keep trying.

CHAPTER NINE

In the days that followed, after his breakfast and morning workout, Morgan continued his explorations of the island, looking for places of interest on the south shore toward the East End. By mid- or late-morning, he would leave the hotel and head out of town, following Route 30 eastward, winding his way alternately through the hills and along the coast. When high up on the hillsides, he would occasionally stop to take in the expansive views of the sea, and sometimes, if the view was particularly spectacular or smaller islands were visible in the distance, he would use his phone to take a few pictures. And when some portion of his drive took him down along the water, he would invariably discover a new cove or beach—some deserted and some with people swimming or snorkeling. Occasionally one of the beaches would have a small food stand or a restaurant where he could have lunch. Afterward, he sometimes went for a swim, and at other times he simply walked on the beach and took in the beauty of his surroundings.

From his first few afternoons at the Harborview's pool, and during these subsequent daily travels around the island, Morgan's skin had gradually taken on a deep, ruddy tan, which seemed to accentuate the muscles of his physique, and his normally brown hair had begun to lighten slightly on the fringes as well, giving him the appearance of one who had been on the island for some time—certainly more than a week or so. And as his tan gradually grew darker, he found he could spend more and more time in the sun without adverse effect.

His most recent daily travels had gradually taken him farther and farther east until, on his third day out, he reached the eastern-most end of the island and the village of Red Hook, with its few shops and restaurants. When he arrived at a yacht basin there, he stopped the Jeep and walked the main street for a time, looking into some of the shops. Among other things, he discovered that from there he could see the adjacent island of St. John, not more than a mile away. Then, after an hour or so of exploring, he returned to the Jeep for his drive back to the Harborview, the Sundowner, and some evening refreshment.

It was always the same when he arrived. He would find his favorite spot beneath the canopy of palm fronds near a particular corner of the bar, from where he could see the band as well as the setting sun. Jerry would greet him with his usual, warm smile, and with a simple, thumbs-up gesture, Morgan would signal that he intended to have his usual drink of rum and Diet Coke, to which Jerry had begun adding a wedge of lime that Morgan found he liked considerably. The small steel band, if not already playing, would begin setting up, and soon the patio would be alive with the sounds of reggae. In the distance, as the sun continued working its way westward, it would invariably cast its soft, pink and orange glow onto the clouds scattered on the horizon.

The evening after his visit to Red Hook and his return to his room for a shower, he descended to the Sundowner and, once again, gave his thumbs-up signal to Jerry, who prepared and delivered to him his rum and Diet Coke—with the now usual wedge of lime.

"Evenin', Mr. Morgan," he said as he placed his drink on the bar. "Another good day out and about?"

"You bet," Morgan said. "Another great day on your beautiful island." Morgan knew he wasn't telling the entire truth. Though he was finding his days here to be more enjoyable than those in Chicago, he still considered them less than great, as he continued thinking of Elaine and finding her killers. Nevertheless, he raised his glass in a brief, unspoken toast to Jerry, and then quaffed off the top half-inch of the drink.

"Afternoons make you thirsty aplenty, eh?"

Morgan nodded affirmatively, the bite of the fresh lime causing him to purse his lips and his jaw to knot up smartly.

As they continued their small talk, a man who Morgan thought to be approximately his own age walked out onto the patio. With black hair combed straight back and a thin, neatly-trimmed moustache, the man exuded an air of authority as he scanned the area, looking as though he were counting the number of diners beginning to gather at the tables. He wore a white, double-breasted dinner jacket, open-collared white shirt, and black slacks and shoes. Morgan judged him to be somewhat shorter than himself, but he could see that, even beneath the dinner jacket, the man was well-muscled. He approached the bar and took a seat across the corner from Morgan.

"Evenin', Mr. Petersen," Jerry said, smiling broadly. "Like a drink, sir?"

"Yeah, I would," the man replied. And without indicating his preference, Jerry began preparing the drink. Morgan focused on the man's surname, Petersen, recalling the brunette of the same name from the art gallery the day he had arrived. He wondered if the two were related—or perhaps married.

Waiting for his drink, the man took a package of filtered cigarettes from an inside pocket of his jacket, shook one from the pack, lit it with a gold metal lighter, and inhaled deeply. Between puffs he pushed with the tip of one finger at the corners of his moustache.

"Here ya be," Jerry said, smiling again as he placed the vodka martini on the bar. "By te way, Mr. Petersen," Jerry continued, "maybe you like to say hello to our hotel guest, Mr. Morgan, a regular here at te Sundowner. Mr. Morgan, tis be te owner of te Harborview, Mr. Petersen."

The two men shook hands across the corner of the bar.

"Please, call me Charlie," Petersen said with a cordial smile.

"And I'm Tom," Morgan replied. There was a moment of silence as Petersen surveyed Morgan's face.

"You a fighter, Tom?" he asked with a wry smile as he gestured toward the cut still slightly swollen and visible above Morgan's eye, despite his tan.

"No, just a survivor," he responded, with a smile of his own. "Can't say much, though, for some of your drivers on this island," he added, hinting at the cause of the cut.

"I can certainly agree with you there," Petersen said. "The way some of my fellow islanders behave behind the wheel leaves a lot to be desired. Have you been with us long?"

"A little over a week now," Morgan responded.

"And how much longer are you planning to stay?"

"Not sure. At least another week, I guess. Maybe more."

"Well, I hope you enjoy the remainder of your time with us. And if there's anything I can do to make you more comfortable while you're here, please don't hesitate to call my office."

Petersen glanced at his watch and then looked toward Jerry serving another customer a few seats away. "By the way, Jerry," Petersen called out, "have you by any chance seen my sister around here this evening?"

Jerry looked up, and it was obvious even before he responded that he saw the young brunette, who Morgan also recognized, coming up behind Petersen.

"Yes, sir, tere be she," he said, nodding in the direction just over Petersen's shoulder. "Right behind you."

Petersen turned and smiled at the young woman, who returned a smile very much like his own. "Hello, Hon!" he said with some surprise in his voice. He gave her a half hug. "I was wondering where you were!" She looked at him, then at Morgan, who had been watching her as she approached, and then again at her brother.

"So, who's your friend, here?" she asked, still smiling and gesturing in Morgan's direction.

"Oh," Petersen said. "Hon, this is Tom Morgan, a guest here in the hotel. Tom, my sister, Vivian."

Vivian smiled warmly and extended her hand. "I see your eye hasn't entirely healed yet," she said. Morgan eased himself off the barstool and shook her hand.

"I guess not. But it's still good for some things," he added, smiling and suggesting the flirtation he intended.

Petersen looked at his sister and registered mild surprise. "You know Tom?" he asked.

"Yes, Charlie," she said, smiling again. "He's the man whose cab ran into the gallery last week."

Petersen paused. "Well, Tom, I think you should join us for dinner. I wouldn't want you to get a totally bad impression of us Virgin Islanders."

Petersen motioned to the maître d', who arrived and took them to a table near one of the patio's exterior walls, with Petersen and his sister on one side of the table and Morgan on the other. Daylight had begun to fade, and the hurricane lamps on the wall's columns had been turned on. As they took their seats beneath the table's umbrella, Morgan could not help but notice the cleavage that hinted at the fullness of Vivian's breasts as she leaned forward. A waiter promptly arrived, presented them all with menus, and handed a wine list to Petersen, who quickly scanned it, made a selection, and returned the list to the waiter.

"So, Tom," Petersen began, "what brings you to the Virgin Islands?"

"Oh, I just wanted a vacation," he said casually, not wanting to reveal the real reason he had come. "It's still a bit chilly in Chicago, and I wanted to get away for a while. I've never been to the Virgin Islands before."

"Well, we've never been to Chicago either," Petersen said. "Although we certainly see on TV how cold your winters are up there. I guess that's one of the reasons we've never been." He smiled, and they all chuckled.

"And what line of work are you in, Tom?" Vivian broke in, smiling as she looked at him from across the table.

Morgan had always felt it prudent never to reveal—particularly to strangers—the truth about his work, and even this far from home he felt no compulsion to tell the entire truth. Instead, he engaged in the same modest subterfuge he often used.

"I work for the federal government," he answered. Then he quickly added, "Department of Agriculture." He was always comfortable that his statement was only a slight divergence from the truth, with the Department of Agriculture being the DOA versus the DEA.

"Oh, glad for that," Petersen said, smiling. "For a moment I thought you might be about to tell us you were with the IRS!" They all laughed.

When the waiter returned with the wine, he uncorked the bottle and poured half an inch of the red liquid into Petersen's glass. Petersen twirled it slowly, sniffed at the bouquet, sipped, and then nodded his approval. The waiter filled each of their glasses half full, and then nestled the bottle into the shaved ice of the wine stand and covered it with a white napkin.

"May I take your dinner order now?" he asked.

They all studied their menus briefly, and after making their selections the waiter departed. Morgan sipped at his wine and then replaced his glass on the table.

"So, tell me about yourselves," he said, looking briefly at Petersen and then turning his gaze toward Vivian. "My guess is that the two of you grew up here."

Petersen paused briefly while sipping his own wine and then responded. "Indeed we did. In fact, our family has been on these islands for at least ten generations." There was a certain permanence and resilience about the way Petersen said it. "But I'm sure you don't want to hear about all that," he continued.

"On the contrary," Morgan said. "I'd like to hear." He looked at Petersen, and then shifted his attention to Vivian, adding, "I'd like to hear all about you." He smiled softly at Vivian and let his eyes stop on her as he ended his sentence.

"I'll tell him about us, Charlie," she said as she touched Petersen's jacket-covered arm. "Our ancestors were mostly Danish…and French," she began. "You've probably already learned at least some of the history of these islands, right?"

"Yes," Morgan said. "At least I know the Danes were some of the earliest settlers."

"Yes. And the Petersens were among them," she continued, "arriving in the seventeen hundreds—initially settling here on St. Thomas, then on St. John, and eventually on St. Croix. We were always told they came because of the land shortages in Denmark. I guess no one told them how small these islands really are," she added jokingly, and once again they all laughed.

As Vivian continued with more detail about some of their earliest ancestors and the difficulties they encountered, Morgan found himself fascinated with her, her sense of history, her expressiveness, and what he could only think of as her charm—to say nothing of her good looks.

"Gradually," she went on, "they cleared and cultivated the land and planted and raised sugarcane—particularly down on St. Croix—for the shipment of raw sugar and for making rum here locally."

"Sounds like they made a good life for themselves," Morgan said.

"Oh, I believe they had a good life, eventually," she continued. "But there was an incredible amount of work along the way; and they had to battle diseases, and hurricanes, and food shortages sometimes too."

"Well, looks like food shortages will not be a problem tonight," Petersen broke in. "I see our dinner has arrived."

The waiter served their meal, brought another bottle of wine, refilled their glasses, and once again nestled the wine bottle into the ice of the wine stand.

"So are you still in the business of raising sugar-cane?" Morgan asked as they began their meal.

"We are," Petersen said. "Not here, of course, but down on St. Croix, where there are fewer hills, and the land is more fertile. We also have a sugar mill down there, producing sugar for the rum distilleries here in the islands."

"Charlie oversees all of that for us," Vivian added, "besides running the hotel, of course. Fortunately, he's managed to maintain control of most of our original land holdings there. But it hasn't been easy."

"I'll add," Petersen said, "that it's because of the sugarcane and the sugar we produce here locally— as well as the relatively low cost of labor, of course— that you can buy a bottle of rum in these islands so inexpensively."

"And I do like the rum," Morgan offered. "Particularly the dark, spiced variety." He looked directly at Vivian. "I like it almost as much as some of the other things I've been introduced to here." He smiled a flirtatious smile at her, and though he did not look away, he caught a glimpse of Petersen eyeing the two of them.

They continued with their meal for a time, and went on with their conversation about the islands, sugar production, and the Petersen family. Finally, Petersen lifted his napkin and placed it on the table.

"So, now you've heard almost three-hundred years of our family history," he said conclusively, as they were finishing their meal. "This is probably a good place to change the subject, before we bore you to death."

Morgan did not speak for a moment. Then he looked at Petersen and again at Vivian "Well, it's certainly an interesting history, and I enjoyed hearing it." He took another sip of his wine.

"Good," Petersen said. "Now, I'm sorry to rush off, but I have some things I've got to take care of before it gets any later." He stood, dropped his napkin into the seat of his chair, and looked at Morgan. "Perhaps I'll see you around the hotel another time." He looked at Vivian and added, "You coming too, Hon?"

Morgan thought Petersen sounded as if he wanted his sister to leave with him.

"No, I think I'll stay for a while and listen to the band," she said.

"Well, then," he continued, "it's been a pleasure meeting you, Tom; and again, if there's anything I can do to make your stay more enjoyable, please don't hesitate to call my office."

Morgan stood. They shook hands, and Petersen departed. It had now been dark for nearly an hour, and Morgan was pleased to have this opportunity to spend some time with Vivian alone. In fact, he could not keep his eyes off her, even when she said nothing. Behind her, a crimson-flowered bougainvillea hung over the patio wall, creating a soft but brilliant background. The light from the hurricane lamps shone softly on her tanned skin and danced in the darkness of her eyes. Her smile captivated him, and when the band started up again, he could not resist asking her what had been on his mind for some time.

"Would you like to dance?" he asked, leaning forward slightly and smiling.

"I'd love to," she answered. She moved gracefully from her chair and took Morgan's arm as they walked to the area in front of the band where a few couples were already gathered. She turned to face him, and Morgan's eyes traced the contours of her body as he took her in his arms.

"Tell me, Tom," she said, looking slightly up at him, "do you have family back in Chicago?"

He could feel the soft yet firm curves of her body, here and there, touching his own. Her breasts delicately yet noticeably brushed against his chest. He imagined that her question might have been a disguised inquiry if he were married, and he wanted to provide her with a satisfactory answer—yet hopefully forestall further questions, at least for the time being.

"No," he said. "I don't have any family anymore. Unfortunately they're all gone."

"Oh, I'm sorry," she said. Then she paused. "Will you be staying with us very much longer?"

Morgan had had two drinks of rum earlier in the evening and two or perhaps three glasses of wine during dinner. That, and the sheer beauty of this woman, made him feel like saying he would stay for as long as she wanted. But he knew he could not say that. At the same time, he was not certain how long he might stay. Finally he said all that he thought he could say with certainty.

"For a little while," he said, hedging at first. Then he added, "Probably another week or two at least. I'm on a sabbatical from work." He smiled as he looked into her eyes, wanting to give her some assurance that he would be around for considerably more than just another few days. She smiled back.

"Would you like me to show you around while you're here?"

Morgan paused, allowing only a second or two to pass. "I'd like that very much," he said. "When can we start?"

"Well, tomorrow," she answered, "if you want. I have some things to take care of at the gallery in the morning, but I can get away by early afternoon. How does two o'clock sound?"

"Perfect," he said. "Shall I pick you up there?"

"Yes, if you don't mind."

"Then I'll see you at two o'clock ," he said, smiling.

The band stopped playing, and as the two of them walked off the dance floor, to Morgan's surprise Petersen had arrived back at the table and was sitting, smoking a cigarette, when they returned.

"Well, I think I'll say good night," Morgan said.

"Leaving, Tom?" Petersen asked.

"Yes, I think so. I've had a long day. But thank you for dinner." Morgan extended his hand once again to Petersen.

"Don't mention it," Petersen replied as he stood and shook Morgan's hand.

Morgan gave Vivian one last smile. "See you tomorrow," he said. Then he left the table and that portion of the restaurant that led to the lobby and the elevator. When he arrived in his room, there was no question that he felt the combined effect of the rum and the wine. But perhaps even more, he was intoxicated with this woman he had just been holding in his arms.

He opened the sliding door at the balcony, stripped off his clothes, and climbed into bed. As he lay there, moonlight sifted through the balcony's sliding screen door, bathing the room in a soft, pale light. The curtains wafted gently in the breeze coming from the harbor, and for a time he could still hear the steel band playing at the Sundowner in the distance. He turned over onto his left side. He knew he would have no trouble falling asleep this night, and in a matter of minutes, as sleep began to overtake him, his thoughts were only of Vivian Petersen, whom he had now encountered for the second time. He could not wait to see her tomorrow.

CHAPTER TEN

In the near darkness of his room, Morgan could not be sure how much time had passed when he thought he sensed the presence of warm, feminine flesh pressing against his own. Full, firm breasts lay softly against his back, and a trim, taut stomach and thighs lightly touched the remainder of his body. A feminine scent surrounded and bathed his senses. He thought he could—just faintly—discern the touch of pubic hair. Was this real?

In his half sleep, he eased his right hand beneath the sheet and over his own hip, to the midsection of this feminine form, and touched the warm mat of hair. Christ, he thought, is this Vivian? As he drowsily pondered the question, he became more aware of the woman's perfume, which pulled and tugged him toward consciousness, and as he began to open his eyes, he suddenly realized this was no dream. No dream at all!

"Tis little pussy be ready for you," the woman half whispered in a dusky creole voice.

Morgan's eyes instantly opened fully, and in a single motion he sat up and turned to face the dark form, which he could see was a young, buxom black woman.

"How in the hell did you get in here?" he asked in a raspy voice as he tried to push more of the fog of sleep from his brain. He surveyed her face as he asked the question.

"I have a key," she responded coyly, dangling the metal object from a length of chain around her neck. "What's te matta? she asked. "You not happy to see me?"

Morgan looked briefly around the room to satisfy himself that he had no additional visitors.

"You're damned right I'm not happy to see you." He grabbed her arm. "Who in the hell gave you that key?"

"Mr. Petersen gives me te key," she said. "You're hurting my arm."

Morgan released her arm, and then stood and retrieved his trousers from the nearby sofa. In a single motion he pulled them on. "Why in the hell would Mr. Peterson give you a key to my room?" he demanded.

"I don't know. He jus' say he want me to come see you and be nice to you."

"Well, when you see Mr. Petersen, you tell him I don't need his favors—or yours!" Turning away, he added, "Now, get the hell out of here!"

"What's te matta?" she asked. "You not like me?"

Morgan turned to face her. He didn't want to insult her by calling her a whore. "Just *go*," he said, this time with greater emphasis, as he gestured toward the door.

The woman stood up from the side of the bed opposite Morgan, pulled on a tight, red knit dress, and found her shoes. "You go to hell!" she said angrily, slamming the door as she left.

Morgan sat back down on the bed and rested his face in his hands, trying to massage more of the sleep from his brain but being careful to avoid the still-tender cut above his eye. Why in the hell would Charles Petersen send this woman to his room? He had just met the man. What could have been on his mind? Morgan continued to massage the muscles of his face, and repeated the question again in his head, as if its repetition might produce an answer. But it did not.

If circumstances had been different, he might have taken the opportunity to have sex with the woman. She was attractive. But years earlier—when he was still in the corps and off base for a weekend of celebrating—he had been with a prostitute, and he had found out exactly what it was like to catch a dose of the clap. After the considerable discomfort of that little experience, he had vowed "never again"—and he meant it.

He walked to the door and flipped the deadbolt closed, which he realized he had failed to secure earlier; then he took off his trousers and returned to bed, again trying to find the comfortable position on his left side—this time with his arm and shoulder beneath the pillow. Why would Charles Petersen send this woman to his room? he questioned yet again...and then once more as well. Maybe Petersen was just trying to be a nice guy and provide him with a little entertainment for the night. On the other hand, Petersen had heard him say he was meeting Vivian tomorrow. Maybe, for some reason, he didn't want the two of them to get together and thought he might interrupt that possibility by interjecting this other woman. Whatever the case, Morgan concluded he couldn't know the answer, short of asking Petersen directly; and he would not do that. If confronted, Petersen would almost certainly deny he had done such a thing. Gradually, he tried to put the matter out of his mind, but his last conscious thought before again falling asleep was, Why would Charles Petersen send this woman to his room?

CHAPTER ELEVEN

It was not quite 2:00 p.m. the next day when Morgan parked his Jeep around the corner from Vivian's gallery, and as he walked toward the front door he saw for the first time the name—La Galerie Petersen—in gold and black lettering on the large, now-replaced front window. Vivian emerged and walked toward him past a group of tourists.

"Hi," she said, almost playfully, as she smiled that same wonderful smile she had given him so often and so freely the night before. "I saw you through the window. Are you always this punctual?"

"Probably not," he responded with a grin, and she laughed.

He took her hand and placed it on his arm, and she continued to smile as they walked the short distance to the Jeep. Morgan was not always especially conscious of women's clothes, but she was dressed so impeccably that he could not help but notice every detail. Her nearly knee-length dress, which was a brilliant gold, had a short, stand-up collar that was open down just far enough to tastefully reveal a modest amount of cleavage, and it was cinched in at the waist by a wide, brown, woven-leather belt that matched exactly the delicate, brown leather straps of her wedge sandals. Her dark-brown hair, with its traces of auburn, moved softly in the gentle afternoon breeze, and with her tan and brilliant smile, he thought she looked absolutely gorgeous. When they arrived at the Jeep, she tossed a large, straw hand-bag—also with brown leather straps—into the back and slid smoothly into the passenger seat beside him.

"So, where would you like to go?" she asked.

"I could make something up," he said. "But I thought you might have a suggestion."

She smiled. "Have you been to St. John?"

"Not yet," he responded.

"Then let's go sailing!" She sounded excited about the prospect. She smiled again and looked at him warmly. "My boat is in the town of Red Hook, on the East End. Do you know it?"

"I do," Morgan said. "I was just there yesterday."

"Great," she said. "Then let's be off!"

Knowing they would drive eastward on Route 30, Morgan made a turn at Dronningens Gada and then turned again out onto Waterfront Drive. He followed it past a new group of cruise ships that had docked the night before and then continued on eastward, out of town, negotiating the road's twists and turns, steep hills, pitches, and dives all quite expertly. As he drove, they occasionally caught glimpses of the sea off to their right, and each time he saw it, he was amazed by its beauty nearly as much as he was by Vivian's. Occasionally too— usually after descending a hill and at a sharp turn at the bottom—he would see, just as he had on his earlier trips around the island, one or more large, green dumpsters, often filled to overflowing with bags of garbage. They were typically surrounded by numerous chickens, some black and some cinnamon colored, pecking and scratching at the refuse.

"Why all this trash?" he asked.

Vivian's hair tossed in the wind. "Not sure," she said somewhat loudly, seeming to try to overcome the noise of the Jeep and the wind. She passed one hand over her hair to keep it from her face. "I guess it's just the island way."

"There are places like this in Chicago," Morgan added, smiling. "Just no wild chickens!" They both laughed.

He continued to guide the Jeep through the road's twists and turns, gradually moving them closer to Red Hook, and within another few minutes the small town was visible a short distance ahead. As they neared the water, Vivian directed him into a parking lot next to the yacht basin, where she pointed to her boat tied at the dock along with several others. Morgan parked the Jeep, and they walked closer. He admired the look of the vessel. He liked the gradual, smooth taper of its hull, the way it sat elegantly in the water, and, as they drew closer still, even its name—*Bon Voyage*, painted in gold-trimmed blue letters that matched the blue of the sail covers.

"Know much about sailing?" she asked.

Morgan had gone sailing perhaps twice. He knew that he was no sailor. "A raw recruit," he said with a grin.

"Well, don't worry. I'll teach you."

They boarded the boat, which she told him was a sloop. "A thirty-five footer," she said, "with a Marconi-rigged main sail. I've just had it updated with the latest navigational equipment."

She showed him around briefly, both above and below deck, and then invited him to take a seat near the helm while she went into the office to pay for the work that had been done. When she returned, she went below and a couple of minutes later emerged barefoot, in tan shorts and a close-fitting, blue midriff top, which snugly covered what Morgan already knew were her ample breasts. As she tested the radio and new SAT/NAV equipment, he continued to scan the curves of her figure. She was truly beautiful.

In what seemed to him almost no time at all, she started the engine and cast off the stern line. Then she asked him to push off from the bow. He gave a solid shove to get the bow headed away from the pilings, and Vivian guided the boat smoothly away from the dock. Slowly at first, they motored out of the yacht basin and into the harbor. Then, as they approached open water, she asked him to take the wheel.

"Just hold it steady," she said. "I'm going to hoist the main sail."

Morgan took the wheel and held it steady as they continued to motor forward. Meanwhile she hoisted the sail, and he watched it billow out full in the mild afternoon breeze. Returning aft, she cut the engine.

"OK," she said. "Let's have some fun!"

Standing beside him, she began pointing out various features of the boat; and as the sloop moved through the water and he felt the bow rising and falling out in front of them, he repeated her words in his mind: "Let's have some fun." It was a suggestion more rich in meaning than she could ever have imagined. It had been far too long since there had been any fun in his life; but now, in her presence—and with the wind carrying them forward across the narrow channel that separated the two islands—he began to feel considerable excitement, not only in sailing but in anticipation of what the remainder of the afternoon might bring. He could hear the wind push on the sail and the flap of water against the sides of the hull, and it felt exhilarating. Vivian continued pointing out features of the boat and some of the basics of sailing—the difference between port and starboard and how to take a compass reading.

"Port is left; starboard is right," she said. Then she took the wheel momentarily, heading them fifteen degrees north of due east, and asked Morgan to take control again while she hoisted the triangular jib. When she did, he could feel it take hold as the wind caught it too and provided additional push through the water.

"I judge we're making eight to ten knots," she said. "We're heading for the little town of Cruz Bay. Should be there in no time."

Morgan remained at the wheel, maintaining the compass heading she had indicated. The bow of the sloop continued moving up and down rhythmically as they pushed through the waves, and he soon began to feel almost comfortable as he scanned the horizon and noted the features of St. John up ahead. The sun, like virtually every day since his arrival, shone brilliantly in an almost-cloudless sky. He put on his sunglasses. Now he could open his eyes fully and try to relax.

They continued east for a time, and as they neared what Vivian said was their intended point of entry to the small harbor of the town, she took the wheel again to bring the sloop slightly about, swinging the bow in the direction of their destination. She then restarted the engine and turned the wheel briefly back to Morgan before going forward to drop the sails. Then, she returned to the helm to retake the wheel and slowly guided them into the harbor, where they joined a number of other boats already anchored or tied at the dock. With the engine reduced to idle, she guided them slowly, smoothly, to an ever-so-gradual stop. Then she jumped off, dropped a bow line over one of the dock's cleats, and returned to the helm to shut off the engine.

"Well, here we are!" she announced with an air of excitement and at the same time some finality. "How'd you like our little sail?"

"I really did," Morgan said. At the same time, he was impressed with how fluidly she had handled everything, even while teaching him. He looked at his watch and was surprised to see that it was only a few minutes past 3:00 p.m. To his amazement, the drive from Charlotte Amalie and the sail to St. John had taken only a little more than an hour.

They stepped off the boat onto the dock and secured the stern line. Morgan took her hand, and they began walking into the perimeter of the little village—which was filled with colorful shops, bars, and restaurants. They explored for nearly an hour, peeking here, looking there; and as they walked up a slight hill on the inland side of town, he noticed immediately ahead a small but ancient cemetery on both sides of the street—its inhabitants ensconced in individual, above-ground tombs or crypts. Seeing it there made him think instantly of his parents—and now Elaine too—lying still and cold in Oakwood Cemetery, and another round of terrible images of her on their last day together began flashing in his mind. He stopped and turned to Vivian.

"Hey, what do you say we go get a drink?" he said, not wanting to let her see what he was feeling.

"Sure! It's nearly Happy Hour," she responded. "Let's go!"

They turned and walked the short distance back into the village, located a restaurant and bar called the Rum Hut, and took seats at the bar, which overlooked the harbor where they had arrived. A female bartender, blond and in her mid-twenties, greeted them with a smile.

"Hi," she said. "Can I take your order?"

Morgan indicated his usual rum and Diet Coke with a wedge of lime, and Vivian, pausing only momentarily, decided on a piña colada. When the bartender returned with their drinks, Vivian turned toward him.

"Let's have a toast," she said. She had a softness in her smile and a brightness in her eyes that made him want to lean forward and kiss her, but he resisted the temptation—at least for the time being—and raised his glass to meet hers. "To a beautiful day and a wonderful time together," she said, looking directly into Morgan's eyes and not taking her gaze from him as they both sipped from their drinks.

"Ohhh...this piña colada is really delicious," she said slowly, almost sensuously. "You should try it!" She handed him her glass, and he looked at her as he drank from it. This was the closest he had been to her lips, and he savored the taste of the drink as well as her scent, which lingered on the glass.

"You're right," he said. "It *is* good!" He continued to look at her, anticipating a time later in the evening when they would return to Charlotte Amalie, where he knew for certain he would kiss her—and hopefully more than once.

When it was time for another drink and some food, they each ordered a burger and decided to share an order of fries. Morgan also departed from his usual rum and Diet Coke and asked for a piña colada for himself as well.

"I told you they were good. You liked it, huh?"

He agreed, and when their food arrived they continued their conversation, looking out onto the bay and its boats at rest in the pale-blue water. It was a totally beautiful and peaceful sight, Morgan thought. He took his cell phone from the pocket of his cargo shorts and asked a fellow patron seated nearby if he would take a picture of the two of them, with the boats and the small harbor as a backdrop. He *definitely* wanted to remember this time with her; and after the man obliged, Vivian produced her phone as well, asking for still more photos of them.

Later, as they finished their meal—and the sun descended farther toward the west—they left the restaurant and boarded the sloop for their return to Red Hook. The light breeze they had encountered earlier in the day had mostly died down, and the water in the channel between the two islands now rolled in broad, smooth waves. Nevertheless, as they were "running with the wind," as Vivian said, they were making equally good time as on the outbound trip.

Arriving back at Red Hook, they sailed into and through the harbor, and, just as they were about to enter the yacht basin, she dropped the sails and restarted the engine, gliding once again slowly, surely, effortlessly to the dock. After taking the cushions from the cockpit and stowing them below, she closed the hatch and took a few minutes to hose down the sloop's hull with fresh water. Then they found the Jeep and left for their return to Charlotte Amalie.

By the time they arrived, it was past eight o'clock and nearly dark. Vivian directed him through some of the old, downtown streets, and then a short distance up into the hills above to her fourplex condo building. The Jeep's headlights showed the building to be a soft beige color, surrounded by lush shrubbery and coconut palms. There was a white Mercedes coupe parked in the short driveway, with the license plate "VIVIAN." He pulled the Jeep up behind the Mercedes and turned off the lights.

"I guess that would be your car, huh?"

"How could you tell?" she said, smiling. "I usually walk to and from work. It's good exercise."

They got out of the Jeep, and Morgan walked her along the lighted walkway to the front door, where she turned to face him.

"I had an absolutely wonderful afternoon, Tom. Really wonderful."

"I was about to say the same thing to you," he said, putting his hands around her waist and gently pulling her close.

She put her arms up over his shoulders, and he leaned forward, kissing her softly. He could tell, though, that it was not only him kissing her. She was kissing him back. And when their lips parted, he continued to hold her close.

"I *really* enjoyed today," he said. "Think we might go out again tomorrow?"

"Absolutely!" she said. She paused momentarily and then added, "Maybe we could go snorkeling. Want to try that?"

"Sure," he answered. He had enjoyed the sail; and he thought he was likely to enjoy snorkeling just as much, maybe more. As a kid he had gone snorkeling on a couple of occasions in the lake waters of the Midwest; and while it had been fun, he knew almost without question that the clear waters surrounding these islands would provide a far more interesting experience.

"Then it's a date!" she said. "But we should probably start a little earlier than today, if that's OK. The best snorkeling is on St. John's north shore, and we'll have to sail a bit farther for a really good spot. What do you think about, say, one o'clock?"

"Sounds good," he said. He smiled and leaned forward and kissed her again, and again she kissed him back. Then he slowly released her and stepped back half a step, still looking into her eyes.

"By the way," he said, "do you suppose I could have your cell number?" He said it in a way that, having just kissed her—twice—made them both smile.

"Oh, I suppose so," she said jokingly. "If you absolutely must." She smiled and recited the number, which he put into his phone, and then he called her to send his number.

"Well, I guess I'll see you tomorrow," he said. "Pick you up at the gallery?"

"Yes. That's probably best."

"OK, see you at one o'clock." He leaned forward and kissed her once more—briefly this time—then turned and walked to the Jeep. Before climbing in, he looked back to see if she had walked inside, but saw her still standing by her door looking at him. He smiled and waved, and she smiled and waved back before walking in. There was something very special about this woman. He knew it. He felt it. And he couldn't wait for the next day.

CHAPTER TWELVE

The following morning, after breakfast and his work-out, Morgan called Vivian to see if he should bring anything for their sail.

"Well, you are going to need some snorkeling gear," she said. "Mine's already on the boat. I thought we could pick some up for you at the dive shop in Red Hook."

"OK, perfect" he said. "Anything else?"

"No, I don't think so."

"All right, then," he said. "I'll see you at 1:00."

As he hung up the phone, however, he thought he should at least get some snacks for the boat, perhaps for after their snorkel. So on his way to the gallery, he stopped at a grocery, picked up a couple bottles of white wine and some cheese and crackers, and then drove down to Waterfront. Again he found a parking spot near the gallery, took the few steps to the front door, and this time walked in. It was still a few minutes before one, and he was greeted by a young woman about Vivian's age, with reddish-gold hair and deep-blue eyes.

"May I help you?" she asked.

"No," he said, pausing just slightly. "Thank you. I'm here to see Vivian."

"Oh," she said, raising her eyebrows. "Well, she's with someone else right now. But feel free to look around while you're waiting." She smiled and returned to her work behind the counter.

Morgan looked toward the back of the gallery, where he saw Vivian with a customer. She signaled that she would be only a minute or two, so he used the time to browse.

The front half of the gallery was two stories high, with white plastered walls. It appeared that the second-story floor had been removed in that area, in order to create an expansive space for displaying the considerable amount of artwork. Throughout the center of the gallery were several open, black iron shelves, all artfully arranged and displaying smaller prints and pieces of sculpture. Skylights in the roof as well as spot lighting from above provided a combination of natural and artificial light, and along one wall was a staircase leading to the second floor, with both the staircase and the floor above having black iron railings that matched the shelving on the floor below. Overall the gallery had a certain elegance, which Morgan thought clearly reflected Vivian's taste and her sense of style.

Many if not most of the paintings displayed on the walls had a tropical theme. If the subject of a painting was a bird, it was a tropical bird. If it was a water scene, it looked like these islands or at least somewhere in the Caribbean. And if the subject involved people, they looked like the locals and tourists browsing and shopping along Waterfront Drive or on one of the nearby side streets.

One painting in particular caught Morgan's attention. Mounted on one of the white, plastered walls, it was of a sailboat, which he thought looked a great deal like the *Bon Voyage*. It was a sizable painting, nearly three feet by four feet, showing the boat under full sail, plying brilliant, blue waters. It was executed in oils or acrylics—Morgan wasn't sure which—with only moderately controlled brush strokes. He liked it because it seemed alive with motion and color. As he studied it, he could almost hear the wind in the sails and the splash of water against the hull—much as he had heard the day before with Vivian.

"You like that one?" Vivian asked as she approached him from behind.

"I do," he said, turning to look at her and showing a bit of surprise. He gave her a warm smile and then looked again at the painting. "I like its style, and it looks alive, like it's really under sail, moving, like the gulls in the air. But mostly," he continued, turning to look at her again, "I like it because it reminds me of our sail yesterday."

"Well, I'd say you have very good taste. This happens to have been done by a really talented local artist by the name of Robert McAdams. And, as you can see, his work commands a pretty good price."

Morgan noted the price tag hanging from one corner of the painting: $12,500. "Yes, I see," he said, nodding his head and registering mild surprise. "This fellow McAdams is talented." Then he looked back at Vivian. "Of course, so are you," he said. He smiled and looked slowly around the gallery, wanting to acknowledge the taste she obviously had in selecting the art she chose to display. "So, are you ready to go?"

"You bet," she answered, showing him once more the smile that he thought so beautiful. She picked up her purse from behind the counter, said a quick good-bye to the clerk, and they left.

Within thirty minutes they were in Red Hook. They stopped briefly at the dive shop to pick up a mask, fins, and a snorkel. Then they drove the remaining short distance to the yacht basin. In a matter of only a few minutes more, they were aboard the *Bon Voyage*. Vivian went below and, like the day before, emerged in shorts and a brief top. Then, after motoring them out to open water, she again turned the wheel over to Morgan and raised the sails. However, this time, instead of directing them to Cruz Bay, she took a heading that would take them around the west end of the island to the north shore.

"There are several nice bays and coves up there," she said. "But this afternoon I want us to try Cinnamon Bay. It's a really beautiful place."

After she had taken a compass reading and set the initial course, she turned the wheel over to Morgan once again and stood nearby. He maintained that initial course as well as others when she made periodic adjustments, gradually steering them around the west end of the island. In little more than an hour, they arrived at the mouth of Cinnamon Bay, with its semicircle of white, sandy beach backed by brilliant-green hills. Vivian dropped the sails. Morgan started the engine, and she took the wheel, guiding them around the several boats already there, to a spot a comfortable distance from the others. Morgan then went forward as she asked and released the anchor, sending it plunging into the water, where it quickly sank to the bottom.

As soon as the anchor took hold, Vivian shut off the engine.

"I'll get the snorkel gear," she said, and she immediately disappeared below. After a couple of minutes, she came back on deck, their snorkel gear in hand; but now she was wearing a bright-yellow bikini.

"This is a marine sanctuary," she said as she handed Morgan his mask, fins, and snorkel. "It's part of a national park that covers most of the water around here. There's no fishing or lobstering. Just looking."

Morgan was already happily doing that. To his delight, the yellow bikini revealed not only the beauty of her tan but also every voluptuous curve of her body; and he saw for the first time what he had previously only more generally imagined. He could scarcely take his eyes off her. Everything about her tugged mightily at his senses; and as he smiled and continued to look at her, she smiled back.

Anticipating their snorkel, Morgan had earlier in the day dressed in his bathing suit. Now, he stepped out of his boat shoes and took off his polo shirt, and after Vivian placed the boat's ladder over the stern, they each put on their masks and snorkel tubes. Finally, with fins held tightly under their arms, they jumped overboard.

The sun was shining beautifully overhead, and in the heat of the afternoon the water felt cool and refreshing on Morgan's skin. After they came to the surface, they put on their fins, placed the masks over their eyes, blew the saltwater from their snorkel tubes, and began their swim.

As they floated on the surface, paddling softly, they looked down into the crystal-clear water—which to Morgan appeared to be not more than twenty or perhaps thirty feet deep. While snorkeling in the freshwater of the Midwest had been at least mildly entertaining in his youth, here, as he had anticipated, it was nothing short of exhilarating. The rays of the sun penetrated the water so thoroughly and perfectly that the colors of the coral, sponges, fish—everything—were spectacularly vivid. From time to time, he pointed to a particular type of coral or sponge or fish about which he had a question, and they would pause and tread water. With snorkel tubes removed from their mouths, Vivian would name what they were encountering. At one point he asked about the sharks they had just seen.

"Just Reef Sharks," she said. "They're fairly common in these waters, but they're pretty docile and generally don't represent a problem. Others, though, like Bull Sharks, can be dangerous," she added. "They're considerably larger—eight to ten feet long—with heavier bodies and broad, flat snouts. If we see any of them, we'll get out of the water. They tend to be territorial, and they can be really aggressive."

As they resumed snorkeling, Morgan continued to take in the multitude of colors. At the same time, he remained watchful for more sharks. He didn't care if they were just Reef Sharks. He had no intention of being lunch for any of them.

At length, after being in the water for nearly an hour, they swam back to the boat, removed their fins, and climbed up the ladder. As Vivian sat toweling her hair, he leaned back against the cushions of the cockpit, letting the sun warm his skin.

"Want to have a glass of wine?" he asked.

"Sure," she said. "Sounds nice."

Morgan went below, retrieved one of the bottles of wine from the small refrigerator in the galley, uncorked it, grabbed a couple of the plastic cups, and, with cheese and crackers on a paper plate, returned above deck. He handed her one of the cups and poured the wine, and together they eased back into the cushions of the cockpit.

"That was a lot of fun," she said as she ran her fingers through her still slightly-damp hair. She took a sip of the wine. "It's been a long time since I've been snorkeling. I'd almost forgotten how beautiful everything is down there."

"Yeah, and up here too," Morgan said, smiling at her.

She smiled in return, and then looked down at her wine before looking up at him once more. "You want to come out again tomorrow?"

"Absolutely," he answered, and he leaned forward and kissed her.

They sipped at their wine, and, after eating most of their cheese and crackers, Morgan returned the remnants of their snack to the galley. Then he came back up on deck.

"What do you say we go to the Rum Hut before heading back? I really liked that place."

"I liked it too!" she said enthusiastically. "Let's go."

He headed for the bow and began pulling up the anchor. Meanwhile, she started the engine and turned the sloop toward open water, where she again suggested that Morgan take the wheel for their sail to Cruz Bay. Half an hour later they arrived, just as the day before, with Vivian guiding them smoothly, effortlessly to the dock. After tying up, they walked the short distance to the bar, where they again ordered piña coladas and—a little later—some dinner.

A light breeze drifted in from the bay, and as they drank the coladas and looked at the boats anchored out in the water, Morgan thought it was, like the day before, entirely beautiful. And with Vivian again by his side, he felt more peace and contentment than he had known in a long, long while.

Later, after they finished their meal, they boarded the *Bon Voyage* for their sail back to Red Hook and the drive to Charlotte Amalie. When they arrived at Vivian's condo, like the evening before, Morgan walked her to her door.

"Want to come in?" she asked. "I can make us some more piña coladas."

"Sure," he said.

"Now, I can't guarantee they'll be as good as those at the Rum Hut," she added as she unlocked the door, "but I'll try."

Inside, she flipped on the lights, and he followed her from the foyer to her living room, with its high ceilings and paddle fans, and then to the kitchen, with its combination of recessed lighting and hanging fixtures over the island. She invited him to have a seat on one of the barstools, and he watched as she gathered the ingredients for the coladas: a bottle of Bacardi Gold from a cabinet and cream of coconut and pineapple juice from the refrigerator. She mixed a batch of the concoction in a blender, along with some ice; then poured the cold, creamy liquid into two short, clear glasses; garnished each with a skewered wedge of pineapple and a cherry; and handed one of the glasses to Morgan.

"OK," she said, smiling. "Tell me what you think."

Morgan raised his glass, inspected its contents briefly and then took a sip. He slowly savored the mixture and then equally slowly licked his lips. He paused. "Terrific," he said. "Absolutely terrific! Where'd you get that recipe?"

"It's a secret," she said, smiling slyly. "But if you're good, maybe one of these days I'll tell you." She smiled again playfully, and then sipped from her own glass.

"Come on," she said, "bring your drink. I'll show you around."

She took him by the hand and led him through the condo room by room: the living room and dining room, her office, the bedrooms—hers and the guest room— the bathrooms and even the patio. Everywhere, he could see her attention to detail. In the living room, the warm, area rug coordinated perfectly with the sofa and side chairs. In the dining room, the fabric of the chairs blended equally well with the drapes. And everywhere there was wonderful artwork. Everything, in every room, reflected not only her sense of style but what Morgan recognized as her undeniable good taste, just like all the things he had seen in her gallery.

As they sat together on the living room couch and continued to sip at the coladas, he kissed her—once, twice, and then several more times. She did not protest. In fact, it was clear to him that she enjoyed each kiss as much as he did. Still, he did not want to push too far, too fast. He truly enjoyed her company; and he didn't want her to think he was interested in her only for sex. So, they simply watched TV for a time, finished the coladas, and finally, as he was leaving, near the front door he pulled her close and kissed her again—and then again.

"Snorkeling again tomorrow?" she asked.

"You bet," he responded, continuing to hold her close. He kissed her a final time, and as he left he thought what a good day it had been. In fact, in the company of this wonderful woman, it had been more than that. It had been a truly *wonderful* day.

CHAPTER THIRTEEN

During the next couple of days, their snorkeling trips became almost routine. After picking Vivian up at the gallery in the early afternoon, they would drive to Red Hook, sail to one of the bays along St. John's north shore, snorkel for an hour or so, and then, in the late afternoon, they would return to the Rum Hut, Red Hook and ultimately to Charlotte Amalie and Vivian's condo. One evening, as they sat together on her couch, sipping more coladas and reviewing the day's sail and snorkel, she asked if he'd like to try scuba diving. Morgan was intrigued. He had never been diving, and he thought it would certainly add a new dimension to their explorations.

"Yeah, I'd like to," he said. "But I know I'll need some lessons. Know where I can get some?"

She was still wearing shorts from the boat, and, smiling, she pushed at his leg with her bare foot. "I'll teach you, silly."

He paused and then smiled back. "Is there anything you *don't* know how to do?" he asked. "You know boating, sailing, snorkeling; you run your own business; and you make *terrific* piña coladas. Is there anything you *can't* do?

"I can't teach you to dive…at least not until tomorrow," she said, smiling again.

He took one of the throw pillows from his end of the couch and tossed it in her direction. "OK," he said. "But there's one thing I've got to know before I agree. Where did you learn to make these great coladas?"

She paused and looked at him. "I got the recipe from the bartender at the Rum Hut. I knew you liked them as much as I did, and I wanted to make you happy." Morgan looked at her and smiled; then he kissed her several times.

"Well, I guess you're going to teach me diving tomorrow, then, huh?"

"You bet!" she said. "We'll get you some dive gear at the shop in Red Hook and be on our way."

They continued to talk for a time about the different bays they had already visited and which one they should try for his first dive. She thought Trunk Bay, where they had gone just the day before, would be best.

It was certainly among the most beautiful, but it was also a bit smaller and shallower than some of the others, and it might be the best choice for his first dive. So it was agreed. It would be Trunk Bay.

CHAPTER FOURTEEN

The following afternoon Morgan picked Vivian up at the gallery at one o'clock, and then drove to Red Hook and the dive shop. While he already had the necessary mask, fins, and snorkel, she said he would also need a dive vest or buoyancy compensator (called a "*bc*" for short, she said), air tanks, a regulator to control the airflow from the tanks, and some weights to aid in his descent. He should also get a dive watch with a bezel, to keep track of the elapsed time at depth, and perhaps a dive knife as well.

"You already know about the sharks," she said. "You never know what we might run into down there, so it's not a bad idea to have a knife."

They looked through all the available equipment, and after selecting the individual items, he also purchased a large, dark-blue duffel in which to carry everything but the tanks. Only a few minutes later, they were aboard the *Bon Voyage*, storing Morgan's gear below deck alongside hers and heading out of the yacht basin and harbor into open water.

For nearly an hour, Morgan stood at the helm, taking compass readings and making course corrections as she showed him, until at length they arrived on St. John's north shore and finally Trunk Bay. There, she took over at the helm, as usual. It was now his turn to drop the jib and main sail. Finally, she turned on the engine, guided the boat around the few others already there, and found an appropriate spot. Morgan dropped the anchor, just as in previous days. He knew he was becoming more proficient in most of the duties aboard the boat, and he enjoyed it.

"OK," Vivian said excitedly. "Here we are. Let's get you ready!"

Together they went below, retrieved the dive bags and tanks, and hoisted everything up through the hatch to the deck. Then they sat together in the cockpit.

For nearly an hour, she showed him in detail how each piece of the equipment fitted and worked together—how to fill the buoyancy compensator, or bc, with air from the air tank and thus float on the surface; how to deflate it at least partially in order to provide for his descent; how to breathe through the regulator; how he should spit into his mask to keep it from fogging up when they were in the water; and even how to blow air through his nose into the mask in order to expel any water that might inadvertently seep in.

"Oh, and one other thing," she said. "I should show you some of the hand signals we might want to use down there." She demonstrated that the palm of her hand, held out flat toward him meant "stop"; that a closed fist, with the thumb pointing left, right, up, or down, indicated the direction they should proceed; and the thumb vacillating quickly back and forth, first in one direction and then the other, indicated the question, "What direction?" Finally, the thumb and index finger pressed together to form a circle indicated the question, "Is everything OK?" And the same sign, given back by the other diver, would indicate all was fine.

At length, she asked him to show her everything and explain how all the equipment worked, as well as its function. When he finished, she asked if he thought he was ready.

He paused briefly. "I think so," he said. "If not, I guess I'll drown," he added wryly.

"Don't worry," she said. They would likely be at the bottom for only thirty minutes or so. He would definitely have more than enough air. "Just remember," she continued, "you can always breathe from my regulator if you have any kind of problem." He could see her eyeing the muscles of his shoulders, his chest and even his legs. "Worst case," she continued, "I'm sure you're more than

strong enough to dump everything and swim to the surface if necessary. If you do, just be sure to bring me with
you! This is the *Buddy System,*" she continued, smiling.
"And we're supposed to always stay together."

Morgan smiled back at her. He wondered if she was
really saying they should *"always"* stay together.

Feeling he was ready, he placed the ladder over the
stern of the sloop. Vivian hoisted a red dive flag with its
white diagonal stripe up the mast, to alert other boat-
ers there were divers in the area; and within a matter of
minutes they had their gear on. Morgan also put on his
dive watch; and, as Vivian suggested, he set the bezel to
reflect thirty-five minutes from the present time. With
that, and with his dive knife strapped to his right calf,
like hers, they both took a few trial breaths through their
regulators and then simultaneously jumped overboard.

After plunging into the water and returning to
the surface, Vivian gave last-minute instructions. They
would swim on the surface to the anchor line; slowly
descend, following it to the bottom or near the bottom;
and then head the short distance to the reef. She said
that, from time to time during the dive, she would give
him an "OK" sign with her thumb and index finger, to
inquire if everything was all right; and if all was well, he
should reply with the same signal.

"You ready?" she asked.

Morgan nodded affirmatively and gave her the "OK"
sign; then together they swam to the anchor line. As they

began their descent—in the water and isolated from any airborne sounds—Morgan immediately became more conscious of his breathing, inhaling and slowly drawing air in through the regulator—uuhhh...and then exhaling and slowly pushing air out with a huuhhh...again... and then again. Hearing these sounds so vividly was an aspect of the dive he had not anticipated; but, as they continued their descent, he gradually became accustomed to them, and in the presence of this beautiful woman his heart raced with excitement.

With the sun shining above and the water entirely clear, he could see not only completely to the bottom, as when they were snorkeling, but a considerable distance up and down the reef as well—again with every color and hue imaginable in the different types of coral and plants, and in the variety of fish that darted through the water nearby and at a distance. As they neared the bottom and he swam along beside her, he noted how effortlessly she moved through the water, as well as the suppleness of her arms and legs in every fluid motion. He tried to mimic the slow rhythm of her movements, which seemed to propel her, almost effortlessly; and for nearly half an hour they explored the reef, first swimming away from the boat for ten to fifteen minutes and then returning in the direction from which they had come. As they explored, Morgan took in every aspect of their surroundings, especially now that he could see everything close-up and in greater detail than had previously been possible from the surface. The Brain Coral, the colorful Fan Coral, and the many different kinds of fish that darted here and there in the water, were all spectacular. Now and then, up ahead or off to one side, he also saw more of the Reef Sharks they had seen when snorkeling, and he invariably pointed to them. But she always gave him the "OK" sign, and indeed, the sharks seemed to pay little or no attention to them and appeared to pose no threat, just as she had said.

After nearly thirty minutes, they had completed the dive and circled back to the boat. From below, Morgan could see the dark shape of its hull as well as its keel projecting deep into the water. As they drew nearer, they swam slowly up the anchor line, the bubbles from their breathing preceding them until they reached the surface. Then they kicked their way to the stern of the boat and the ladder, removed their fins, and somewhat clumsily climbed aboard. Morgan felt himself breathing harder than usual as he removed his gear.

"Well, how'd you like it?" she asked. She removed her gear as well, and they settled into the cushions of the cockpit.

"Fantastic!" he said between breaths. "Even better than I imagined! Although I'm still not used to the sharks," he added with a slight laugh. He continued to breathe somewhat heavily, and Vivian picked up his pressure gauge.

"I understand," she said. "I see you used your air pretty fast. But that's normal. Every new diver uses air fast. Actually, I think you did great. Even *better* than great! Not one preliminary lesson in a pool or in the shallows. Just instant submersion." She smiled. "You were terrific, Honey." She leaned forward and kissed him.

He noted it was the first time she had called him that, and he kissed her back.

The water during their dive had been relatively warm, even at the bottom. At the same time, it was considerably cooler than body temperature, and the sun now felt comfortable and warm on Morgan's skin. He was a bit thirsty, and hungry. He took a sip from a bottle of water and watched Vivian towel her hair.

"What do you say we have some wine and a snack?"

"Sure," she said. "I'll get it." She toweled her hair a bit more, ran her fingers gingerly through it, and went below.

When she returned through the hatch, she had one of the bottles of wine and two, clear-plastic cups in one hand, and in the other a small basket lined with a red and white checkered cloth napkin and filled with cheese and crackers. She poured the wine, first into Morgan's cup and then into her own. He smiled, showing the pleasure he felt in simply watching her. Not only was she beautiful; she was knowledgeable about a great many things. Even more, she seemed eager to help him and to please him.

"Tell me," she said, as she took a sip from her wine, "I've been curious. You said you have no family back in Chicago. Does that mean no parents? Or anybody?"

Morgan listened to her question. He knew it was time—perhaps past time—to tell her more about himself. But he had purposely waited until she broached the subject, and now she had.

"Yes," he said. "Except for an aunt and uncle and a couple of cousins, there's no one else. My mom died from breast cancer not long after I graduated from college, and my dad was killed in a car wreck just over a year later, while I was in the marines."

"Oh, I'm so sorry, Tom. So sorry." She paused briefly and then added, "You were in the marines?"

"Yeah, for four years."

"Where were you stationed?"

"Several places," he said. "Quantico, Virginia, for a while. Then I did a couple of tours in Iraq."

"Oh my," she said. She reached out her hand and slowly smoothed her fingers through his hair. "I'm glad you made it back."

"Me too," he said with a slight smile. "But I lost some good friends—and my very best friend, Adam Wells—while over there in that hellhole. Adam was a hell of a warrior, and the best friend anyone could ever hope to have. I watched him die right in front of me. They say that Iraq is the location of the Garden of Eden, supposedly somewhere between the Tigris and Euphrates

Rivers. Well, I can tell you for a certainty. It's no damn Garden of Eden anymore."

"And you didn't have any brothers or sisters?"

"Oh, no, I had a sister," he said. "Elaine. But unfortunately I lost her too just a few months ago." He paused and took a deep breath. "I've been pretty torn up about it." He exhaled audibly. "That's the reason I'm down here, really" he continued. "I needed to take a break and get away for a while." He looked down at his cup of wine, his bare feet, and the deck.

"Who of us ever knows what will happen to us in our lives?" she said. "Sometimes wonderful things. And sometimes absolutely terrible things. I haven't mentioned it, but I lost both of my folks too—or I guess I should say Charlie and I lost them. My mother died when I was a senior in high school. It was terrible, and I still miss her every day. And my dad died in a plane crash a few years ago. He was a wonderful father; and after we lost him, Charlie had to step into his shoes to keep the businesses running. He flies back and forth between the islands all the time. But I hate flying." They sat sipping their wine for a time, and then she continued. "And what about girlfriends? Got any of them back home?"

Morgan hesitated. He didn't know where the conversation might be headed at this point, and he hoped she wouldn't start asking about his work.

"I guess I've had a few over the years," he said. "But nobody now. How about you?" he continued. "You're a beautiful woman. You must've had at least a few men in your life."

"Well, I was in love once," she said. "And like you I've had a few relationships. But you know how it goes. Sometimes things just don't work out." She looked directly into his eyes.

"I know," he said, looking back at her and studying the soft contours of her face. "But I keep hoping that one of these times it will." He smiled and kissed her, hoping she knew how much he cared about her, and for her.

"I have another question," he said. "I've heard you can't really say you know someone until you know their middle name. What yours?"

"Marie," she said. "Vivian Marie. I think both names were a kind of nod to the French side of my mother's family. So what's yours?"

Morgan paused. "Andrew," he said. "Thomas Andrew. My mom said she never expected me to be a saint, but she could at least give me the names of a couple apostles." He smiled wryly, and she smiled back.

Gradually, they settled into the cushions of the cockpit. She nestled her head onto his chest, and they sat together, continuing to drink their wine. When it was finally finished, he suggested they again go to the Rum Hut for some more piña coladas.

"Sure," she said. "Let's go." She stood and took the remaining wine and left-over snacks below. When she returned, she started the engine, and Morgan raised the anchor for their departure. It was sad to think that Vivian had lost her parents, as he had. They obviously had a great deal in common—more than he had known and more than he could have imagined. Maybe she was the reason he was here. Now, he knew without any question, he'd have to extend his stay.

CHAPTER FIFTEEN

First thing the following morning, before leaving his room, Morgan called the front desk to ask about staying on for another couple of weeks. If he couldn't, he'd have to start looking for another place. The clerk advised that while the hotel was running close to 100 percent occupancy, he could extend for another two weeks if he wished.

"Fine," Morgan said. "Let's do that." It was expensive to continue in the hotel, but he had no mortgage payment at home; he was comfortable at the Harborview; and he was still getting paid. So, he would continue to stay where he was.

During the next few afternoons, he and Vivian also continued sailing to St. John, and Morgan grew more and more confident onboard, whether at the wheel or some other task. He certainly knew port from starboard. He also now knew how to take a compass heading and keep it, even if it became necessary to tack because of wind direction or shifts. He knew the difference between running with the wind, sailing close-hauled almost directly into the wind, and how to sail on a beam reach, at right angles with the true wind. She had also shown him how to raise and lower the main sail and jib; how to crank the slack out of a halyard in order to draw a sail up snug and tight to prevent it from luffing in the wind; even how to properly curl the lines on deck, and more. He also knew where the vessel's gear was stowed, *and* he'd learned the cardinal rule of sailing: never lose track of where you are, for without knowing your present position you cannot know in which direction to sail for your intended destination.

He also became more and more at ease in their afternoon dives. He no longer had to follow the anchor line down to the bottom. They could simply swim down freely. He also became almost unaware of the sound of his breathing, and he didn't use his air as fast. Likewise, he could now, almost without thinking about it, equalize the pressure on his ears, and clear water from his mask by simply exhaling through his nose.

And not only did his confidence below the surface increase with their repeated dives, he learned to identify more of the different kinds of coral and other marine life they encountered, such as Staghorn and Basket

Coral, and others, including the not-to-be-touched Fire Coral. Likewise, different types of sponges such as Tube and Stovepipe and others became readily identifiable, as did virtually every type of fish, from black and white striped French Angels, to unique Fairy Fish—purple on the front of their bodies and bright yellow behind—to Lion Fish, with their many strange, tentacle-like fins which looked very much like the ragged manes of adult male lions. He also learned the several types of so-called "bait fish," such as Shiners, Scad, and Jack Fish, which Vivian said provided the main food source for the Reef Sharks and others.

On their third day of diving, they dropped anchor once again in Cinnamon Bay; and, after descending, they swam along the top of the reef. A little more than twenty minutes into the dive, out of nowhere, it seemed to Morgan, a swarm of bait fish—all Shiners—suddenly appeared in his peripheral vision, and in less than a second they surrounded him like a thousand glistening mirrors. Then they darted swiftly off, pursued, he saw immediately, by a shark eight or ten feet long, with a broad snout, only feet from him. *Christ! A Bull Shark*, he thought. Then there was a another one immediately behind the first, and then a third—headed directly toward him, its mouth open. Morgan had already instinctively grabbed the dive knife strapped to his calf, and he jabbed in the direction of the third shark, gouging a deep hole just behind its gaping mouth. Blood gushed

into the water, and as the shark swam off, Morgan looked
for Vivian, who was already giving him exaggerated gestures that they should head for the surface. Immediately
they began kicking their way to the top, and as they did,
Morgan repeatedly scanned the waters below them for
more sharks, but thankfully he saw none. As soon as
they reached the surface, they sought the stern of the
sloop and the ladder.

"Damn!" he said as he stepped onto the deck and
dropped his dive gear. "That son-of-a-bitch came out of
nowhere. I thought he had me!"

"Yes, I know," Vivian said. She dropped her own gear
and hugged him, hanging on to him for several seconds.

"I think I could use a drink," he said, exhaling audibly. "You have anything stronger than wine?"

Vivian went below and made a rum and Diet Coke for
each of them. She made Morgan's a double, and when
she handed it to him, he took two sizeable swallows.
With the death of his high school friends all those years
ago, later his mom and dad, and later still his friends in
Iraq and then Elaine too, he had come to feel there was
almost no place safe in the world. Now he knew for sure
there wasn't. Not even here.

CHAPTER SIXTEEN

When Morgan picked Vivian up at the gallery the following afternoon, they decided they'd both had enough diving, at least for a while; but they would sail again to St. John and simply enjoy an afternoon at one of the island's beaches. Vivian said she knew a great spot on the south shore not far from Cruz Bay. They could sail there easily, and then afterward go to the Rum Hut. Morgan agreed. He drove them again to Red Hook and the yacht basin; and, like the days before, in no time they were motoring out of the harbor and into open water. When they arrived at the small cove just south of Cruz Bay, he dropped the anchor as usual. Then they inflated the raft Vivian brought up from below and rowed ashore.

It was another beautiful day, with the sun shining warmly; and when they pulled the raft onto the beach, they spread out their towels and lay for a time in the warmth of the sand. Morgan had now been on these islands for almost three weeks. With his daily exposure to the sun, the depth of his tan was nearly equal to hers, and the fringes of his hair had continued to lighten, now to a copper-like, cinnamon color. They talked and laughed. Vivian confessed that she definitely had been attracted to him since that first day they had met, but joked she hadn't known that sharks would be attracted to him as well. They laughed still more, and they kissed several times. She had brought some bottled water and a clump of grapes from the boat; and as they lay there, she offered him one of the grapes, then another. But each time Morgan opened his mouth to receive one of them from her, she quickly pulled it back and popped it into her own mouth. She teased him this way several times, with both of them laughing, until finally she stood and tried to run away with all the remaining grapes. But Morgan chased her and caught her, with both of them laughing and tumbling onto the sand, where they kissed still more, ultimately with passion.

There was almost no one else on the beach, and the few others who were present were a considerable distance away. Morgan reached for one of her breasts; then the other; and then her crotch. She moaned, and he knew if they had been alone, or if it had been dark, they would have had sex then and there. But the fact was, they were not alone, and it was not dark. So he reluctantly allowed the passion to subside, kissed her a few more times, and then he stood. With one hand, he pulled her to her feet. They had been on the beach for nearly an hour, so after arriving back at their towels and the raft, they returned to the *Bon Voyage* and sailed the short distance to Cruz Bay.

When they arrived at the Rum Hut, they sat at a table; and after ordering their usual piña coladas, Morgan excused himself. Once out of Vivian's line of sight, he left the restaurant, hoping to be away for only a few minutes. For the past several days, he had been thinking of a necklace he had seen in the window of a jewelry store, when browsing during their first visit to the town. If it was still there, he *had* to buy it for her. He went quickly to the store he remembered; and when he did not see the necklace in the window, he walked inside and described it to the female clerk, who took him to one of the display cases some distance from the front.

"Is this the one you're talking about?" she asked.

To Morgan's delight, it was. The main body of the necklace was made of very small pieces of pink coral, each rounded and polished to a smooth sheen, like a tiny pearl; and there were strands upon strands of them, strung together and then twisted, giving the necklace the appearance of a soft, languid rope of nearly an inch in thickness. Its two ends were held together at the back with a strong clasp, and opposite the clasp, in the center of the necklace, was its most striking feature—a single, perfect, white sand dollar nearly two inches in diameter. When he had first seen it in the window, he thought it was not only unique, but absolutely beautiful. And viewing it again now, he thought it was both of those things, and more.

"How much is it?" he asked.

She took the necklace from the display case and turned over the small, white tag attached to the clasp with a piece of string. "$1,595.00," she said.

Morgan had prepared himself for a potentially higher price, so he did not hesitate. He produced a credit card; and after completing the purchase, the clerk placed the necklace in a white gift box, which, at Morgan's request, she speedily gift wrapped in some silver paper. Afterward she put the wrapped box in a plastic bag with the store's name on it, and Morgan quickly retraced his steps to the Rum Hut. When he arrived, he did not try to hide the bag, but simply placed it on their table in such a way that the store name was hidden. Vivian looked at it inquisitively and then at Morgan.

"So what's in the bag?" she asked.

He smiled slightly, knowing he had piqued her interest and that he had a secret he would not reveal—at least not for a while. "Oh, just a little something I picked up at a store."

"What kind of store?" she asked.

"Oh, just a store down the street," he said playfully.

"Aren't you going to let me see what's inside?"

"Maybe, if you're good," he said, smiling and teasing her, as she had teased him with the grapes. "I'll show you when we get back to the boat."

His piña colada was there on the table, still untouched. He picked it up, raised his glass between them, invited her to do likewise, and then he offered a toast.

"To us," he said. And they sipped from their glasses.

During their dinner, he noticed that she looked repeatedly at the bag. In fact, it appeared to him she could hardly keep her eyes from it. So when they stepped aboard the boat, he asked her to join him on the cushions of the cockpit; and when she was seated beside him, he took the box from the plastic bag and handed it to her. "I hope you like it," he said.

Vivian took the box in her hands, carefully removed the wrapping paper, and lifted off the top, revealing the necklace nestled on some white velvet.

"Oh, Tom," she said slowly. "It's beautiful!" He could hear the earnestness in her voice. She took it from the box and held it up with both hands. "I absolutely love it!" Then she clutched it to the top of her chest near her throat. "Here," she said, handing it to him and turning slightly. "Help me put it on!"

Morgan took the necklace from her, separated the clasp, placed it around her neck, and latched it.

She looked down and placed her right hand on it, and then turned to face him directly. "Tom, I absolutely *love* it!" she said once again, with even more emphasis than before, and she leaned forward and kissed him—enthusiastically at first, and then once again, more softly, and finally, very tenderly. She looked into his eyes. "It's the most wonderful, beautiful gift anyone has ever given me."

Morgan doubted the full truth of her statement, but he was definitely pleased that she liked it.

"I liked it," he said. "And I hoped you would too."

"Oh I do, I do!" she repeated. She kissed him again, and they sat without talking for a moment, her head against Morgan's chest and her right hand continuing to touch the necklace. "There's just one thing I have to ask," she added. "This isn't some kind of good-bye gift, is it? I mean, you haven't decided to go back to Chicago, have you?"

Morgan sat up straight so he could look directly into her eyes, and he placed his hands on her upper arms near her shoulders.

"Oh, no," he said, continuing to look at her earnestly. "Not at all. In fact, I have to tell you, Vivian, I've started thinking I just may not go back. Things being how they are now, here with you, I'm not sure how I can. I've been thinking about moving out of the hotel and getting a place of my own—at least for a while, so we might see how things go."

"Oh, Tom," she said. She leaned forward and kissed him. "You have no idea how much I've been hoping you'd say something like that." She kissed him again, and he kissed her back. Then she nestled under his arm even more snugly than before, and with her head on his chest, she held his hand close to her heart.

They sat this way for some time, not moving and not speaking, and he thought about her words. Perhaps he had not known how much she had been hoping he would stay. On the other hand, what she did not know was that, for him, these past few days had been more wonderful than he could ever have imagined. While from time to time he'd had thoughts of Elaine and her killers, just being with her had eased the ache in his heart, and she had, without knowing it, provided a kind of passage for him, not unlike the cruise ships he knew at this very moment to be languishing at the docks in Charlotte Amalie. Just as they take their passengers from one place to another, she had carried him out of the darkness and misery that had been his life and brought him to this new place, giving him a kind of peace he had not known, perhaps ever, and he thought he was starting to truly love her. As they continued to sit motionless, the afternoon light was beginning to fade. Then, suddenly, she sat upright, as if startled.

"Oh my God," she said. "I almost forgot."

"Forgot what?" Morgan said, sitting up straighter himself.

"Charlie invited us to come over to his place this evening and—I hope you don't mind—I accepted without asking you." Morgan responded that he did not mind. At the same time, he was uncertain how another meeting with Petersen might go, considering he knew that he was responsible for that midnight visitor to his room.

"Well, I guess we should get going, then," he said. "Why don't you give him a call? I'll get us ready to push off."

CHAPTER SEVENTEEN

Arriving back in Charlotte Amalie, Vivian gave directions to Petersen's house, which was high up on one of the hillsides above downtown. It was well past dark when the headlights of the Jeep shone onto the iron gates at the entrance to Petersen's drive. Morgan pulled up near the call box, and Vivian reached across him to push the button and let her brother know they had arrived.

"OK, we're here, finally," she said.

The gates slowly swung open, and they drove up the short remaining distance to the house, which had a commanding view of the city lights and the harbor spread out below. There were three cars already parked in front of the house—one of which was a large, black Mercedes sedan, which Morgan thought was almost certainly Petersen's, since the other two automobiles were more modest by comparison. He could not anticipate what this meeting with Petersen would be like. While he did not feel at all timid about it, he had found this wonderful woman, and he did not want to have any kind of confrontation with her brother that might affect his relationship with her—or the way she was obviously beginning to feel about him. He parked alongside the other cars, turned the Jeep's lights and engine off, and together they walked toward the front door.

The house was a two-story stucco, which in the darkness appeared to be light-gray or perhaps white, with black or very dark shutters at the windows and heavy stones inset at the corners and around the front doorway. The outside lights were on, softly illuminating the shrubbery and walkway.

"I just love this house," she said. "This is where Charlie and I grew up. Then, after Daddy got killed, Charlie moved back in. We both own it, but I think Charlie figures it's his now—especially since he's running the businesses."

Vivian opened the front door and announced, "Hey, it's us!"

When they walked inside, Morgan surveyed the sizable foyer with its two, matching, curved staircases and white tile floor that led to a large and comfortable-looking family room with several couches. Off to one side, Petersen called back.

"Come on in," he said. "We're in the kitchen."

They walked across the tile of the foyer. Vivian dropped her purse onto one of the sofas in the family room, and they turned into the kitchen, where Petersen, a blond woman, and two other men were sitting at a large, granite-topped center island.

"Hi, Hon," Petersen said from his seat on one of the barstools. Then he quickly added, "Hi, Tom. How you been?" His voice was neither sarcastic nor particularly friendly.

"Just fine, Charlie. We've been having a lot of fun." Morgan put his arm around Vivian's shoulders as she stood beside him, and he pulled her close. She smiled and looked up at him.

"So I hear," Petersen said. "Here, let me introduce you to everybody. This is my fiancée, Allison," he said, gesturing to the blond, who was half standing and half sitting on Petersen's lap. She was wearing white shorts and a tight-fitting, red top that ended just below her sizable breasts, and she smiled an engaging smile. Morgan nodded and smiled a pleasant hello in return.

"And these two guys, Jim…and Mike here…are good friends. Guys, this is Tom Morgan."

Morgan shook hands with the two men and again nodded and smiled hello. Both appeared to be somewhere in their thirties. The one Petersen had called Jim was the larger of the two, heavier muscled, with a crew cut and a noticeable scar on his jaw. The other one, who had his hair buzzed off in a sort of boot-camp crop, had a big nose and tattoos on his forearms. Both men looked as though they lifted weights, as did Petersen, especially now that Morgan could see him with his jacket off.

"So, can we get you something to eat?" Petersen asked. "We've already eaten, but we can warm something up for you."

"Actually, Charlie," Vivian said, "we've already eaten too. We were out on the boat all afternoon, and I forgot about our plans for tonight until just a while ago when I called. I think we'd both like to get freshened up, though, if we could. Can I show Tom to one of the bathrooms?"

"Sure, Hon, go ahead." Petersen sipped at his drink, and then pushed at the ends of his moustache with his index finger.

Vivian took Morgan by the hand, and together they walked to the foyer and up one of the stairways to a large, lavish bath, where she pointed out the soaps, shampoos, and other toiletries.

"Make yourself comfortable," she said. "I'll make you a drink while you get your shower."

"Sure you don't want to stay and wash my back?" he asked, smiling a flirtatious smile.

"I will...one of these days," she said with a smile mimicking his own. Then she ducked out of the room and pulled the door partially closed behind her.

Morgan took a quick shower, dressed again, and returned to the kitchen, where Vivian had a rum and Diet Coke with a wedge of lime waiting for him.

"Here you go, Honey," she said.

Morgan noticed immediately that she had now called him that for a second time, and now in front of her brother. He wondered if the word had just slipped out, or if it had been an intentional signal to Petersen about how close they had become.

"OK, it's my turn," she said, and she started toward the foyer and the stairs.

Morgan watched Petersen's eyes follow his sister as she left the kitchen. Then he saw Petersen gesture to Allison that she should follow.

"I'll come too," Allison called out, "and get you some fresh towels." She stopped leaning on Petersen and headed for the foyer, her large breasts bouncing as she walked quickly from the room.

Petersen looked at his two friends. "Why don't you guys go on and take care of those things we were talking about earlier? Maybe I'll get Tom here to play a game of pool."

As the two men left the kitchen and walked toward the front door, Peterson stood up.

"C'mon, Tom. Let's have a game."

Morgan picked up his drink, and they walked across the foyer, beneath one of the stairways to a set of double doors, which, when Petersen opened them, revealed a game room with a pool table at its center. Petersen turned on the lights, adjusting them with the rheostat to a dim glow. Then he flipped on the low-hanging light fixture, which, with its shade, cast a bright light directly down onto the table's smooth, black felt. There was a triangle of balls already in place, and Morgan could also see a fully-stocked bar as well as several trophies of Marlin, Dolphin, Barracuda, and a small Hammerhead Shark decorating the walls. He sat his drink down on the granite-topped bar.

"So, how have we been treating you at the hotel?" Petersen asked, looking at him with what Morgan thought might have been a knowing smile.

"Just fine," Morgan said. "Although I did have a strange visitor in my room—later the same night I met you, as a matter of fact." Morgan had not actually planned to bring the subject up, until Petersen mentioned the hotel. But then, having said it, he eyed Petersen to catch his reaction.

"Oh?" Petersen responded casually. He removed the triangle from the rack of balls, then walked over to the cue sticks mounted on the wall, selected one for himself, and handed one to Morgan, tip first. Then he walked with his cue to the other end of the table, opposite Morgan. "What kind of visitor?" he asked as he applied some chalk to his cue and then tossed the chalk cube to Morgan.

"I think you know," Morgan said unflinchingly as he caught it with his left hand. He applied the chalk to his own cue, then lifted the butt of the stick off the floor and held it horizontally in both hands, as if ready to do battle.

"Really?" Petersen asked.

"Well, she said you sent her." Morgan paused without saying more for the moment.

"Me?" Petersen said as he leaned forward to break the nest of balls. His black hair shone in the low-hanging light. "Eight Ball," he added, just before he drew back and stroked firmly with his stick, making the cue ball hit the others with a loud crack. The balls ricocheted back and forth across the table, with the one and the seven dropping neatly into two of the table's pockets.

"Yeah, she said you gave her a key." Morgan eyed Petersen steadily as they both moved around the table.

"Really," Petersen said again as he circled to the other side, and Morgan moved as well, as if sparring with him, maintaining a position opposite Petersen. Again Petersen leaned forward, preparing to take a shot. "Why would she say a thing like that?" Again he stroked firmly, sending the cue ball swiftly toward the three, which was perched precariously close to the pocket nearest Morgan. But the shot was delivered too forcefully, and the three did not drop but instead rebounded from the pocket.

With a clear shot on the fifteen, Morgan circled the table, continuing to eye Petersen carefully. Then he leaned forward himself, his head low, and took aim at the ball, the light from above accentuating the cinnamon-colored fringes of his hair. He fired a shot that smashed the fifteen hard into the corner pocket directly in front of Petersen.

"She said you wanted her to be nice to me." Morgan looked up and continued to eye Petersen.

"And what did you say?"

Morgan circled the table again, considering the potential shots, and then he leaned forward once more, the intensity of the light from above again accentuating the cinnamon-colored fringes of his hair. "I told her to get the hell out." He stroked the cue hard, this time hitting and dropping the eleven. He stood up.

"Tom, let me be frank," Petersen said. "Guys like you come down here thinking you're going to have a good time, and I don't object to that. I just don't want it to be at my sister's expense."

"What do you mean, at her expense?" Morgan said, glaring at him.

"Look, don't play innocent with me," Petersen said. "I'm sure it hasn't escaped your attention that my sister's got money. And I don't want somebody trying to take advantage of her. It's happened before, and I don't want to see it happen again."

"I don't care about your sister's money!" Morgan fired back quickly. He circled the table and took aim once again, this time sending the cue ball racing in the direction of the ten, which grazed another ball on its way to the pocket, and it did not drop. He stood again.

"You must be kidding," Petersen said. "Everybody cares about money. And what can you possibly give her, with your little government job?" He leaned forward, his black hair shining once again under the light. He took aim at the six, slamming it into the side pocket nearest the bar. "And knowing what I know of my sister," he continued, "if I should tell her about that little visitor you asked me to send up to your room, that would be the end of you." Petersen stood and leaned firmly on his cue stick. "So, my advice to you is go on back to Chicago. There's nothing for you down here in the Virgin Islands."

Morgan felt his face growing red and anger welling up inside him. He thought he might explode if he didn't get some release. He clenched his teeth tightly, trying to maintain his composure, and watched Petersen scan the balls still on the table and then lean forward. He stroked the cue, this time sending the five ball speeding straight into the pocket in front of Morgan. Morgan's eyes followed him as he stood up, and for a moment he felt like going over to the man and grabbing him by the throat. At that very moment, however, he saw Vivian and Allison returning from upstairs, approaching the doors to the game room.

"OK, all cleaned up!" Vivian announced, sounding as refreshed as she looked. "By the way, Charlie," she added, "what do you think of the necklace Tom got me?" She put her hand up to the necklace, and Petersen looked briefly in her direction.

"OK, I guess. Looks a little cheap," he said.

"Charlie!" she exclaimed, almost yelling at him. "I think it's beautiful!"

Morgan looked briefly at Petersen, still wanting to throttle him, and then back at Vivian.

"You know what, Charlie?" she said. "I think we'll just leave."

"You want to leave?" Petersen asked. "Just because I told you what I think?"

"You're damn right!" she said. "I don't know why you had to say such a thing. We're out of here!"

In a way, Morgan was disappointed that he would be leaving the game before dealing with Petersen. At the same time, he felt no small amount of contempt for the man, and he was happy to leave his presence, and his home.

"Maybe we can pick this up another time," he said to Petersen. He replaced his cue stick in the rack on the wall and walked toward Vivian, trying not to show his anger, as well as the disdain he felt for the man, his money, and his bad manners. He walked with Vivian toward the front door.

"Well, I guess we'll see you later," Petersen called out behind them.

"Yeah, see you," Allison added, sounding as if she were genuinely trying to remain friendly. Morgan did not respond to either overture, and when they arrived outside, he and Vivian sat in the Jeep without speaking. Ultimately she broke the silence.

"I hope you can forgive my brother," she said. "He can be really nice, but sometimes he can be an absolute jerk."

For a moment Morgan said nothing. He now knew that Petersen was not only ill-mannered, but a real son-of-a-bitch. He could, of course, when the occasion called for it, put up a façade and sound gentlemanly and sincere. But in reality, Morgan knew he was, as his sister had said, an absolute jerk, to say the very least.

"Where would you like to go?" he asked as he turned the Jeep's headlights on and started slowly down the driveway.

"I don't know. I just want to get out of here. Tell you what," she added, "there's a local hangout called the Purple Parrot not far from here. It's a little hole-in-the-wall kind of place, but it can be fun. Let's go there."

Morgan drove down the road several hundred yards and made a few turns as Vivian directed, eventually reaching Waterfront Drive. There he turned right, and after only a couple of blocks, he turned left and arrived at a dingy, dark-green, one-story building that looked as if it had not been painted since it was built—most likely decades earlier. He pulled into the gravel parking lot, where there was an ancient streetlight that seeped soft, yellow light out into the night air and onto the cars already parked there. A purple neon sign on top of the building flashed the words "Purple Parrot" as well as an outline image of the bird itself. Other neon signs in the bar's windows advertised a variety of beers, but there were no other lights in the immediate area. Morgan found a parking space.

"You sure this place is OK?" he asked.

"Oh, it's fine," she said. "I know the people here."

He shut the Jeep off, and they walked to the front of the building, through a screen door that slammed behind them, and then across the worn linoleum floor to the bar, where there were a number of round, swivel stools covered with red vinyl—most of which were cracked or torn from age or wear, or both. The conversations of the customers, mostly black, filled the air, and a jukebox played lively music in the background. They sat down on two of the vinyl-covered stools.

"Good evenin', Miss Petersen," said the heavyset black woman standing behind the bar. "Long time since we see you." She smiled, looking at Vivian and then at Morgan. "What can we get for you?" Her voice seemed genuinely friendly.

"How about a couple of beers?" Morgan said, looking at Vivian and wrinkling his forehead into a question as he looked at her. She nodded affirmatively.

"You got it," the woman said. She turned to one side to gather up two bottles of beer, which she produced, dripping water from the cooler. She wiped the bottles on the white apron that hung from around her neck, popped off the tops, and sat them on the bar.

"Glasses?" she asked.

"No, these will be fine," Vivian said, smiling at her kindly. Morgan handed one of the beers to Vivian and picked up the other one for himself. He looked into her eyes, then at the necklace he had given her only a few hours earlier, and then back into her eyes. He raised his bottle and offered a toast.

"Here's to the most beautiful woman in the Virgin Islands," he said. Then he drank from his beer and lowered it, keeping it in his right hand, which he rested on his thigh. Vivian was holding her beer in one hand as well; and, leaning forward, she placed her other hand on the red vinyl top of his bar stool, carefully, almost teasingly, between his legs.

"And how would you know a thing like that?" she asked, smiling, close to his face. "You haven't seen all the women here."

Morgan looked more deeply into her eyes. True, he had not. But there was no mistake. In fact, she was not only the most beautiful woman in the Virgin Islands. To him she was the most beautiful woman in the entire world, and he knew he loved her. But as much as her beauty, he loved her strength, her character, her candor, her willingness to stick up for him with her brother, even the playfulness she was now showing. In fact, he couldn't think of anything he didn't love about her. The jukebox was now playing a slow, romantic melody in the background.

"Let's dance," he said.

They placed their beers on the bar. He took her hand, and they walked between the few tables to an area near the jukebox, where he took her in his arms. But unlike that night when they danced for the first time at the Sundowner, she placed her head softly against his chest, and he could feel all the curves of her body close to his own. They moved as if they were one, and when the music stopped, they kissed before returning to their barstools. With a temporary lull in the music, Morgan thought he heard cheers and shouts coming from what he could only guess was a back room.

"What's that?" he asked, nodding in the direction of the sounds, but only half expecting she might know the answer.

"Oh, they have cock fights back there sometimes," she said. "Sounds like they're going tonight. Want to see?"

Morgan looked at her inquisitively. "Sure. Why not?" he said.

They stood and walked from the bar to the back wall, where there was a heavy door with a metal pull handle. They opened it and walked into the room, joining no fewer than thirty or forty people crowded into the space. In the center of the room, suspended from the ceiling, hung a single, green-shaded lightbulb, which shone downward, illuminating the floor below, where there was painted a black circle eight to ten feet in diameter. Against the wall opposite the entrance were stacked several wood and wire cages, which Morgan could see were the quarters for the combatants.

The smell of smoke and sweat filled the close, hot air of the room, and two combination barkers and referees stood in the ring. One, a black man approaching middle age, had a thick build and wore a white ball cap. The other, also black but thinner, wore a T-shirt with a pocket that held a package of cigarettes. Morgan pressed as close as possible at the back of the crowd of onlookers, and Vivian peeked over the shoulders of some as well.

The first cock, brought out by the handler with the thick build and white cap, was a vigorous-looking bird, Morgan thought, with reddish-brown or cinnamon-colored feathers that included flashes of black at his neck and in his tail feathers—the latter of which arched nicely and shone brilliantly beneath the light. His large, red comb flopped over handsomely to one side, and his spurs extended nearly two inches from the backs of his legs. His handler held him up in the air with both hands, and, amid the cheers and shouts of the crowd, he walked the bird around inside the circle so that all might see and admire him. He was obviously a fighter, and Morgan liked the bird instinctively.

The smaller, thinner handler, with the pack of cigarettes in his shirt pocket, brought out the second bird—this one coal black in color. And while this bird appeared to be slightly smaller than the first, it too had a large comb that flopped to one side and the long, spiked spurs of a fighting cock. As the second handler held the bird up and carried him around inside the ring, Morgan noted that his plumage, despite its overall blackness, here and there appeared greenish-purple, giving him an almost regal appearance. His tail feathers crested and hung elegantly, and the crowd cheered at the sight of him, simultaneously giving out thunderous claps and whistles. Morgan thought the black bird showed a kind of arrogance that he did not like, and while he would undoubtedly prove a worthy opponent, Morgan wanted all the more to see the first bird win.

Some members of the crowd began to place bets. Morgan took a twenty-dollar bill from his pocket and pressed it into the hand of the handler with the white cap. The man smiled at Morgan and returned to him four, round, green tokens.

In the growing excitement and close heat of the room, Morgan could feel the sweat building on his forehead and under his arms. His eyes caught Vivian's as she watched with interest that seemed keen but somewhat less than his own.

When all bets had been placed, the two handlers paused momentarily opposite each other within the circle and began baiting and teasing the birds, moving them into close proximity to one another, circling and encouraging their excitement and anger. With the first pass, the neck feathers of the cocks raised instinctively, and though their wings were clasped firmly against their bodies by their handlers, the birds nevertheless tried to lash out with their beaks and spurs. The first attempted attack came from the black, which was immediately returned by the cinnamon-colored bird. There appeared to be a fury in the eyes of both, as they kept their neck feathers furled out full and kicked vigorously with their legs, each in a futile attempt to reach the other. After three or four such passes, the handlers bent down, quickly dropped the birds inside the black-outlined circle, and immediately stepped back.

The cocks eyed one another unflinchingly, with their heads moving up and down beneath the light, only inches from the floor, neck feathers furled and wings spread. As one bird raised its head in order to gain some advantage, the other immediately mimicked the movement. Then, suddenly, both birds sprang up and forward, simultaneously pecking wildly and lashing out with their long, spiked talons. Time after time they repeated their attacks, and for a while neither gained an advantage. The black would lash out, striking sharply at the other bird, but he would be met instantly with a series of counter moves of equal or greater fury from the cinnamon-colored bird, jumping and gouging with his spurs, trying to drive them into the smaller bird's face. But as the smaller, black cock launched yet another attack, in one quick slash of a talon he left a gash over the left eye of the cinnamon-colored bird. The cut began to ooze blood, and the bird instinctively shook his head as if to shake off the sting of the wound. As a few drops of blood splattered onto the floor inside the circle, the cinnamon-colored cock suddenly bounded upward once again and attacked the other bird, toppling him backward and bloodying his face. The handlers instantly retrieved both birds, grabbing them and collapsing their wings against their sides in a single motion.

Morgan was startled at how swiftly the fight had ended, but at least the cinnamon-colored cock had retaliated, and won. As Morgan collected his winnings, he thought how much the fight reminded him of his exchange an hour earlier with Petersen. He only wished he'd had the opportunity to unleash his anger on the man, as the cinnamon-colored cock had on the other bird.

CHAPTER EIGHTEEN

The following morning Morgan awoke early, showered and shaved, and left the Harborview to begin looking for an apartment. He was determined to stay on the island with Vivian. But he would not stay in Petersen's hotel another day. He drove into downtown, picked up a magazine advertising apartments and houses for rent, and began scouring the ads, focusing on those that were furnished and within the city. When he had narrowed his search to the two or three that fit his criteria, he called about the one at the top of his list—a small bungalow that appeared to sit somewhat close to the street but nevertheless looked reasonably hospitable. The agent verified that indeed it was still for rent, and it was furnished, just as advertised. He agreed to meet Morgan at eleven o'clock and then provided directions to Symington Street, where the house was located. Within only a few minutes, Morgan was on Symington, looking for the house number and sign in the window, as the agent had described.

Some of the houses in the immediate area were small, stucco bungalows, while others were ancient, two-story structures built of stone. All sat close to the street, without front lawns. Many, however, did have potted flowers or bougainvillea or wisteria clinging to their exterior walls, which added both softness and color to the area, despite the general absence of lawns.

Suddenly, there was the house number Morgan had been looking for, with a "For Rent" sign in the window bearing the name and telephone number of the agent to whom he'd spoken. The house looked as if it had recently been painted a soft, yellow-cream color, and it had a reddish, terra cotta tile roof. To one side stood one of the ancient-looking, stone, two-story homes, built in the style of the old Danes, with strong, impenetrable-looking shutters at the windows and doors. On the other side was a paved parking area, barely large enough to accommodate the Jeep and one other vehicle—and beyond that, yet another ancient, two-story home. Morgan pulled the Jeep into the parking area and scanned the exterior of the bungalow, which included a purple bougainvillea clinging to the wall near the front door and four, perfectly-matched, arched windows, two on each side of the entrance.

When the real estate agent arrived, he showed Morgan through the interior, which Morgan liked immediately. Just inside the front door and on the right was a living room, with a set of arched windows that looked out to the street, a comfortable-looking couch, a coffee table, a couple of overstuffed chairs, and a television. On the opposite side of the entry, a bedroom with windows matching those of the living room also looked out onto the street in front. In the rear, behind the living room, a kitchen was outfitted with all the necessary appliances, including a refrigerator, oven, microwave, toaster, and coffee maker. The cabinets even held dishes, pots and pans, and silverware. Next to the kitchen, the single bath that served the house had a tub with a shower, and on the other side of the bath the second bedroom had French doors, which, like the single door from the kitchen, led out onto a patio. Beyond the patio's short perimeter wall stood a cluster of trees that very nearly blocked the view of the houses behind. While it was more than adequate for Morgan's needs, he indeed liked it.

The agent said the house had most recently been used as a seasonal rental, and if he wished—with an adequate security deposit—he could rent it for one, two, or three weeks, or a month, his choice. However, the monthly rate was considerably less, especially since it was now June and the beginning of the off-season. Morgan definitely wanted out of the Harborview. Furthermore, when the agent told him the monthly rate, he quickly calculated that it was barely one-fourth the cost of staying in the hotel, *and* it was less than a half mile from Vivian's condo. It seemed perfect. He signed the lease for a full month, gave the agent a check covering the deposit and first month's rent, and in return he received a set of keys. Now, he had only to go back to the hotel and collect his things, which he determined he would do in short order. Then he would call Vivian and tell her about his new place.

Back at the Harborview, he packed; and before closing his larger bag, he called the front desk, advising the male clerk that something had come up. He now needed to check out earlier than expected and asked if he would get his paperwork ready. After the call, he closed his bag and walked once more out onto the balcony. In one direction he could see the city, still spread out colorfully along the sweeping arch of the harbor. In the other direction, cruise ships continued to be moored at their docks, just as every day and night since his arrival. Smaller boats also moved about. The view was as beautiful as ever. But he could not continue to stay in Petersen's hotel. He *would not*. He picked up his bags and went to the front desk to complete his checkout. Then he drove to the bungalow and called Vivian.

"Hello!" he said, allowing his voice to convey the excitement he felt.

"Hi!" she responded. "I was wondering when I was going to hear from you. Where are you?"

"I'm standing in my new place on Symington."

"What? You're kidding!" she said, sounding both surprised that he had found a place so quickly and gleeful at the same time.

"No, I'm not kidding. I just rented it this morning."

"You'll be so close to me!" she said. "What's it like?"

Morgan briefly described the house, acknowledging that it was small but, at the same time, really all he needed.

"When can I see it?"

"Whenever you want," he said. "Now, if you like!"

She said she had some things to finish at the gallery, but she would be there in less than twenty minutes. Then she added, "I have a surprise for you too!"

"What kind of surprise?" he asked.

"Oh, just a surprise," she said whimsically. "I'll tell you when I get there."

They hung up, and he took his bags to the back bedroom to start unpacking. When Vivian arrived and he opened the door, she kissed him immediately.

"I just can't believe you've found this place—and so soon!" she said excitedly. "And so close to me!" She almost squealed when she said it, and she jumped into his arms and kissed him again.

He showed her around the bungalow, including the small patio out back. "What do you think of it?" he asked.

"It's really cute," she said. "I love it."

Morgan grinned, feeling some sense of satisfaction at having found such a relatively nice place. In fact, he could hardly believe it, since it had happened so quickly. It was also good to be sharing the excitement with her. And he was out of the Harborview!

"Now, what's the surprise you have for me?" He paused and waited.

"Well, the weekend is coming up," she began slowly, "and I thought it would be fun if we sailed down to St. Croix. I haven't been down there for some time, and I'd like to show it to you, if you'd like to see it!"

"Are you kidding?" he said. "I'd love to!" It would give him another opportunity to exercise his newly-acquired sailing skills and to see another of the islands. Besides, it would put some distance between himself and Petersen, if only for a couple of days. In any case it should make for an interesting weekend with her.

"Oh, wonderful!" she said. "Now, I want to get back to the gallery for a little while, but I'll come back later; and then let's go out and celebrate. What do you say?"

"Sure!" he responded. He had this new place, and they were going to have an exciting weekend. He definitely felt a celebration was in order.

She left, giving him another kiss, and he used the afternoon to finish unpacking, go to the grocery for a few staples, and get ready for their evening. It was just a little past five o'clock when she arrived back at the bungalow, and she let herself in.

"I'm here," she said as she opened the door. And as Morgan came from the bedroom and walked toward her, she dropped her purse onto one of the living room chairs, rushed toward him, and kissed him.

"I'm so excited," she said. "Do you have anything to drink?" Clearly she was in the mood to celebrate.

"I have both rum and wine," he said. "You want some wine?"

"Yes, I'd love some." She followed him into the kitchen.

"Red or white?" he asked.

"How about red?" she said.

Morgan pulled a bottle of merlot from the refrigerator, opened it, and poured the deep-red liquid into two short, clear glasses without stems. She smiled, and they sipped at the wine.

"Now, I've got something to show you," she said. "I brought a sailing chart for us to look at." She nearly ran into the living room and retrieved a sizable piece of folded paper from her purse. Then she returned to the kitchen and unfolded it on top of the small table. They stood looking at it and both sipped again at the wine.

"OK. Here we are up here," she said, pointing to St. Thomas and St. John. "And here's St. Croix, down here, about forty miles south." She gestured with her right hand, smoothing her fingers in a southerly direction along the surface of the chart, indicating a destination along a line of longitude due south. Morgan scrutinized the lines of both longitude and latitude as she spoke.

He was entirely familiar with map reading. He'd done plenty of it in the corps. But he had not known that St. Croix was forty miles away.

"With the trade winds coming mostly from the east," she continued, "we'll obviously have to do a bit of tacking. But if we can maintain at least eight to ten knots, we should get down to the port at Christiansted within four to five hours. If we leave Red Hook fairly early, say by eight o'clock or so, we should get there by one, or maybe a little after. Worst case scenario, if we have to do a lot of tacking, we'll still arrive by mid-afternoon. Then we'll have the remainder of the day and night to explore, and at least a good part of Sunday." She drank again from her glass. "What do you think?"

"I think it sounds great," Morgan said.

They took their wine into the living room and sat on the couch, continuing to talk about the upcoming sail. After a time Morgan looked at his watch, noting it was already past six o'clock, and he was getting hungry.

"Tell you what," he said. "Let's go get something to eat—and we'll celebrate! Where would you like to go?"

"Let's try the Sea House," she said. "It's nice, and it has a great view of the harbor."

When they finished their wine, they left in the Jeep and made their way through the twists and turns of the few short blocks leading down to the harbor. Then they turned right on Waterfront and traveled another few short blocks. They found a parking space and walked up the flight of steps to the restaurant—on the second floor, above some shops. Morgan had not been there before, but he asked that they be seated near one of the front windows, which, as Vivian had said, gave them an excellent view of the harbor. He pulled one of the chairs out for her, seating her across from him, and then seated himself. He thought their celebration required that they each have at least two glasses of wine, so he ordered a bottle. And when the wine arrived, they toasted heartily—to his new home *and* to their sail to St. Croix. They clinked their glasses together, and while it caused him to think for a moment about Elaine, he knew this was a night for celebrating, so he forced himself to think only of this time, in this place. The waiter came once again, and after giving him their dinner order, they continued to sip their wine and talk until the meal arrived.

Gradually, the sun began to set; and with daylight growing dim, the waiter returned, lit the small candle on their table, and poured the remainder of the wine into their glasses. They held hands, and in the soft glow of the candlelight, Morgan thought she looked as radiant as on that first night during dinner at the Harborview—only now he loved her, and he was pretty sure she loved him.

"Here's to us," he said as he raised his glass, "and to a wonderful weekend." Again they clinked their glasses together and drank deeply.

Finally, the waiter returned with their check. Morgan paid the tab, and they finished the last of their wine and left.

Back at his place, they stood close together outside, holding on to each other between the Jeep and her Mercedes. "Want to come in for a nightcap?" he asked. He hoped she would say yes—and perhaps even spend the night.

"Oh, I'd love to, Tom, believe me," she said softly. "I'd love to. I want to be with you. But of all things, it's just not a good time of month right now, you know. But everything should be back to normal in a day or so, and I want things to be perfect for us. Can I give you a rain check?"

Morgan paused. "All right," he said finally, with some reluctance. "A rain check. But I'm holding you to it," he said as he continued to hold on to her and tug at her waist. He smiled faintly, but he couldn't hide the fact that he was disappointed, nor did he want to. At the same time, he knew he had to acquiesce. "What time shall I pick you up in the morning?"

"If we're going to leave Red Hook by eight, I'd say not later than seven thirty."

"OK. I'll be there by seven thirty."

She got into her car, and he leaned forward and kissed her through the open, driver's-side window.

"I'm so happy you're here, Tom. I really, really am. We'll have a wonderful weekend. I promise."

He kissed her once again. Then he stood while she backed the Mercedes out of the parking space. He watched the car's taillights disappear at the end of the street, and inside the bungalow, as he prepared to turn in, he thought more about their sail to St. Croix. He hoped it would be a fair day tomorrow, and he looked forward to it being the wonderful weekend she'd promised.

CHAPTER NINETEEN

The anticipation Morgan felt about their upcoming weekend made him sleep somewhat uneasily. He awoke at daybreak, fixed a pot of coffee, and walked out onto his patio. Looking up, he could see no clouds in the early-morning sky. He went back inside; showered; dressed in a pair of cargo shorts, a polo shirt, and boat shoes; then tossed his shaving gear, his bathing suit, and a change of clothes into his carry-on and called Vivian to let her know he would be there in just a few minutes. When he arrived, she came out with a small bag of her own and a cooler. She had made sandwiches for the trip and packed a few soft drinks. He loaded her bag and the cooler into the back of the Jeep; then they drove down to the harbor and Route 30. It was just after 8:00 a.m. when they pulled into the parking lot at the yacht basin in Red Hook.

"Looks like a great day for sailing," she said.

Except for a few thin clouds scattered in the east, the sky was an uninterrupted, endless blue. They unlocked the cabin and went below. Vivian put the sandwiches and drinks in the galley's refrigerator, and then checked the weather report on the local weather channel. All appeared clear.

Before leaving the yacht basin, they stopped at the fueling station to top off the tank, and by 8:30 they were motoring out into the bay toward open water. She asked Morgan to take the wheel; then she hoisted the main sail and jib. Both sails caught the wind and billowed out full. The trade winds were coming easy from the east.

"You want me to stay at the helm, or you want to take it?" he asked.

"Why don't you keep it, at least for now?" she said. "You're doing fine."

Together they set the sloop on a course ten degrees west of due south. The gentle breeze felt invigorating and slightly cool at this relatively early hour, and the sloop moved along nearly silently, with the sails filled and the bow cresting and falling lightly over the steady stream of oncoming waves. Vivian made coffee below, poured some into two Styrofoam cups and then came up topside and handed one to Morgan. They were making good time, and, after a little more than an hour, St. Thomas and St. John were beginning to disappear behind them.

They had anticipated that as long as the winds continued from the east, they probably could continue to sail close-hauled, with the sails nearly parallel with the centerline of the sloop. In this way they should be able to maintain their heading mostly south, without the necessity of a great deal of tacking. But after an hour or so, the wind began to shift—only a little at first, but then more, and then more still—until it came nearly directly from the south, making it necessary to adjust their heading considerably. Now they changed course and sailed in a southeasterly direction for nearly half an hour; then they came about so as to head in a southwesterly direction for an almost equal period of time. These course corrections meant sailing a greater distance overall, and since they were also traveling at a reduced speed—tacking as they were toward a windward objective—Morgan knew without her saying anything it would now take considerably more time to complete the trip. Nevertheless, from sailing around St. John during the previous days, he had gained some proficiency in tacking this way; and with assurance from Vivian on the foredeck that they should again adjust their course, he would do so, calling out to her.

"Ready about!" he would say. Then she would take the line controlling the jib and stand at the ready.

"Hard alee!" he would then call out, just before swinging the bow into and then past the direction of the wind, forcing the jib to the other side of the mast, where it and the main sail would once again take up the wind.

They continued tacking in this way, making course corrections from time to time, and at those times they would watch each other—Morgan at the helm and Vivian on the foredeck. She would smile in his direction, and he would smile back, pleased with the way they were working together as a coordinated team of two.

By mid-morning the sun was warming the air noticeably. The sloop continued pushing through the water, and Morgan motioned for her to join him at the helm. The wind had picked up, and he judged their forward speed to be close to eight knots.

"You still OK with me at the wheel?" he asked somewhat loudly.

"Sure. You're doing fine!"

"OK," he said. "So why don't you tell me what we're going to do when we get to St. Croix?"

She smiled. "Well, first of all, I want to show you around Christiansted," she said, letting the wind push her hair back, away from her face. "It's a beautiful old town with lots of history. There's an old fort and a number of other historical buildings. But there are also modern hotels and shops and restaurants. I made a reservation for us at a quaint little inn that I know right in town. It's really very nice. I also want to take you out into the countryside and show you the plantation and the Great House there, built by my great-great-grandfather.

It's a beautiful old place, although Charlie did tell me he's been using it as a warehouse sometimes to store some of the sugar we've been producing. I'd also like to take you over to the town of Frederiksted."

"Well, I'm anxious to see it all," Morgan said. "Sounds like a good time!"

As noon approached, they ate the sandwiches Vivian had prepared, and as they continued to slowly zigzag their way southward, Morgan suddenly noticed on the southeastern horizon a sizable mass of dark clouds. He looked again to make sure his eyes weren't deceiving him.

"Where in the hell did that come from?" he said, pointing toward the southeast.

Vivian looked in the direction he had pointed. "I don't know. There was nothing like that mentioned on the weather channel this morning. I'll go below and see what they're saying now."

Morgan continued at the wheel. There was no question in his mind. Clouds like that could spell trouble, and when Vivian emerged from below and he saw the expression on her face, he knew she was at least mildly concerned.

"Now they tell us!" she said.

"Tell us what?"

"That there's a line of thunderstorms coming from the southeast. It's pretty big too, they say, and it's moving over water at a speed of about ten miles an hour."

Morgan could see that the mass of clouds was huge. And not only did it cover the entire southeastern horizon, it already appeared larger than when he had first viewed it only minutes earlier. He thought it was definitely big enough to give them a hard time if it overtook them. Vivian went below again briefly and then returned.

"The SAT/NAV shows us just a little more than halfway to St. Croix," she said. "It's about as far in one direction as in the other. I guess we'll just have to push on."

The air was growing slightly cooler now, and as the clouds continued to swell higher and move closer, they looked increasingly darker and more ominous. Morgan knew there was no way they could outrun this thing. Still, despite his concerns, he wanted to sound as optimistic as possible.

"Maybe we'll get lucky, and it won't be that bad," he said.

As the minutes passed, the wind continued to pick up speed and pushed harder on the sails; and though he could not calculate how far away the storm was, he knew it would not be long before it reached them. They made some course adjustments based on the direction of the wind, and he continued to watch the clouds as they grew higher and closer.

"Why don't you take the wheel?" he said somewhat loudly. "I'll go below and get the raincoats."

Vivian took the wheel, and as he headed below she called out to him. "Might as well get the life jackets too. Best to be prepared!"

When he returned, he put on one of the life jackets and a raincoat and then held the wheel while she did likewise. Then he returned the wheel to her.

"These summer squalls can come up pretty fast sometimes," she said, speaking loudly in the increasing wind. But we're seaworthy; there's probably no reason to be truly concerned. Often a storm like this will pass in twenty to thirty minutes."

Morgan wanted to believe her. But there was just something about the look of these clouds. He'd seen clouds like this back in the Midwest, and the storms they brought with them were almost always mean and spiteful.

"I've left the weather channel on," she said. "I just hope this wind doesn't push us too far west."

Morgan had never been in a storm at sea, but he knew perfectly well that if they got hit hard enough, they could indeed be blown too far west and possibly miss St. Croix altogether. And even though he thought the sloop to be seaworthy, as she had said, it was after all only a thirty-five footer; and the prospect of being driven out into the open sea beyond St. Croix in a boat of this size had no appeal whatsoever. As he thought about the approaching storm, he also realized they had not seen another boat for some time; and as they continued to make their way southward, the wind increased even more. The sea began to roll in large, broad swells, with the bow of the sloop rising and falling three to four feet at a time—and then four to five feet. The clouds, which previously had been only ahead of them, were now above as well and rapidly continuing northward. The sloop began to list considerably, and he knew the storm would soon be upon them.

"Here," she said. "You take the wheel again for a minute. I'm going forward to lower the sails a little."

He had previously estimated their forward speed while they were tacking at perhaps five to six knots. At the same time, it was already past 2:00 p.m.; and with the speed and direction of the wind, the pitching and rolling of the boat, and now the sails partially down, he thought it could be another two or three hours before they might reach Christiansted, maybe more.

In the distance he saw flashes of lightning and heard the accompanying crack of electricity followed by the ominous rumble of thunder. Vivian went below again to listen to the weather channel.

"Oh my God," she said loudly as she came back topside. "Looks like we're really in for it. The storm's been upgraded to tropical storm status, with wind speeds approaching fifty miles an hour!" A look of true concern covered her face, and after she retook the wheel, Morgan stood near her and held on to the sloop's rigging.

The wind was now coming at them stronger than ever and almost cold. The clouds in the distance and above churned menacingly. Then, the rain came. Only a few large drops at first. But in less than a minute, it was pouring down on them; and the wind blew even more fiercely, whipping at the sails and making the boat list considerably.

"I'm going to have to take the sails the rest of the way down," she said loudly. She returned control of the wheel to Morgan and again went forward to drop the sails, completely this time. Suddenly, though, with the sails down, they were bobbing and rolling uncontrollably in the sea. Morgan started the engine, hoping it would propel them through the water; but even at high throttle, he could not be sure they were moving forward.

The wind was now pushing the sea into swells of six to eight feet. The bow of the sloop pitched even more wildly, and as the squall line overtook them, torrents of rain pounded them, their raincoats, and the deck, creating a thunderous roar. Lightning flashed and cracked, and the wind and rain, now unbelievably cold, sent chills over Morgan's body. He could feel the hair on his arms and legs stand up beneath his clothes and the raincoat, and as the boat continued to rise and fall in the waves, he struggled to stay on his feet. He saw Vivian struggling as well. As she made her way back from the foredeck, she held on to the rigging.

"I'm going to bring up the life raft," she yelled as she approached him. "Just in case!" She went below, and when she returned with the raft and closed the hatch behind her, a sudden pitch of the boat sent her sprawling face first, crashing hard onto the deck in front of him.

Morgan couldn't take his hands from the wheel, but he called to her. "Honey, you all right?"

For a moment she said nothing. Then she pulled herself up, and, holding on to the boom of the main sail, she sat on top of the cabin, facing him, her right arm tight around the boom and her left arm hanging by her side.

"I've hurt my shoulder," she yelled above the sound of the wind and the rain. She grimaced and rocked back and forth slightly, the look of pain clearly visible on her face. "I think you're going to have to stay at the helm for a while."

As he continued to fight with the wheel and tried to keep his balance, he realized he had lost track of the time. It had probably been at least an hour since he had looked at his watch—and now he was too busy with the wheel even to try. But he knew it had to be approaching five o'clock, and because of the clouds and the pounding rain, he estimated visibility to be only twenty yards or so in any direction. He had no idea how near they might be to land, if they were approaching it at all. He could only try to hold the sloop as steady as possible and not allow her to lay over in the water. Hopefully they would see Christiansted somewhere up ahead.

The rain continued to pour down, and the sloop continued to rise and fall between the swells, which were now even greater than before. The wind and waves were coming at them so violently that he could no longer read the compass in front of him. It was all he could do to hold on to the wheel and hope they would see land before daylight disappeared completely.

Nearly blinded by the storm for another hour, he still had not seen land—or anything other than the fear on Vivian's face as she continued to hold on to the main sail boom. Her lips were purple, and she looked almost sick. He could not be sure with the rising and falling of the sloop, but he thought she was shivering.

"I'm really scared, Tom," she called out as she continued to cling to the boom. "We should've seen land before now! I'm afraid we might've missed it altogether!"

Morgan hoped that what she had guessed would not be true. It had grown increasingly dark; and though it was not quite nightfall, the sky and sea were now only shades of black and gray and green. Visibility was no more than a few yards. Ahead he could barely see beyond the bow, and the only thing that gave him any sense of their position was the direction from which the wind and rain continued to come. At least that one thing had been constant for some time, and on that single fact he based his conclusion that they must still be headed south, or perhaps southwest, depending on how hard the wind and current were pushing them.

The waves continued to come in swells, sometimes washing over the sides of the boat and into the cockpit. More and more he felt that they might, at almost any minute, be swept overboard—especially if the waves came in a certain way or if they experienced a sudden shift in their direction. He considered the possibility of tying a line to both of them to prevent them from being washed away, but he dismissed the notion as quickly as it occurred to him, knowing it would be better to be swept off the boat entirely than to be helplessly drowned in a tangle of lines.

"Can you see anything at all?" he shouted to her.

"Nothing," she yelled back, continuing to cling to the boom.

"Well, keep looking!" he shouted again. It was nearly dark, and he knew it was unnecessary advice. Of course she would keep looking. She had been doing so all along, just as he had. Then, suddenly, out of nowhere, he heard a sound that sent a shockwave through his body. It was a single hard and jarring BANG, which immediately flipped the sloop onto its starboard side and sent the mast hurling toward the foaming sea. He could not see what they had struck, but he knew it was a reef—or something *very* hard and *very* solid. If he had known for certain that it was land, he would have been happy. But what if it was merely a pillar of coral that they had smashed into somewhere offshore, tearing a hole in the hull? Or what if they had been carried west, past the island, hit some rocks, and were now about to be swept away from the very land they had tried so desperately to reach?

In an instant the impact tore the wheel from Morgan's hands; and, unable to grasp any portion of the rigging, he reached for the rip cord of the raft, hoping to inflate it as he and Vivian were tossed overboard and into the sea, waves crashing about them. In a matter of seconds, the raft inflated, but in the process he lost sight of Vivian. He kicked and struggled to hold on to the raft, and at the same time he tried to locate her. For a moment he could see nothing but the raft and the raging waves. But then, in a brief flash of lightning, he caught a glimpse of her yellow raincoat, perhaps ten feet from him. He thought she did not see him, or maybe she was unconscious. He kicked and struggled, trying to make his way to her as the waves carried them farther away from the sloop. He fought and kicked still more, and at length he reached her, exhausted from the weight of water in his clothes. He had swallowed some saltwater, and for a moment he felt sick. Then he grabbed her arm and pulled her to him.

"Here! Hold on!" he yelled, as he put her right arm over the top of the raft and showed her the line to hold. She was obviously dazed, and at first she did not respond. Then she looked at him somewhat blankly.

"OK," she said feebly.

With the force of the waves, there was no way to climb or crawl into the raft. Morgan knew they were both too exhausted. So they simply clung to its sides as they shifted and bobbed helplessly in what he hoped was not the open sea. It was now past dark, and he could see nothing but the yellow of the raft and their raincoats when lightning flashed.

"Are you all right?" he yelled to her as he continued to kick and struggle. He did not know if she heard him. Then, suddenly, before she answered, his foot struck something hard that did not move, and then he struck it again—and then again! My God, he thought, it must be a reef! Perhaps land was close at hand!

"Vivian!" he shouted. "I think we're on a reef!" She looked at him in a way he thought was more alert now. "I think we're on a reef!" he repeated.

The sea continued to toss them uncontrollably, and the rain continued to beat down, and still he could see nothing. He thought if he were watchful, with the next flash of lightning he might see land—somewhere—if they were near enough. He knew that the reef could run a considerable distance offshore, but if luck were with them, it might be fairly close. Here and there lightning continued to flash, and then suddenly there was a triple flash of sufficient duration that he was able to look around. Yes! There it was! Land! He could see the dark profile of hills with trees, perhaps less than a hundred yards away. The image stuck in his mind, and he reasoned that if the hills looked that near, perhaps the shore was closer still.

"Vivian, it's land!" he yelled. "I've seen land!"

The very thought of approaching land again, of actually touching it, walking on it, feeling it beneath him, charged him with a new energy; and, continuing to hold on to the raft, he kicked more vigorously, hoping to propel them in the direction of the shore. Then she joined him in the effort, and together they tried to urge the raft forward. The sea continued to churn and toss them, but then Morgan's right foot landed on something less solid. And then his left foot did as well. It was a sandy bottom! They continued until Vivian said that she too touched it. And then, finally, half floating and half walking and falling, the sea, in one last surge, swept them onto the shore, where they wobbled wearily a few more yards and together collapsed on the soft, inflated sides of the raft.

Morgan lay there beside her, exhausted, gasping for air, trying to catch his breath. They had never managed to climb into the raft. But it was all right. It was quite enough now simply to lie on the softness of it and feel the solid, unmoving earth beneath them. He raised his head for a moment and let his arm drop over her. He was too weak to speak. He could feel his heart pounding and his pulse racing; and, even with the rain pouring down upon them, with lightning flashing and the crashing sounds of thunder all about them, he was content to continue lying there. It did not matter. None of it mattered. They had reached St. Croix.

CHAPTER TWENTY

They continued to lie on top of the raft until they finally caught their breath; and when Vivian agreed she had strength enough to walk, they abandoned the beach for the cover of some nearby trees. Sitting there on the sand, Morgan pulled the raft partially over them, and it felt good to have at least some protection from the wind and rain, which continued to tug and lift at the raft and pound it noisily. For some time they watched the sea throw itself onto the land; and then, gradually, the thunder and lightning began to subside, as did the wind and rain. After half an hour, only a light breeze remained, slightly swaying the trees above them.

"Do you have any idea where we are?" Morgan asked.

"None," she said. She looked up from the sand beneath them and gave him a faint smile. She still looked almost pale, and very likely she cared no more than he did about where they were specifically. They were somewhere on St. Croix, and that was really all that mattered. He put his arm around her, pulling her closer, and she looked at him and smiled. It was the first time he had seen her smile, even faintly, since hours earlier, and he smiled a reassuring smile at her in return.

"We're going to be all right," he said, and he kissed her tenderly on the forehead.

When it appeared the storm had finally passed, they stood and for a moment looked back in the direction from which they had come across the sand. Vivian said she hoped they might catch a glimpse of the *Bon Voyage*; but after scanning the shoreline and the waves for a time and seeing nothing, they turned to begin making their way up the hill behind them.

"Maybe we'll be able to find her tomorrow," she said simply. Morgan could hear the sadness in her voice.

For several minutes they slipped and struggled their way up the hill, and when they finally reached its crest, they paused. Vivian said she thought their most likely location was somewhere west of Christiansted. The only question was, how far west?

A full moon was now peeking here and there through the clouds that drifted slowly above, and Morgan was surprised by how well he could see in the intermittent moonlight. It gave him some hope that Vivian might somehow recognize where they were—and perhaps they'd even find shelter somewhere. She took his hand, and together they walked toward a low, adjacent hill, pausing once in a while in order that she might gain a sense of their position. They had kept their raincoats and life jackets on, since they provided at least some protection from the remaining breeze and helped to preserve body heat. As they walked, Morgan could see no lights in the surrounding countryside. He surmised that any power that might previously have been supplied to the area had long since been knocked out by the storm. All he could see was the slight rising and falling of the land in broad, gently-rolling fields. When they had walked perhaps half a mile, they stopped, and Vivian looked around slowly once again.

"I think I know this area," she said, hesitating only slightly. "Everything looks vaguely familiar." She scanned the fields and the horizon. "Yes! There it is!" she said excitedly. She looked at Morgan.

"What?" he asked.

"The Great House!" she exclaimed. "The Great House!" She pointed off toward a dark silhouette, located on a slight hill some distance from them. Morgan thought he could perhaps see what she was pointing to, but trees at the perimeter of what he supposed could be a structure blurred any distinct lines of a building, and he could not be certain.

"Are you sure?" he said, as she began to lead them in the direction she had pointed.

"Pretty sure!" she said.

They continued to plod through the soft mud of the fields in the direction of the object she had pointed out; and, as they grew nearer, Morgan began to see in the moonlight a dark, two-story building, with a considerable pitch to the roof, sitting atop a small rise in the surrounding landscape.

"Is that it?"

"It is!" she said excitedly. "It is!"

She smiled, and she took Morgan's hand once more. They walked briskly the remaining distance to the house and then up several steps to the heavy, double front doors. Vivian took a large key from the pocket of her shorts.

"I hope this still works," she said; and as she placed the key in the lock and turned it, Morgan heard a click. She pushed on the door, and its hinges groaned as it swung slowly inward.

"At least it's dry and will keep us out of the wind," she said, as she stepped in and onto the stone floor. "And soon there will be light." She reached around to a shelf just inside the doorway and produced, to Morgan's surprise, a lantern and matches.

"Here!" she said, handing him the lantern. "Hold this." She closed the door behind them, struck one of the matches, and carefully lit the lantern's wick. After adjusting it and lowering the glass globe, they stepped farther into the room.

The light cast a dim but warm glow all about them; and, as Morgan held the lantern up and looked around, he saw two broad stairways—one on each side of the room—leading to the second floor and a balcony above, all beneath a ceiling perhaps eighteen to twenty feet high. It reminded him of the Petersen house back on St. Thomas, as if perhaps this had served as a model for it. Straight ahead of them on the cut-stone floor was row after row of large, brown paper bags, stacked five or six tiers high on pallets. Vivian had said the building was being used as a warehouse for the storage of sugar, and clearly there was a great deal of it here.

"Think we could find someplace to build a fire and try to get dried out?" he asked.

She led them through a huge archway to another, even larger room, also filled with multiple rows of the stacked sugar, and then to another, smaller room toward the back of the house. There, along an outer wall, was a fireplace, in a room Morgan presumed had to have been, at one time, the kitchen.

"I'll try to get a fire started," he said; and, after taking off his raincoat and life jacket, he began gathering together bits and pieces of paper that were scattered about, as well as wood from a stray pallet in the adjoining room. Then, from the flame of the lantern, he started a small fire. Afterward, he walked to a nearby pallet load of sugar, and one by one he carried a number of the bags and placed them on the floor in a sizable, single layer near the fireplace. He knew they would make a bed that was at least somewhat softer than the cut stone of the floor. Vivian took her raincoat and life jacket off as well, and together they sat on the bags of sugar and warmed themselves, holding their hands out toward the flames. On almost any cool night, Morgan thought, a fire like this would have felt warm and comforting, but it was especially so this night.

"I guess we should get out of some of these wet clothes," she offered after a time. Morgan had been thinking the same thing, but he had wanted to see if she might say it before he suggested it himself.

"Good idea, I suppose," he said. Then, standing up and stepping a few feet away to a nearby pallet of sugar, he began taking off his clothes: first his boat shoes, caked with mud from the fields, and then his shirt and finally his cargo shorts. As he undressed and laid his shirt and shorts out on top of the stack of sugar, he could not help but glance occasionally in Vivian's direction. As she removed her blouse and shorts and laid them out, he focused on how the sheer, damp fabric of her underwear clung to her body—revealing, he imagined, more than she might have wanted him to see. He returned with her to the fire, where they sat once again, and for a time she said nothing. Then she moved closer to him and leaned her head onto his shoulder.

"You know," she said softly, "you saved my life out there tonight." He turned his gaze from the fire toward her, and she looked directly into his eyes. "You know you did."

Morgan wasn't sure. He might have saved her. Maybe. But that wasn't what was important to him.

"The only thing I care about," he said, "is that you're here, and we're together." He continued to look into her eyes as they reflected the firelight. Then he eased her back gently onto the bags of sugar, where he kissed her—softly at first, and then lovingly, and then passionately. The fire in the fireplace continued to flicker; and there, on the sacks of sugar in the Great House of her ancestors, she gave herself to him.

CHAPTER TWENTY-ONE

The following morning Morgan was awakened early by a thin, orange line of sunlight that sliced silently through a crack in the closed shutters of one of the kitchen windows. Like a laser, it cut across the stone floor, finding first his shoulder, then his neck and cheek, and finally his eyelids. He tried to ignore it, but the light pursued him, forcing his eyes to open. He rolled over on one side. The fire in the fireplace had long since gone out, but so too had the damp chill of the night before gone from the room. He looked over at Vivian, partially covered by one of the raincoats. The sunlight had not yet reached her, still sleeping just inches from him. He slowly, quietly stood, retrieved his clothes from the stack of sugar, dressed, and made his way through the rooms of the Great House to the front doors and stepped outside. He squinted in the brightness of the morning light.

Above, the sky was a perfect, cloudless blue that held no trace of the storm the night before. But as he scanned the countryside, he could see wind damage to some of the trees, where, here and there, a limb had been wrenched off; and out in some of the cane fields there were places where the sugarcane had been nearly flattened, as if some marauding giant had tramped through the area in the night.

A hundred yards or so away, where the land was nearly flat and covered with grass, he spotted a large shed, painted a soft green that nearly matched the color of the surrounding landscape. It was completely open on the side facing him, and he could see it was being used as a hangar. The nose and part of the fuselage and wings of a small, yellow plane were clearly visible. A portion of the shed's metal roof had been partially torn off, with pieces of it flapping slightly in the light morning breeze. Lucky for the plane's owner, he thought. The plane itself appeared to have suffered little or no damage, covered as it was beneath the protective shell of the building.

As he turned to walk back inside, where he thought he might find Vivian awake, he paused for a moment as he saw, now in the daylight, the beauty of the stones that had been selected for the walls of the Great House, which had remained perfectly straight and plumb through all the decades since their construction. And with every window covered by heavy, wood shutters fitted with wrought-iron hinges and clasps, the building had obviously survived many storms like that of the night before—and no doubt other, even stronger storms as well—virtually unscathed. The Danes certainly knew what they were doing, he thought, when they created this near-perfect building. It had obviously been designed to last for centuries.

When he returned to the kitchen and found Vivian still asleep, his curiosity about the remainder of the place got the better of him. So he took the lantern and began exploring. Adjacent to the kitchen, in the main room they had passed through the night before, and through which he had also walked again this morning, were the rows and rows of palletized sugar; and as he casually walked down one of the aisles, noting the heavy timbers that supported the ceiling, he also noticed that one of the stacks of sugar was somewhat disheveled, as if it had been bumped into and haphazardly reconstructed.

He examined it more closely in the light from the lantern and discovered that not only was there a lopsidedness to the column, but it indeed appeared to have been restacked, since some of the bags, unlike those on the other pallets, had been positioned with their printed side down instead of up. He looked up and down the height of the column and noticed at its base, where the wood pallet met the floor, there was no mortar between two of the stones, but, instead, a gap of perhaps a fin-ger width. He squatted and, placing the lantern on the floor, traced an index finger along the several exposed inches at the edge of one stone. It was level with the adjoining stones of the floor, but he was curious about the lack of mortar here, while it was evident everywhere else. He paused, then stood, and, setting the lantern aside, he began to slowly but deliberately take down the stack of bags, placing them in the aisle.

Bag after bag came down, gradually reducing the height of the stack until, finally, he neared the bottom and at length set the last bag aside. He reached slowly down to the pallet and slid it into the aisle as well. Now he could see in their entirety, two square stones, each of which was approximately two feet in diameter—and again with no mortar—as evident elsewhere throughout the house. Morgan knelt on one knee, fitted his fingertips into the space separating the two stones, and lifted, try-ing to pry one stone from its seat. It resisted considerably, so he increased the distance between his hands and tried again, this time pulling back and upward. Gradually, he lifted one edge of the slab, which he discovered, as its bottom cleared the surrounding stones of the floor, was nearly two inches thick. He slid the first slab of stone— and then the second—off to one side, and with the lan-tern he peered into the darkness of the hole below.

There, down little more than two feet below the floor, were several black, nylon duffel bags. Moving them around with one hand, he quickly counted: one, two, three, four…at least eight in total. He pulled one of the bags out and placed it on the stone floor. With no dust or mold on it, it could not have been in this hiding place for long. His fingers deftly sought and then found the bag's zipper, and he opened it, revealing several clear plastic bags, each filled with a white, crystalline powder, which he knew was not sugar. He took one of the bags from the duffel and held it in his hand. Even without a lab kit to test the substance, he knew what it was. He knew by the way it looked, by its weight and texture, and by the fact that it was hidden in this secret place beneath the floor. With his teeth he created a pin-sized hole near a corner of the bag, and with his finger he tasted the substance. No, it definitely was *not* sugar. Damn! With this many bags, he reasoned, there was probably three or four hundred pounds of the stuff, maybe more.

But why would anyone leave a quantity of cocaine, especially an amount as large as this, buried and unattended? A series of images began to flash in his mind like numerous, color photographs laid out in front of him. The plane. The hangar and runway—all at this relatively remote location. Had the plane been used to bring in the cocaine? Or was it here to take it away? Or both? Almost certainly it was involved. How else would the drugs have come to be here? His mind flipped through more images. He knew the entire population of St. Croix, or for that matter all of these Virgin Islands, was not sufficient to consume this much cocaine within any reasonable period of time. It must be in transit, moving toward the mainland U.S. in all probability—certainly not away from it. And this relatively remote island, with its out-of-the-way hillsides, provided a practically unobservable entry point. His sense of geography told him that all these islands were closer to South America— and perhaps Colombia in particular—than to the mainland United States. And while he could only guess at the flying radius of the small plane he had seen in the hangar, even if it could not make the flight from South America in a single hop, it should be possible, even relatively easy, with one or two island stops, to bring it this far north. But how would it be moved from here to the U.S. mainland? And by whom?

His mind leaped toward an answer to this last question as soon as he thought it. Who but Charles Petersen? This was, after all, Petersen land—*and* the Petersen Great House. Who else but he would have knowledge of this hiding place beneath the floor? For a moment his thoughts shifted to Vivian. Surely she was not involved. Nothing she had ever said or done suggested involvement in anything like this. Furthermore, if she were part of it, why would she bring him here to where the cocaine was located, at a time when he might discover it? No. Clearly, she was not involved.

But Petersen was another matter. He had not known they were coming to St. Croix. And even if Vivian had mentioned it to him, there was no way he could have anticipated their arrival at the Great House while the coke was here. But again, why had it been placed here?

As his mind pondered the question, more photographs lined up for review. He saw again the broken tree limbs and downed cane from the storm the night before. Was it possible that whoever had the coke—again, most likely Petersen—had arrived just before the storm hit and needed a quick, secure place to stash it? And now, as Morgan pondered the subject, perhaps an even better question was what, if anything, would *he* do about it? He knew he could simply ignore it and go on his way, as if he had seen nothing. But then his mind flashed back to those friends so long ago in high school, and to Elaine and those final images of her, pale and unmoving on that sidewalk. As he thought of her, and of all the anguish he had felt for months and the anxiety he had tried to escape by coming to these islands, he knew there was no question what he would do—what he was trained to do; what he *had* to do.

Quickly he placed the plastic bag back into the duffel, zipped it closed, and dropped it into its stone hiding place with the others. After reseating the square stones, he dragged the pallet carefully back into place as well, with a portion of the two stones exposed, just as before. Then he restacked the bags of sugar in a somewhat tilted column, picked up the lantern, and walked back toward the kitchen.

"Hi there," Vivian said, smiling brightly when he arrived. She had put her underwear back on and was sitting on the bags of sugar in front of the fireplace. "I was wondering where you were."

Morgan smiled, walked toward her, and sat down on one of the bags next to her. "I've been trying to figure out," he said, wrinkling his forehead and seeming to grow serious, "where the shower is around this place."

She laughed. "Well, one of those is going to be hard to find here," she said. "This house was built long before indoor plumbing, and no one has lived in it for a hundred years. But we're only three or four miles from town," she went on. "Let's see if we can get a ride. We'll go to that inn I told you about."

She stood and walked to her clothes still on top of the stack of sugar where she had placed them the night before.

"How's your shoulder feeling this morning?" he asked.

"I think it's fine, now," she said. "But you didn't seem very concerned about it last night." She gave him a wry smile.

"I guess I wasn't thinking about your shoulder at the time," he said, smiling back at her as he began returning the bags of sugar from in front of the fireplace to the pallet from which they had come. He was careful to keep the stack straight and upright. Then he shook the creases out of the raincoats, folded them over his arm, and retrieved the life jackets from the floor. He saw Vivian watching him.

"I thought you were a neat guy," she said, smiling at him again and hinting at the double meaning in her words. "But are you always this neat?"

"Of course," he said. "I thought you knew." The complete truth was, however, that he wanted to leave as little evidence of their visit as possible. None if he could. He reasoned that if Petersen discovered they had been there, he might become wary—and all the more secretive in his actions. But without any suggestion of a visitor, he'd go about his business as usual, with no increased reason for concern. The only thing was, if the cocaine was here on St. Croix, perhaps Petersen was as well.

Vivian picked up the lantern, and together they walked to the front door, where she replaced the lantern and the box of matches on the shelf along the inside wall; and as they stepped outside, Morgan reflected quickly on how he had left everything. Almost nothing had changed except for a few ashes in the fireplace. Within a few hours they would be cold, if they were not already, and virtually undetectable. He was confident that no one was likely to suspect their visit—not even Petersen. He closed the door tightly behind them, and Vivian locked it before they walked away.

"I'd like to go back to the coast before going into town," she said. "Maybe we can find the *Bon Voyage*, or at least see what's left of her."

"Sure," Morgan said. He understood her feelings about the boat. He took her hand, and together they walked out into the adjacent field, following their tracks from the night before, which were still quite visible in the drying mud. In the distance, he viewed the hangar and the plane once again, and he asked Vivian about it. If it belonged to her brother, he wanted to know.

"Whose plane?" he asked simply, trying to sound as casual about the inquiry as possible.

"I don't know," she said. "But it's probably Charlie's. You know, he has to go back and forth between the islands all the time."

Morgan thought about her answer. That would certainly give him plenty of cover for moving the cocaine around.

They continued to walk north for a time, still retracing their tracks. Finally, they mounted one last hill, and at its crest they looked out onto the sea. There in the distance, piled up on a peninsula of jagged rocks that jutted out from the land perhaps a hundred yards, they saw the *Bon Voyage*, her hull smashed and motionless, like a huge, white swan, lying lifeless where she had drowned.

"God, it makes me sick to see her like this," Vivian said, as tears welled up in her eyes.

Morgan put his arm around her shoulders. "I know," he said, pausing for a moment. "But she got us here. She was one hell of a boat."

"Yes, she was, wasn't she?" Vivian agreed. "One hell of a boat." She paused. "I guess I'll have to call a salvage company. I can hardly believe it." She wiped at her tears with her fingertips.

They continued to view the boat for a time, and then slowly turned and headed eastward along the coast. Vivian said she thought that within a mile—or perhaps a little more—they should find a road, and a ride, that would take them into Christiansted; and within ten to fifteen minutes they arrived at the road she had predicted. At first there were no cars or other vehicles, but she was confident some kind of ride would show up.

"If we just wait here," she said, "a car or taxi-bus will come by. I know it." And again, just as she had predicted, within a matter of minutes a multicolored, midsize motorcoach, with open windows, approached. They flagged the driver down and boarded. Morgan reached into the front pocket of his cargo shorts, paid the fare with a few, still-damp bills from his wallet, and, with their raincoats and life jackets in their arms, they took their seats among the few other passengers.

As the vehicle rumbled off in the direction of Christiansted, he leaned toward her. "I am really hungry," he said quietly but with considerable emphasis.

"Me too," she said. "And the inn will be perfect. They have absolutely terrific food. But can I please take a shower first? My hair is a mess, and I feel awful." She sounded almost pleading.

Morgan readily agreed. The wreck of the *Bon Voyage*, the moonlight trek through muddy fields, and a night on sacks of sugar had made him feel less than terrific himself. A shower would feel good to him as well.

As they reached Christiansted, the taxi-bus made a couple of stops before reaching the small inn. They got out and walked the few steps to the front door, and in the lobby they approached the desk clerk, a young man of mixed race, with closely-cropped black hair.

"Good morning," Vivian said. "My name's Vivian Petersen. I had a reservation for last night, but unfortunately we didn't make it because of the storm. Any chance that room might still be available?"

The clerk looked briefly at his computer screen. "Indeed it is, Miss Petersen. Sorry you didn't get here last night. But the room is still yours." He handed her a key over the counter. "Checkout time isn't until noon," he said. "Room 212."

When they arrived in the room, Morgan suggested that she shower first. He was content to wait his turn; and, as he waited, he thought about the possibility of going into the bathroom and offering to wash her back—and perhaps other parts as well. He knew that she cared deeply about him and perhaps she even loved him. At the same time, last night had been a combination of circumstances. And if circumstances were different today, he felt almost certain she would want to revisit their lovemaking. But she had been through a lot in the last twenty-four hours; and if he knew anything at all about women, likely she would not be interested— at least until sometime later, after they got back to St. Thomas and she had an opportunity to get fixed up in her own environment. Finally, he could hear her using the hair dryer, and he imagined she would be feeling at least somewhat better.

"You can come in and start your shower if you want," she called out over the sound of the dryer.

Morgan walked into the bathroom and saw her, again in her underwear, fluffing and pulling at her hair with one hand as she moved the dryer back and forth with the other. No lipstick; no makeup; she was still beautiful. He took off his clothes, and while she seemed not to notice, he thought she did. He stepped into the tub and turned on the shower.

"I'm going to make this quick," he said. "I'm starving."

When they left the room and arrived in the lobby, Vivian directed them toward the back of the inn and out onto a small, open-air courtyard dotted with tables and chairs, all beneath one large tree that dominated the area and shaded it as well. It looked as though everything had been restored to normal since the storm the night before. Each of the tables had a freshly-pressed, white tablecloth and a tiny clump of flowers in a small, clear vase as its centerpiece. As it was past mid-morning and between normal mealtimes, there was only one other couple present. Morgan and Vivian selected one

of the tables, and a waitress—a young black woman—
appeared with menus. He asked her to please stand by,
and as he studied the menu he quickly made his breakfast selections.

"I'll have a ham and cheese omelet, please, plus bacon *and* sausage, hash browns, wheat toast, orange juice,
and black coffee."

"That sounds terrific," Vivian added. "I'll have the
same—except no bacon or sausage please."

When the waitress brought their coffee, they sipped at
it less than contentedly, awaiting their food, and when it finally arrived, they began consuming it in a way that would
have made any onlooker know they were indeed extremely
hungry. It did not take long for most of the meal to disappear, and when they had finished the last of it, the waitress
brought some croissants and strawberry jam.

"Compliments of the inn," she said.

As they lingered over their dessert and more coffee,
sunlight drifted softly through the tree above, where
two or three sparrows chirped, seemingly happy, as
they jumped from limb to limb. Morgan took a piece
of his croissant and tossed it to the floor, where the
birds descended and pecked vigorously at the diminish-
ing crumbs. He could not help but think how peaceful
the morning was, especially compared with the raging
storm that could have so easily taken their lives less than
twenty-four hours earlier. But there was no place safe
in the world. He knew that. And storms like yesterday's

were just one more thing that made life tenuous, at best. He eyed Vivian lovingly, and when she looked at him, he smiled. He was happy simply to be alive and here with her. At least they were safe, for now.

The other couple, with whom they had shared the courtyard, finished their meal; and as Morgan watched them leave, he saw, to his complete astonishment, Charles Petersen walk out onto the patio, accompanied by a stoutly-built, blond-haired man.

"Vivian! Tom!" Petersen called out, sounding not only surprised but strangely friendly, Morgan thought, given their confrontation of a few days earlier. He walked toward them.

"Oh my goodness! Charlie!" Vivian exclaimed. She stood and gave Petersen a warm smile and then a hug. Morgan imagined she had chosen—at least for the moment—to ignore their earlier conflict, and he stood and managed a smile as well, but only because he chose not to reveal his true feelings about the man while in Vivian's presence. Petersen gave her a hug, and then extended his hand to Morgan. He took Petersen's hand and shook it firmly. He could hardly believe the man's feigned friendliness, as if there were no acrimony between them. Clearly he was an insincere and treacherous bastard. Nevertheless, Morgan participated in his charade, in order not to reveal the contempt he felt for him—at least not yet. He then looked in the direction of the blond-haired man accompanying him. He had a tattoo of a coiled snake on one side of his neck.

"Oh, and this is a friend of mine," Petersen said, stepping back slightly and gesturing with one hand toward his companion. "Bill Hamilton. Bill, this is my sister, Vivian, and this is Tom Morgan. Bill's also my pilot sometimes," Petersen added. Hamilton extended his hand, and Morgan shook it as well, thinking that, with his snake tattoo, he was definitely a suspicious-looking character, not unlike the two other individuals he had met at Petersen's house. It wasn't difficult to imagine any of them involved with drugs.

"We flew down yesterday," Petersen went on. "But we got trapped by that storm and wound up having to stay over—here in the inn. When did you two get here?" He addressed his question to Vivian.

"Oh, Charlie, you won't believe it," she said, sounding somewhat dejected. "We came down yesterday too, on the *Bon Voyage*. But we got caught in that storm, and I'm afraid the boat is no more. She got us here—obviously. But she's cracked up out on some rocks, west of here."

"Wow!" Petersen said. "Well, at least you're all right." Morgan imagined Petersen's comment was sincere as far as his sister was concerned, but he knew damn well the man had no such feelings about him.

"Yes," Vivian said, "we're OK. But after being swept ashore, we wound up trudging through the mud for quite a while last night, until we found the Great House. That's where we spent the night."

There was a momentary pause in the conversation, and Morgan thought he detected at least mild concern on Petersen's face, as he wrinkled his forehead questioningly. "Well, how'd you get in?"

"Oh, I still have a key," she answered earnestly. "You know. Grandpa gave me one too. I had planned that Tom and I would go out there sometime while we were here, just so I could see it again and show it to him as well. We just made it there a little earlier than I had expected."

"Well, was everything all right?"

"Oh, yeah," she said. "And we saw all the sugar. There was sure a lot of it stacked up all over the place. I guess production is going really well!"

The look of concern that Petersen had shown moments earlier had not entirely disappeared, and he glanced momentarily at Morgan, then back at Vivian.

"We built a small fire in the kitchen fireplace," she added. "But I'm sure it was out before we left. And I was also sure to lock the front door behind us, just so you know."

Morgan wished she hadn't spoken about their visit to the Great House, since it might start Petersen wondering if anything had been disturbed or discovered.

"No worries," he said at length, his look of concern somewhat diminished. "So, what are you going to do today?"

"I don't know," she said, looking briefly at Morgan. "We'll probably look around town for a while. But that storm has pretty much ruined our trip. We'll probably catch a plane this afternoon and head back—as much as I hate to fly." She looked again at Morgan.

"Well, I'd invite you to go back with us," Petersen said. "But our plane is just a two-seater." Morgan thought it just as well. He didn't like being in the man's presence, let alone the thought of riding with him in a plane.

"Oh, I was wondering," Vivian interjected. "Is that your plane we saw out in the hangar at the plantation?"

"Yeah. Did it look all right?"

"I think so," she said. "We saw it only from a distance, but it was still there. Looked like it was probably OK."

"Good," Petersen said, sounding somewhat relieved. "I hope so." He glanced at his watch, then continued. "Unfortunately, Hon, I can't visit more right now. With that storm, I want to get out to the mill and see if everything is all right there." He looked at Hamilton. "I guess we better get checked out." Then he looked again at Vivian. "You two enjoy your afternoon," he said. "I'll see you back home in another day or two." He hugged her briefly. "See you, Tom," he said.

"Yeah, see you," Morgan responded. He knew for an absolute certainty he would see Petersen. In fact, he was going to do everything he could to keep a close eye on everything he did from now on, starting just as soon as they could get back to St. Thomas. He watched as

Peterson and Hamilton departed. In his mind, he could see the two of them, yesterday afternoon as the storm approached, placing the bags of cocaine beneath the stones in the floor of the Great House and then hastily restacking the bags of sugar so they might get to Christiansted before the full force of the storm struck. He hoped he had done an adequate job of mimicking the loosely stacked bags, so Petersen would not suspect his discovery. If he did suspect it, he knew there would be a problem. And not just any problem, but a big problem!

It was now late morning, nearing noon. The sun was continuing to shine brightly in a clear, blue sky. Morgan's cell was still in a pocket of his cargo shorts, but he knew it had been damaged by their dousing at sea, and Vivian's was still in her purse on the *Bon Voyage*; so they returned to their room to call the local airport and book seats on an afternoon flight back to St. Thomas. As they prepared to leave the room, Morgan looked at the raincoats and life jackets on the bed.

"Think we should take these with us or just leave them?"

"I think we should take them," Vivian said. "Without the life jackets, we probably wouldn't be here. I'd like to keep them—for the memory of how they saved us, and how you saved me."

They left the room with the raincoats and life jackets in their arms and spent the next couple of hours exploring Christiansted. As they walked through the town's cobblestone streets, they saw some of the debris left by the storm—here and there a broken branch on a tree, a few small limbs and leaves scattered about, a torn awning—but otherwise, relatively little evidence of the storm that had been so severe for them at sea. The mostly stone and stucco buildings, despite their obvious antiquity, were unaffected. Unquestionably they, like the Great House, had seen hundreds of such storms.

Likewise, shopkeepers, tourists, and others were moving about the streets, coming and going to and from the stores, now open for business as if nothing of consequence had happened. Morgan and Vivian looked into some of the shops as they browsed. She also pointed out a number of buildings and other structures of particular interest—an ancient church; another small inn; the old Danish fort, somewhat like the one on St. Thomas. While Morgan thought it pleasant enough to tour the town, he could scarcely concentrate on his surroundings. His mind kept drifting back to Petersen and his friend, Hamilton. He imagined they were at the mill or perhaps in the hangar, checking out the plane, or at the Great House retrieving those duffel bags from beneath the floor. Maybe they were even beginning their flight back to St. Thomas—although he hoped not. His instincts told him that Petersen was almost certainly involved with the cocaine. He didn't know how it could be otherwise. He only wished he could see firsthand what he was imagining.

"So, what do you think?" Vivian asked, breaking into his thoughts. "Do you like the place?"

"I do," he said. "It's very nice. Maybe another time, when we haven't had quite so much excitement, we can come back and see more."

"Oh, I hope so," she said. "I like coming down here—at least once in a while."

Morgan looked at his watch. It was getting close to the time of their flight. "I think we better get to the airport, though," he said. "OK?" He was definitely anxious to get back to St. Thomas as soon as possible.

"Sure. OK," she said. She smiled but looked slightly concerned. Morgan thought she was probably apprehensive about the upcoming flight, so he took her hand as they walked out onto a main street and hailed a taxi. Within thirty minutes they were at the airport, boarding the small plane with fewer than a dozen other passengers.

"You know I hate flying," she said as she sat in the seat beside him.

"I know," he said. "But we'll be fine. Honest." He took her hand again, and she held on tightly as the pilot began taxiing to the runway.

Morgan didn't know what he would do—or, perhaps more importantly, what she might do—if he found Petersen guilty of what he suspected. He could only hope it wouldn't destroy his relationship with her. He didn't know how he could make it all work out, but somehow he had to. He loved her.

CHAPTER TWENTY-TWO

B ack on St. Thomas, Morgan and Vivian caught a cab from the airport into Charlotte Amalie and stopped at Vivian's condo to drop her off. She was anxious to get further cleaned up, she said, and get her hair fixed. He would go on to Red Hook to retrieve the Jeep.

"Will I see you later this afternoon? Or this evening?" she asked.

Morgan paused. "Let's plan on this evening," he said. "After I get the Jeep, I want to go to the bungalow and get cleaned up myself; and I want to try to get a new phone—and get my data transferred if I can—before the stores close. So I'll plan to see you after that, OK?" He knew he wasn't telling her the real reason it would be later when he returned to her. The truth was, he wanted to get back from Red Hook as soon as possible and go to the airport, where he hoped he might yet catch sight of Petersen and Hamilton coming back from St. Croix—and perhaps follow them to see what they might do with the coke. That could easily take the remainder of the afternoon, or more. He didn't like *not* telling her the truth. But he couldn't think of any practical way to tell her what he suspected—or thought he knew—about her brother.

"OK," she said, "I'll see you a little later then." She picked up the raincoats and life jackets, leaned across the seat, kissed him, and stepped out of the cab.

"Oh," he called to her through the cab's open window. "Have you got a key somewhere?" He didn't want to drive away and leave her stranded.

"Oh, yes. I have one hidden outside."

"OK," he said. He smiled and waved, then blew her a kiss as the cab rumbled off.

It was already nearly 3:00 p.m. It would take him an hour to get to Red Hook and back. He still had the keys to both the Jeep and his bungalow zippered safely in the left front pocket of his cargo shorts, and his now waterlogged cell phone was in the other. But there would probably be no time to get a new phone today. He only hoped that Petersen and Hamilton had not already arrived back on St. Thomas.

He urged the cab driver to get to Red Hook as quickly as he could, and when they arrived Morgan jumped into the Jeep and raced back through the twists and turns of Route 30 to Charlotte Amalie. With any luck, he reasoned, it had taken Petersen and Hamilton at least some amount of time to get to the mill—if in fact Petersen was planning to go there, as he had said. Then it would take more time to get to the plantation and the Great House, unstack the bags of sugar, carry the cocaine to the plane, and then fly to St. Thomas—*if* they were going to do so today. But when he thought of it, he remembered Petersen saying to Hamilton that they should check out of the inn. So, unless they were planning to spend tonight somewhere else, it was almost certain that—if they had not already arrived on St. Thomas—they would be on their way back, now or very soon.

Morgan pushed the Jeep hard toward the airport. He parked in a lot just outside the airport grounds and began watching arrivals. Nearly five hours had passed since he had seen Petersen and Hamilton. They'd had more than enough time to return in the plane. He could only hope they had not already done so. He waited and watched.

It seemed somehow odd to him to be sitting here now—not quite a month since his own first landing—waiting for a plane full of cocaine. But here he was nevertheless. The heat of the late-afternoon sun bore down on the top of the Jeep, and as he sat there he realized he was sweating. He started the engine and pushed the air-conditioning all the way to cold.

Plane after plane landed. He was glad that Cyril E. King was not another O'Hare Field. There, he could never have hoped to see all the arrivals. Here, he was certain he had seen every last one—and none of them was the yellow two-seater from the hangar on St. Croix. Nearly two hours passed. It was approaching 6:00 p.m., and soon he would *have* to get back into town to see Vivian. More planes arrived, but still no yellow plane. He hated to give up and just leave, but he still had to get back to his place and change clothes. And if he didn't return to Vivian soon, she'd almost certainly question where he had been during so much time. He reluctantly put the Jeep into gear, left the airport grounds, and headed east toward town.

When he had traveled no more than a mile, something in the sky, fairly high up and well ahead of him, caught his attention. It was a small plane, and the sun's rays, coming from behind him, glanced off the aircraft, or its windows. For a time he couldn't determine the color. But it was a small plane to be sure, propeller driven, and the more he looked at it, the more he thought it might be yellow. It was tending northwest, and he thought it was descending. As quickly as he could, he made a U-turn, watching the plane as it tended toward the center of the island. Yes. He was almost certain it was yellow. In any case, he had to follow it to be sure.

As soon as Route 38 appeared, he turned onto it and continued in a northwesterly direction, keeping the plane in sight as best he could. When he was almost directly behind it—perhaps a mile or so back—he could tell that it was indeed descending, and he continued to watch, pushing the Jeep ahead as fast as possible given the twists and turns of the road. Finally, as he drove over the crest of one last hill, he saw the plane touching down in the distance on a patch of green. He recognized immediately that this was the island's West End, or at least very near the West End—the same area he had visited on his first day out in the Jeep. With its gently rolling fields between hillsides, it was perfectly adequate for landing a small plane. And of course! It was much better to use a remote landing spot like this rather than the airport. Here there'd be little if any chance of being detected. He turned the Jeep onto a gravel country road, parked in the shade of a large tree, and watched.

Two figures—both men, he thought—began walking back and forth between the plane and a dark-colored automobile, carrying what looked very much like the black duffels he'd seen in the Great House. At this distance he couldn't be sure, and he couldn't determine the make of the car, but he continued to watch. After perhaps five minutes, the plane took off, and immediately afterward the automobile pulled out onto Route 38 and began moving in his direction. As it passed up ahead of him, he could see it was a dark—probably black—sedan. My God, he thought as he studied the automobile. That was Petersen's car—or, at least, it looked like it could be. He remembered the black Mercedes sedan parked in Petersen's driveway the night he and Vivian had visited him. Now, as the car drove by up ahead, he was sure it was a black sedan. He just couldn't tell if it was a Mercedes.

After the car passed, he pulled out onto Route 38 as well, but stayed back far enough not to be detected; and when the driver turned to go east on Route 30 toward Charlotte Amalie, he continued to follow. He *had* to see if this was Petersen. If it was, Morgan felt something must have guided him to be at this right place and this right time. Maybe it was his instincts. Maybe divine providence. Or maybe just dumb luck. But something had brought him here.

He continued to follow the car into Charlotte Amalie, down along Waterfront Drive, but he remained well behind, sometimes allowing several cars to get in between them. Ultimately, the sedan—which he was beginning to believe had to be Petersen's car—pulled into a parking lot between the Harborview and the harbor, where a number of boats, some of considerable size, were berthed at a pier that jutted well out into the water. Morgan pulled into the parking lot as well, but continued to maintain a comfortable distance. He shut the Jeep off, and when a man emerged from the sedan, Morgan squinted. The evening light had started to fade slightly, but even at this distance he was now certain. It *was* Petersen. Same black hair, combed straight back.

Same shirt and slacks he'd seen him wearing earlier in the day. Yes, it was him all right. He watched as he locked the automobile with his remote key, causing the car's lights to flash in acknowledgment. Then he saw him walk up the slight hill toward the hotel.

But why had he parked down here near the water, especially if his destination was the Harborview? He continued to watch, trying to be patient. He felt time passing, and he looked at his watch. It was nearly 7:00 p.m., and he began to wonder how he might explain his hours of absence to Vivian.

Within a few more minutes, however, two men appeared and unlocked the Mercedes, again making its lights flash. Morgan could not be certain, especially given his distance from them, but he thought they were the same two men he had met at Petersen's house. He watched them open the automobile's trunk, and each pulled out two duffel bags. Then they walked—almost casually—down to the pier and out of sight. Within two or three minutes, they reappeared, wrestled four more of the black duffels from the trunk, and returned once again down the pier. When they appeared from their second trip, to Morgan's surprise, they retrieved four *more* bags—for a total of twelve—and carried them somewhere down on the pier. That was four more bags than he had estimated in the Great House. Obviously he hadn't managed to count them all; but he now knew they probably represented five- to six-hundred pounds of coke! When both men finally returned from their third trip, they relocked the car, again making its lights flash, and walked in the direction of the hotel, just as Petersen had. He now knew that the cocaine from the Great House on St. Croix was—at least for the time being—stowed somewhere on that pier. Or, more likely, it was on one of the boats there, and he had to find out which one.

As soon as the two men disappeared up the hill, he left the Jeep, walked down to the pier himself and then along its length. Every slip was occupied. But, as he walked, one boat in particular caught his eye—a sizable fishing boat with a tuna tower and the name *Charlie's Change* painted in gold script on the boat's transom. This had to be Petersen's boat. And it was just like him, Morgan thought, to suggest he had purchased it using only the change in his pocket. So, this was where the bags of cocaine were now stowed! But where were they headed? And when? He couldn't stay here day and night, watching. And even if he could, he had no boat to follow. He had to get a phone and call Blackburn, and he had to do it soon. Tomorrow would be Monday—and he would definitely call as early as possible. Hopefully, the coke wouldn't move before then. Meanwhile, he had to get to Vivian's.

He started the Jeep, went straight to his place, quickly changed clothes, shaved, and drove to her condo. He knew he had to construct some kind of alibi to explain this absence for more than four hours. It would have taken no more than an hour to go to Red Hook and back. Likewise it should not have taken him more than an hour to go to his place and get cleaned up, and no more than an hour—two at the most—to go to the phone store, pick out a replacement phone, and have the data transferred. That would make the time match. But that would mean he would have to lie again. He hated not telling her the truth, but he couldn't tell her he was with the DEA. He knew from past experience what that could do to this relationship. She might even hate him for not being truthful from the beginning. And if he couldn't tell her the truth about his job, there was no reason to tell her what he knew about her brother. He decided that the technicians at the phone store had worked diligently to complete the data transfer to a new phone, but so far they'd found it impossible to finish the task because of the water damage to the old phone. They would have to continue working on it tomorrow. That was what had taken so much time.

When he arrived at Vivian's and she opened the door, she looked totally refreshed, as if a wreck at sea and an overnight stay on bags of sugar on a stone floor had never occurred.

"Hi," she said, greeting him with a smile and a kiss. "I was beginning to wonder what had happened to you." She was wearing the coral necklace he had given her, and it pleased him to see her have it on again.

In the dining room, she had already provided place settings for two on the table. "I've made us some dinner," she said. "I hope you're hungry."

"I am," he said, rubbing his hands together to show his enthusiasm. He had not eaten since their meal late that morning. "Actually, I'm starving," he added.

She pulled out the chair at the head of the table, invited him to sit, and then leaned over the back of the chair and kissed him on the cheek. She lit the candles in the center of the table. "Give me just a minute," she said, "and I'll be back."

She returned first with salads, and then with the rest of their meal from the oven. To Morgan it looked and smelled totally delicious, and he hoped she would not ask him about his afternoon and evening. As it turned out, she did not. It seemed she wanted to talk only about their troubled sail to St. Croix, the loss of the *Bon Voyage*, and again how he had saved her.

In the candlelight, she looked as beautiful as ever. But there was always so much more to her than her beauty. He had always appreciated her sense of history, her knowledge of sailing and so many other things. And he loved her energy and her enthusiasm. At the same time, she was gentle, thoughtful, and kind, and he was attracted to her femininity, her softness, and even her vulnerability, like her fear of flying.

When they finished their meal, she turned to him. "You know," she said, pausing slightly, "I'm so happy we're together. The day you arrived on the island and I watched you drive away in that cab, I was really upset. I thought I might never see you again. But then, that next week, when I saw you at the hotel with Charlie, I was so excited I can't even describe it. I've had that same feeling, Tom, every day since. And then last night, after the storm, I knew I…" Her voice trailed off without completing her sentence.

He reached across the corner of the table and placed his hand on hers. He clasped her fingers gently and smiled as he looked into her eyes. "Would it make it easier if I told you how much I love you?" he said. "Finding you has meant more to me than I can say, and you've made me happier than I've ever been. That's why I rented the house. That's why I'm here, Viv. And that's why I don't ever want to leave." He leaned forward and kissed her, softly at first, and then passionately.

Without words they walked to her bedroom and, like the night before, he eased her back—but this time on a bed that was considerably softer than the bags of sugar. There was no doubt in his mind that he loved this woman. He loved everything about her. Everything. He just didn't know how he was going to handle this thing with her brother.

Then he heard her say, "I love you, Tom."

CHAPTER TWENTY-THREE

The next morning Morgan awoke still in Vivian's bed and still naked from the night before. She lay close to him, breathing softly. He carefully lifted the sheet, just enough to peek beneath it and see the smooth flow of her tanned skin, interrupted here and there with small patches of white, where the sun had rarely if ever shone. God, she was gorgeous.

"Like what you see?" she asked, opening her eyes and smiling playfully.

"Oh jeeez! I thought you were asleep!" he said, both startled and somewhat embarrassed.

"I was, until you lifted the sheet." She smiled again and then bounded out of bed and headed for the bathroom. "What do you want to do today?"

"I don't know for sure, but I'd like to get a new phone."

"I thought you already got one yesterday," she said, calling out from the bathroom.

"I tried. But they had problems with the data transfer and told me to come back today."

"I need to get one too," she said. She peeked around the corner, seemingly more modest than before. "Who's your carrier?

"AT&T."

"Oh, darn," she said. "I thought we might go together. I'm with Verizon. Tell you what," she continued, again from the bathroom, "why don't you get yours; I'll get mine; and then let's meet over at the hotel and hang out at the pool this afternoon. Just make a lazy day of it. What do you think?"

Morgan could hardly believe his ears. From his first days at the Harborview and his afternoons poolside, he knew that from the pool deck it was not only possible to see the entire harbor, but more specifically to see the pier where he now knew Petersen's boat was docked. Her idea was perfect! He could keep an eye on the boat and see if it moved or not. Hopefully it would not.

"Sounds great!" he called back to her.

He heard the water running in the shower, and after a few more minutes she came out of the bathroom, this time with a towel around her body and another encircling her hair.

"OK," she said. "Your turn. As soon as I get dressed, I'll fix us some breakfast. Afterward we can go see about some new phones."

Morgan got out of bed and walked unceremoniously to the bathroom. No sense in displaying any false modesty. She'd already seen it all.

"By the way," she said to him, "I put a new toothbrush and some toothpaste out on the counter for you. You can take your time. It'll take me a while to get everything ready."

He showered leisurely, brushed his teeth, dressed, and then met her in the kitchen. She had prepared a wonderful breakfast: eggs, bacon, wheat toast, orange juice, and coffee—all of which he consumed with considerable vigor.

"Oh, I just realized," he said as he was finishing. "I'll have to get a new bathing suit too. Lost mine on the boat."

"No problem," she answered. "Let's just plan to meet at the pool around noon. That'll give me some time to clean up around here and get a phone myself. I want to call a salvage company about the boat and maybe even go to the gallery for a bit."

Again, it was perfect. This would give him plenty of time to get his phone, call Blackburn, and pick up a bathing suit before heading to the hotel. He kissed her good-bye and then drove directly to the AT&T store, where he picked out a phone and got his data transferred. Back in the Jeep, he called Blackburn immediately. If he couldn't get him at the office, he'd try him on his cell. The phone rang.

"Hello, this is Blackburn," the voice on the other end said perfunctorily.

"Hey, George, it's Tom."

"Hey, Tom! Good to hear from you. You having some fun down there now?"

"Yeah, I am, George. But you're not going to believe this. I've uncovered some important stuff down here. Several hundred pounds of coke, for starters. It's on a boat owned by this guy Charlie Petersen, and it's docked near me right now."

"Whoa! How'd you come across that?"

"Long story," Morgan said. "Problem is, I don't know when it might be moved, or where. And if it moves, I can't follow it. I need some help! Like today!"

"Wow! I don't know, Tom," Blackburn said, seeming to mull the circumstances over in his mind. "I'd have to get the Miami office involved. I can't promise anything, but I'll give 'em a call and see what they say. Can I assume you're calling on your cell?"

"I am," he said.

"OK, I'll call Miami and get back to you as soon as I can—hopefully within an hour or so."

"Oh, just one more thing," Morgan said. "I don't have a weapon down here, and I'd feel a whole lot better if I had one. If you can get somebody to come down and help out, will you see if they can bring me a .45? I'd appreciate it."

"Sure, Tom. I'll see what I can do. By the way," he added, "what else you been up to since you been down there, besides chasing coke?"

"A lot," Morgan said. "For one thing, I've met this really terrific woman."

"Really?" Blackburn said. "What's her name?"

"Vivian," Morgan answered. "Vivian Petersen."

"Isn't that the same name as this guy with the coke?"

"Yeah…she's his sister. But she's not involved in any of this. She doesn't know anything about it."

Blackburn paused. "All right," he said. "If you say so. Well, I'll get back in touch with you—like I said, hopefully within an hour or so."

They hung up, and Morgan placed the phone on the Jeep's seat, between his legs. OK. He needed to buy a new bathing suit and get to the hotel as soon as possible. He wanted to get there before Vivian, and hopefully Blackburn would get back to him before she arrived.

He started the Jeep and drove to the nearest store where he thought he could find a bathing suit, located one, and went to his place and put it on—plus a fresh shirt and his flip-flops. Then he drove to the parking lot near the pier and Petersen's boat. He parked and walked down the pier to satisfy himself that the boat was still there. It was. He only hoped it hadn't moved sometime in the night. He also hoped Blackburn really understood the urgency involved here and that the people in Miami would understand as well—and respond.

He walked up the hill to the Harborview. It was nearly eleven o'clock when he arrived on the pool deck, and a few people were already starting to gather for their day of sunbathing. He selected a couple of chaise lounges near the pool's perimeter railing and repositioned them, so that he would only have to turn his head slightly to one side for a clear view, through the railing, down to the pier. If anyone moved that boat, he would know it. Now, all he needed to do was wait for Blackburn's call.

He took his shirt off, kicked off his flip-flops, and settled back onto the chaise, glancing occasionally toward the pier. A few people arrived and departed, but no boats moved. Half an hour passed, and then forty-five minutes. It was almost noon, and still no call from Blackburn. The minutes dragged. He took his phone from his pocket and placed it on the chaise next to him. He hoped he was going to hear from the old man before Vivian arrived. He continued to watch those on the pool deck and at the pier. Finally, after another few minutes, his cell rang.

"Hey, George," Morgan answered quickly.

"Good news," Blackburn said. "I just talked to some guy in Miami by the name of Jim Trumbull. He says they'll have two, maybe three men down there sometime early this evening. Will that help?"

"Sure will, George. Thanks." He paused. "By the way, I assume you gave them my cell number."

Blackburn chuckled through the phone. "Sure did, Tom. They'll give you a call as soon as their plane lands."

"Great," he said. "Oh, and be sure to tell Dan and Scott what's going on down here, will you? Tell 'em I've been thinking about them, and I'm sorry I haven't called. But I'll call them in a day or two."

"OK, will do, Tom."

"Thanks again, George, for everything."

They hung up and Morgan resumed his vigil. The minutes continued to tick by. If all went as Blackburn said, he thought agents from Miami should be there by five or six o'clock. He just hoped Petersen's boat wouldn't move in the meantime.

It was only a few minutes past noon when Vivian arrived. He waved to her from across the pool deck. She waived back and walked toward him.

"Hey, how long have you been here?" she asked with a pleasant ring to her voice.

"Just a few minutes," he said, not wanting to tell her he'd been there for more than an hour. She was wearing a white cover-up, step-up sandals, and a large, big-brim straw hat. She carried an equally large, straw beach bag and a couple of towels.

"Here," she said, smiling and handing him one of the towels. "I brought one for you." She smiled again.

"Thanks," he said, realizing that in his haste to get there he had failed to think of bringing one. She put her beach bag on the pool deck, took off her sandals and hat—and finally her cover-up, revealing a deep-red bikini. Her lipstick matched it perfectly; and she smiled as she sat down and reclined on the chaise beside him.

"Did you get your phone all right?"

"Sure did," he said. "Got it right here." He held it up for her to see. "How about you?"

"Yes, no problem for me. I had no data to transfer. But I looked up a salvage company and called about the *Bon Voyage.*"

"Oh, good," he said. "Are they going to be able to pull her off those rocks?"

"They thought they probably could. They're going to see about raising her tomorrow, and they'll call me when they've got her in their yard. Then I'll be able to call the insurance company."

"What about everything onboard? Your purse, the dive gear, and everything?"

"They said they'd send it all." She paused. "Meantime..." she said, pausing slightly more, "do you suppose I could have your number?" She asked, pretending to almost beg.

"Oh, I *suppose*," he said, mimicking the way she had said the same words to him when he had asked for her number the evening after their first day of sailing. He recited his number. She entered it, and they sat talking casually for a few minutes.

"By the way, I haven't had lunch yet," she said. "You haven't eaten either, have you?"

He hadn't eaten, of course, and he knew as soon as she asked that she would probably want to go up to the Sundowner. He didn't want to leave the pool deck, but at the same time he saw no way of *not* having lunch with her.

"No, I haven't. You want to get something?"

"Yes," she said. "I'm hungry." She stood and began putting on her cover-up. Meantime, Morgan slipped on his shirt and flip-flops, and they left the pool deck, heading up the steps to the Sundowner. He calculated that if they proceeded at a somewhat less than leisurely pace, they should be able to have lunch and return in less than an hour. He just hoped Petersen's boat wouldn't leave during that time.

As soon as they finished lunch and returned, Morgan looked immediately in the direction of the pier and the boat. It was still there, and in the approximately forty-five minutes they had been in the restaurant, he doubted anyone had had time to move it and return. They ordered piña coladas and spent the remainder of the afternoon relaxing, reading magazines, and talking—with Morgan glancing occasionally toward the pier to confirm Petersen's boat was still present.

As the hours passed, a few people arrived at the dock. A workman came with a truck and a toolbox, apparently to make some repairs to one of the boats. A sailboat arrived as well—with the owner spending considerable time washing the boat down before departing for his car in the lot where Morgan had parked. But there were no boat departures. He had to remind himself that it was, after all, Monday. Most of these boat owners were probably at work, with no plans for boating today. Nevertheless, he continued to watch.

A few minutes before five o'clock, his cell rang. "Hello," he said, "this is Tom." He listened as one of the agents from Miami explained that they had just arrived at the airport. They had picked up their luggage and were waiting to get their rental car. He wanted to know where and when they could meet. "Yes. Yes," Morgan said. "Listen, I know this is going to take some time. Can I call you back in a few minutes?" He waited for the agent's response; then he hung up and looked at Vivian.

"My office," he said, trying to sound disappointed. "I'm going to have to talk with them, and it's almost certain to take a while."

"They're not going to try to get you to come back to Chicago, are they?"

"No, I don't think so. At least not yet anyway. And if they do," he continued, "I'll just have to tell them I'm not going." He smiled reassuringly.

"Well, OK," she said, smiling back, but with a hint of distrust still in her voice. "I suppose I've had enough sun anyway, so I guess it's time to go." She stood and began putting on her cover-up and sandals and picking up her things. Morgan stood as well and put on his shirt and flip-flops.

"I'll walk you to your car. I've had enough sun too." When they reached her Mercedes, he kissed her.

"You coming over for dinner?" she asked.

"Sure. As soon as I finish with these people at the office, I'll go back to my place and freshen up. Then I'll come over."

"OK. I'll pick up some things at the grocery and see you in a little while."

He watched her drive away; then he walked quickly to the Jeep. As soon as he sat behind the wheel, he returned the Miami agent's call.

"This is Tom Morgan," he said when the agent answered. "Where are you now?"

"We're still at the airport," he said. "But we're about ready to leave." He explained that there were three of them. Before leaving Miami they had arranged to rent a boat as well as a car. They would drop one of them at the boat rental, and the other two would drive to meet Morgan.

"Where can we meet up?" the agent asked. Morgan gave him directions to the Harborview, and described his location in the parking lot, adjacent to the hotel but down near the water, not far from the pier.

"I'm in a red Jeep with a tan convertible top," he said. They hung up, and Morgan waited.

CHAPTER TWENTY-FOUR

I n half an hour, a gray Honda sedan pulled up in the parking space beside Morgan. The passenger in the vehicle, a man with a shaved head in his late-thirties, rolled down his window.

"You Tom Morgan?" he asked.

"Sure am," Morgan responded. "Man, am I glad to see you guys!"

The two agents, dressed in casual, plain clothes, left their car and approached Morgan, still seated in the Jeep.

"Tom, I'm Bill Cavanaugh," the driver of the Honda said, extending his hand. Cavanaugh, in his mid-forties, with a deep, husky voice, was just over six feet tall with a medium build and visible strands of gray in his black, wavy hair. He flipped open his badge wallet to show

Morgan his identification. "And this guy here with the bald head is Bob Brady. Ain't he a beaut?" Cavanaugh smiled.

Morgan smiled in return and shook their hands as they nodded hello.

"Your other partner's bringing the boat over, I guess."

"Yeah," Cavanaugh responded. "That's Ricardo. He should be here before long. He knows to look for us out here near the hotel. While we're waiting, though," Cavanaugh continued, "why don't you fill us in on what's been happening? We want to be sure we've got the story straight."

Morgan described briefly how he had discovered the cocaine beneath the floor in the Petersen family Great House on St. Croix, how yesterday he had caught sight of the plane from the hangar landing a few miles west and north of the St. Thomas airport, and how he had followed Petersen—owner and general manager of the Harborview—down here, where some of his men had carried the coke onto his boat, *Charlie's Change.* Morgan gestured toward the pier, explaining he'd also kept an eye on the boat this afternoon, until now.

"Sounds like you've been pretty busy," Cavanaugh said. "So, any reason we can't take a walk down there and see what this boat looks like?"

"No reason I can think of," Morgan answered.

"OK, I'll call Ricardo" Cavanaugh said, "and have him meet us down at the end of the pier."

Cavanaugh made the call. Ricardo said he was on the boat in the middle of the harbor, and he could see the hotel and the pier in the distance. He'd be there in just a couple of minutes. As Cavanaugh and Brady walked with Morgan down the length of the pier, Morgan casually called their attention to Petersen's boat as they passed by, and within minutes after they reached the end of the pier, Ricardo pulled up in a speedboat. He cut the engine and tied the boat off. Cavanaugh made the introductions.

"Tom, this is Ricardo Alvarez. Ricardo, Tom Morgan." The two men shook hands and said hello. Alvarez was about five-feet nine, with a stocky build, and though he was clearly Latino, with black hair and dark eyes, he had no accent. He wanted to walk down the pier to take a look at the boat as well, and when he returned, Morgan said first thing he wanted to do was establish their plan.

For privacy, and to avoid drawing attention to themselves, they boarded the speedboat and anchored some distance out in the harbor. Once there, Morgan explained that he specifically did not want to simply grab the coke and arrest a few locals. Rather, he wanted to follow Petersen's boat, wherever it might go, and hopefully follow the coke up the pipeline, so they could find out who was involved, and where.

Since Petersen could move the boat at any time, it was agreed that Cavanaugh, Brady, and Alvarez would stay on the speedboat 'round the clock, and, working in shifts, they'd be ready to follow Petersen's boat whenever it might move. Of course, it was also recognized that, despite the fact that the cocaine was on the boat now, it could still possibly be moved over land to yet another location. Therefore, Morgan would remain in and around Charlotte Amalie at all times, and if they saw the coke being transferred back onto land, they'd call him immediately. He'd then have to get to the parking lot and pier fast, in order to trail its movement on land. He just needed to stay nearby—and ready. That was it. And that would work. The three of them exchanged cell numbers with Morgan and agreed they would stay in touch occasionally throughout each day.

"Just a couple more things before we go back," Morgan said. "Petersen has a sister, Vivian, and she's not involved in any of this. I'm certain of that, since it was actually because of her that I came across the coke in the first place. Also, she has no idea that I'm with the DEA, and I want to keep it that way—at least for now. So if you guys should come into contact with her for some reason, she's not to know about me. Agreed?

"Sure, Tom," Cavanaugh said. "As far as I'm concerned, you're in charge here." The other two nodded their heads in agreement as well.

"And one final thing," Morgan said. Did you bring me a weapon? I've got nothing down here, and I'd feel a whole lot better if I had something."

"Sure did," Cavanaugh said. "It's back in the car."

"OK. Well, I think that covers everything," Morgan said, "at least for now. If anything else comes up, we can discuss it at the time."

Alvarez started the engine and dropped the three of them back at the pier, agreeing to stay with the boat while Cavanaugh and Brady went shopping for food for the next couple of days. In the parking lot, Cavanaugh retrieved a locked metal box and its key from the trunk of the Honda and handed it to Morgan.

"It's a .45," he said, "with an extra clip and a couple boxes of ammo. Hope you won't need all of it," he said, smiling slightly.

"Yeah, hope not," Morgan said, smiling back.

He took the box, shook hands with both of them, and gave them directions to a nearby grocery. After they drove away, he thought about calling Blackburn to let him know the Miami guys had arrived, but it was already 6:30, and he had to get back to his place and then to Vivian's. He'd send Blackburn a quick text for now, and call him in the morning with more details.

CHAPTER TWENTY-FIVE

The following morning, as Morgan helped Vivian clean up their breakfast dishes, he rinsed the plates, cups, and glasses, and placed them in the dishwasher. She closed it and turned it on.

"So, what are you planning to do today?" she asked.

"Well, I thought I'd meet you for lunch. But before that I'm going to get some fishing gear and go fishing. I started thinking about it last night, and I want to give it a try. I think I'll go down to the harbor somewhere."

"Wow! Well, good luck," she said, as she picked up her purse from the island. "Maybe you'll catch us something for dinner." She smiled.

"We'll see," he said, smiling back. "Shall I drop you at the gallery?"

"I guess, if you want. I was going to walk."

"No, come on," he said. "I'll drop you."

They left the condo, and he drove her down the hill to Waterfront and then the gallery. He stopped the Jeep and leaned over and kissed her. "See you at noon," he said.

"OK," she said as she stepped out. "See you then!" She smiled, blew him a kiss, and walked toward the front door. He watched as she went inside; then he drove off.

He knew there was a bait and tackle store only a few blocks away. He'd go there now and buy some gear, just as he'd said—at least a rod and reel, some lures, a bait bucket, and maybe a cooler and some ice. Even if he caught nothing, it would give him something to do for the day, and it would keep him near the water and not far from Petersen's boat, in case he got a call from Cavanaugh or one of the others. But he also wanted to get back to Blackburn and make sure the old man got his text. When he pulled up in front of the bait and tackle store, he called Blackburn's cell.

"Hey, Tom," Blackburn said when he answered. "Got your text. I see the guys from Miami got down there all right."

"Yeah, we got 'em all set up. They've been on a boat, out in the harbor, since last evening, providing surveillance on Petersen's boat. I'm on standby, in case the coke gets transferred back onto land."

"Well, sounds like you've got the bases covered."

"I think so," Morgan said. "By the way, did you let Dan and Scott know what's going on?"

"Yep, sure did, Tom."

"Well, I'm going to give 'em a call myself. It's been too long since I've talked with them."

"OK," Blackburn said. "Just be sure to keep me up-to-date about what happens."

"Will do, George."

They hung up, and Morgan went into the store and made his purchases. Then he drove to the harbor, tossed a line in the water, and called Weber.

"Hey, Buddy!" Weber said enthusiastically when he answered his cell. "We been wondering what the hell you've been up to. George tells us that you've come across a stash of coke down there—and you've got some guys from Miami helping you keep an eye on it."

"Yeah, that's the situation," he said. "And when it moves, I'm hoping we can follow it. I want to see where it winds up."

"Sounds good," Weber said. "Say, Scotty's here, and he wants to talk to you too. I'll put you on speaker."

"Hey, Scott, how you doin'?"

"Good," he said. "Say, George also tells us you've found yourself a special lady down there. Is that right?"

"Yeah, she's pretty terrific all right."

"Well, why don't you send us a picture?"

"OK, I can do that. I'll send you one as soon as we hang up."

"She doesn't know you work for the Agency does she?" Sullivan asked.

"No. I haven't been able to tell her yet. It's her brother who's running the coke."

"Oh, man! Sounds like you're really in the middle of it. Well, keep us up to speed on what happens. Give us a call or a text once in a while."

"Will do, Scotty. I'm sorry I haven't been in touch. I guess I've just had a lot on my plate."

When they hung up, he forwarded both of them a copy of the photo of himself and Vivian taken during their first afternoon at the Rum Hut. He knew they'd like it. They'd also probably wish they were here with him.

Morgan fished for the remainder of the morning but caught nothing of consequence. Then he met Vivian for lunch. She wanted to go to a little street-side café on Radets Gada. It was only a couple of blocks from the gallery, so they walked, and as soon as they were seated she asked about his fishing.

"So, how did it go this morning? Did you catch anything?"

"Oh, I got a couple of bites and hooked one," he said. "But it was small, so I threw it back."

"Well, maybe you'll have better luck this afternoon."

"I hope so," he said. "But maybe I'm not much of a fisherman."

"Well, give it a chance," she said encouragingly. "Remember, you just started."

"You're right," he said. "I'll try to be patient about it." The thing he was really impatient about, though, was Petersen's boat—and when it might move. He was more than anxious to see where it might go and what would happen with the coke when it got there.

When they finished their lunch, he walked her back to the gallery, and then drove to the parking lot near the pier, just to make sure the boat hadn't moved—and that Cavanaugh and the others hadn't somehow missed it. But it was still there. Afterward, he looked for another location on the harbor, where he thought he might have better luck with his fishing.

CHAPTER TWENTY-SIX

Morgan continued fishing this same way during the next few days. Each morning after dropping Vivian at the gallery, he'd drive somewhere along the harbor, find a spot that looked promising, and fish for a few hours. Then, after meeting Vivian for lunch, he'd fish for the remainder of the afternoon. Once in a while he'd get a nibble or a bite, and occasionally he'd drag some poor, undersized creature to the shore or to the dock he sometimes frequented. But nothing ever seemed worth keeping. From time to time, he would receive a call from Cavanaugh—or Morgan would call him just to relieve his boredom and confirm that none of them had seen anything. But, though several days passed, neither they nor Morgan saw anyone approach Petersen's boat.

Then each evening Morgan and Vivian would have dinner, either at his place or hers, and watch TV or perhaps play cards or some board game. One evening she said the salvage company had called about the boat. They had retrieved it—or at least what was left of it. She had called the insurance company also and filed a claim. They were sending an adjustor to check the boat out and provide an estimate of the damage—although the salvage company said it was a total loss. Other than that, nothing of consequence occurred. Morgan and Cavanaugh continued their daily contacts, and at night Cavanaugh, Brady, or Alvarez—whoever was on duty— used night-vision binoculars to keep tabs on Petersen's boat, but no one visited, day or night. One evening, however, when Morgan was out on Vivian's patio after dinner, he received a call.

"You're not gonna believe this," Cavanaugh said quickly. "A couple of guys showed up at the boat a while ago and started bringing *more* coke onboard!"

"You're kidding," Morgan said. "How much?"

"Not exactly sure. We couldn't see everything because some of the other boats were in the way. But it looked like they made three or four trips from a car in the parking lot. So if they were each carrying two bags on each trip, it looks like somewhere around a dozen bags."

"Damn," Morgan said. "That's maybe another five- or six-hundred pounds! I wonder how much they're going to put on that boat before they move it."

"Well, one thing's for sure," Cavanaugh continued jokingly, "they've got to be hoping like hell it doesn't sink!"

His comment made Morgan smile, and he was curious about the two men who had brought the coke onboard.

"What'd these guys look like?"

"Well, at this distance we couldn't get a real good look, but they were both white and looked like they were pretty husky. One of 'em was wearing a ball cap; the other one had his hair buzzed off short. Other than that we couldn't tell much."

Morgan thought it might have been the same two he had seen at Petersen's house and who later had put the first shipment onboard—if what he had seen *was* the first shipment. More likely, however, there had been other shipments before that, and he just happened to have seen one in what was almost certainly an ongoing stream of shipments.

"Well, you're obviously keeping your eye on things out there," he said. "Something else has got to happen. We'll just have to wait and see." As they ended the conversation, Morgan wondered how many more shipments there might be before Petersen moved the boat. He opened the slider and walked back inside.

"Did I hear you talking with somebody out there?" Vivian called out from the kitchen.

"Yeah, it was my boss again."

She came from the kitchen and walked up to him, put her arms around his neck, and stood close. "Now, he's not trying to get you to come back to Chicago, is he?"

"No," Morgan said. "He was just checking to see how I'm doing. He said he's glad I'm enjoying myself."

"So, you're enjoying yourself, are you?" she asked, looking into his eyes and smiling. He felt her push up against him in a way that left no question what she had in mind.

"You might say that," he said, smiling back.

"No, I want to hear *you* say it."

"Yes, I'm enjoying myself," he said. He smiled again and leaned forward and kissed her.

She kissed him back. Then she took him by the hand, and they walked toward her bedroom.

CHAPTER TWENTY-SEVEN

Still more days passed, and Morgan's daily routine
continued much as before. Some mornings he would
drive to the pier and watch Petersen's boat for a while—at
least until he got bored watching nothing occur. Then he
would go somewhere else around the harbor and throw a
line in the water. Occasionally he would drag in another
miniscule fish, which he would invariably throw back before going to meet Vivian for lunch.

Each afternoon would be a virtual repeat of the
morning, and he as well as Cavanaugh and the others were growing impatient with the lack of activity.
Cavanaugh continued to call each day, at least once
and sometimes more; and Morgan was always grateful
when his phone rang. Likewise, he would occasionally
call Cavanaugh, especially if he was growing anxious

at having heard nothing from him. Initially they had all agreed they would follow the coke, find out where it was going, and hopefully make enough arrests to interrupt at least this part of the supply chain. But Brady and Alvarez especially were beginning to say they wanted to move in and arrest Petersen and his men, just to get this thing over with, so they could return to Miami.

But then one night about 9:30, while Morgan was out picking up a bottle of wine to take back to Vivian's, he got a call from Cavanaugh, who was speaking in a near whisper.

"You're not going believe what the hell's happening out here now," Cavanaugh said. "A little bit ago, four men got on Petersen's boat, motored across the harbor to a spot not far from one of the cruise ships, and after a few minutes they began putting some kind of submersible devices into the water."

"Submersible devices?" Morgan questioned.

"Yeah, they look sort of like torpedoes."

"How big?" he asked.

"Pretty big. They look like they're probably five or six feet long and maybe a foot in diameter. Two of the men got in the water with scuba outfits, and…. Oh, there they go again!" Cavanaugh continued. "They just disappeared with the *fourth one!*"

Morgan's mind raced over what Cavanaugh was telling him, trying to make sense of it. If these submersibles were shaped like torpedoes, they were obviously made to travel easily through the water. They certainly weren't intended to blow up the ship. But if they were big enough—or there were enough of them—they could hold the cocaine from Petersen's boat. Maybe they had some way of attaching these devices to the hull of the ship, and that's how they were getting the coke into the States. No need to risk flying it in or running it in aboard some speedboat. Just quietly, surreptitiously sneak it in, unseen and unsuspected by anyone. Pretty damn clever, he thought.

"Can you get the name of that ship?"

"Yeah," Cavanaugh said. "I can see it right now. It's the *Caribbean Princess*."

"OK," he said. "You go ahead and monitor what's going on out there. I'll check online later tonight and find out where this boat's headed, and I'll call you in the morning."

He went into the store, completed his wine purchase, and then returned to the condo, where he and Vivian snuggled on the couch for a time. After an hour or so, they went to bed. He lay there close beside her, listening until he could hear her breathing softly, rhythmically. When he was convinced that she was asleep, he slowly eased himself out of bed, took his phone from its charger cord, and went into the bathroom, quietly closing the door behind him. He could have waited until the next morning to find out where this *Caribbean Princess* was headed, but he couldn't help himself. He had grown so anxious during the past few days, when nothing had happened, that he had to find out, now!

He got online with his phone, but had to look at several cruise lines that traveled the Caribbean before he discovered the *Caribbean Princess.* As it turned out, her next port of call after St. Thomas was San Juan, *tomorrow,* and then Grand Turk Island in the Turks and Caicos the day after that, and finally Miami, three days from now. It was difficult to imagine Puerto Rico as the final destination for the coke, and it certainly would not be the Turks and Caicos, as they were too small to use almost any amount over a handful. Miami had to be where it was headed. To be certain, though, he'd call Blackburn tomorrow morning and see if he could get somebody to check the ship out while it was in Puerto Rico. Maybe, for some reason, the coke was going to be transferred to yet another ship while it was there. Either way, he'd call Blackburn first thing. He shut his phone off and then quietly returned to bed, carefully pulling the covers over himself. He could hear Vivian still breathing softly, just as before.

CHAPTER TWENTY-EIGHT

The next morning after breakfast, Morgan again dropped Vivian at the gallery and departed for one of his usual spots around the harbor. First, though, he stopped again in the parking lot near the pier to check on Petersen's boat. There it was, back in its slip, as if nothing whatsoever had occurred. He would call Blackburn in another hour or so. But first he wanted to talk with Cavanaugh to find out if anything else had happened after their conversation last night. He pulled his cell from his pocket and punched up Cavanaugh's number.

"Morning, Bill," he said when Cavanaugh answered. "Anything interesting happen after we talked last night?"

"Yeah, we saw them put two more submersibles in the water, for a total of six. Got some pictures too, and afterward we managed to get a good look at all four of these guys."

"Really," Morgan said with some surprise.

"Yeah. After they headed back to the pier, we did too and tied up down at the end. We got off and walked up the pier just about the time they were getting off of their boat. That's when we saw them, under the lights. I'm pretty sure we could identify 'em in court."

"That's terrific!" Morgan said. "I've got to tell you what a great job you guys have done, not only last night but in all the days and nights leading up to this. Where are you now?"

"Well, we were tired of that damn boat, and we were able to get rooms over here at the Windward Passage."

"So what's your plan for the rest of the day?"

"We thought we'd try to fly back to Miami this afternoon. We figured our work here was done, at least for now. In fact, Brady just signaled me that he can get us on a flight that leaves about 2:30, if that sounds OK."

"Sure," Morgan said. "But I'd like to see you guys before you go. Obviously I couldn't have done any of this without you."

"Why don't you come on over and join us for breakfast?"

"Will do," Morgan said. "See you in just a few minutes."

They hung up. Morgan drove to their hotel and then sat with them in the restaurant. The waitress, a young woman who said her name was Sherry, came with menus and then returned to take their order. Morgan explained that he'd already had breakfast but he would have some coffee.

As the others sat eating, he said, "I'm guessing that last night was probably the first decent night's sleep you guys have had since you've been here." All three heartily agreed.

"Yeah," Brady jumped in. "It was pretty damned hot and crowded on that boat!"

"And the food wasn't all that good either," Alvarez offered. "No rice and beans. I got tired of cold cuts and soft drinks." They all laughed.

"Well, I can't thank you all enough for what you've done, especially with the heat and cramped quarters— to say nothing about the lousy food." They all laughed again.

"After a few days out there on the water," Cavanaugh said, "we talked about the possibility of one or two of us at a time spending an occasional night in a hotel, but we never knew what might happen—or when. So we just toughed it out."

"Well, again, I can't thank you enough. And just so you know, the *Caribbean Princess* is scheduled to dock in Miami in a couple of days. I'm going to be there to meet it; and I hope you guys might be able to get yourselves assigned to continue working with me on this. Think you can?"

"Yeah, I'm pretty sure we could do that," Cavanaugh said.

"Well, I hope so. And if it works out, we'll have to find some time to go out and have a drink or two after I get there. And I'll buy! OK?"

They all smiled and shook hands. Morgan left the restaurant, and waved back to them as he departed. It was now a little past 10:00—8:00 in Chicago—and he needed to call Blackburn. As he walked to the Jeep, he called the old man's cell.

"Morning, Tom. How are things going down there now?"

"Well, I've got some good news. Some interesting developments."

"What's that?"

"A few days ago, Petersen's men put five- to six-hundred more pounds of coke on his boat, and then last night—now get this—it looks like they loaded the coke into some kind of submersibles and somehow mounted them, below the waterline, on the hull of a cruise ship."

"No shit," Blackburn said. "Is it still there?"

"No, that's the problem, George. It left here later last night, bound for San Juan. It'll be in the Turks and Caicos tomorrow and then Miami day after that. I don't know if somebody might off-load the stuff in Puerto Rico or if it'll stay onboard all the way to Florida."

"I hear you," he said. "Most likely it'll make it all the way to the States, but just to be sure, I'll contact Miami again and see if Trumbull can get somebody down there with a scuba outfit to check it out. What's the name of this boat?"

"The *Caribbean Princess.*"

"And how long is it supposed to be in San Juan?"

"Just today," Morgan said.

"All right. I'll see what I can do. I'll get back to you as soon as I know something."

They hung up, and Morgan began what he calculated would be a wait of probably several hours. To fill the time, he decided to go fishing again, but first he went back to the bait and tackle shop where he'd made his original purchases and bought some live shrimp. Afterward, he looked for a good spot along the harbor's edge to drop in a line, thinking this time he might actually catch something worth keeping.

By noon, however, he had not caught a single fish; and when he hadn't heard from Blackburn, he packed his gear back in the Jeep and went to the gallery to meet Vivian. They walked together along Tvaer Gada street and found a sidewalk café where there were sizeable trees, which made the area at least somewhat cool in the mid-day heat. They sat at one of the umbrella-shaded tables and ordered.

"Did you catch anything this morning?" she asked.

"No. I even bought shrimp for bait," he said, "and didn't get a single bite. I guess the fish here just don't like shrimp!" They both laughed.

"Well, maybe you'll be luckier this afternoon," she said. He could tell she was trying to sound hopeful.

After their meal Morgan walked her back to the gallery.

"Call me when you're ready to leave," he said, "and I'll come get you." He kissed her good-bye, and then returned to the harbor to resume fishing.

He had only a couple of bites the entire afternoon, and neither produced a fish worth keeping. When it was almost five o'clock and he had not yet heard from Blackburn, he decided to call him to see what, if anything, had been discovered.

"I was just getting ready to call you," Blackburn said when he answered his cell. "Trumbull had some people in San Juan check out your boat, and sure enough there are submersibles of some kind stuck on it. They didn't say how they were attached, but they're still on there, so it looks like they're going all the way to Miami."

"Great!" Morgan said. "Then I'm going too! I've got to be a part of this!"

"I thought you'd probably say something like that," Blackburn said. "So I talked with some of the people upstairs a little bit ago, and based on all the work you've been doing since you've been gone, they've agreed we should cover your expenses while you've been down there—and for this whole adventure, wherever it leads. That's in addition to your salary, of course."

"Hey, that sounds terrific, George. Thank you!"

"Just be sure to take care of yourself while you're in Miami, and keep me informed."

"I will, George. I will."

They hung up and within a few minutes Vivian called, saying she was ready to leave the gallery. He sent a brief text to both Weber and Sullivan, to let them know he was following the coke to Miami. Then he drove to the gallery to get Vivian. He knew that after they arrived at her condo, they would fix dinner; and either during dinner, or after, he would have to tell her he was going to go to Miami—or rather *Chicago*, he corrected himself. He couldn't let her know Miami was his destination, so he'd book a flight to Chicago that stopped in Miami; and he'd get off there. He didn't know how he was going to pull this off. But he knew he had to, somehow.

CHAPTER TWENTY-NINE

After dinner that evening, as they sat together on the couch, Morgan decided it was time to bring up the subject of his planned trip.

"By the way, my boss called again this afternoon," he began.

"Oh?" she said, sounding a little concerned. "What'd he want?"

"Well, apparently some issues have come up now, which only I can help resolve, and he wants me to come back for a few days."

"Why does it have to be you?" she said, in what sounded like a mixture of disappointment and anxiety over him leaving, and the prospect of him perhaps not coming back.

"Well, it involves a lot of crop issues in the Midwest," he said. "And, of course, that's my region, so I guess I'll have to go."

"Well, are you sure it's just for a few days?"

"Yeah, I'm sure. At least it won't be for more than a week, at most."

"Maybe I could go with you!" she said, suddenly sounding excited at the prospect. "You know I've never been to Chicago."

"And this from a woman who doesn't like to fly?"

"I don't," she said. "But I'd do it to be with you."

"Look, we'll go to Chicago...sometime. But this trip isn't the right time. I'll be working long hours, I'm sure; and you'll be bored just sitting around my place or otherwise waiting for me. Let's plan to go when we can spend some quality time together, and I can show you around the city. Meanwhile, I promise to call you all the time, every day I'm away."

"You promise?"

"I promise," he said; and he kissed her—twice. "Now, I better book my flight." He picked up his phone. "You want to look with me?"

"No, you go ahead," she said. She got up from the couch. "I'll clean up the kitchen. Then maybe we can watch a movie...or something." She smiled coyly and looked at him in such a way that he knew almost certainly what the "something" was that she had in mind.

When she left the room, he got online to begin his search. Sure enough, he found a flight leaving the next afternoon at 2:30. It stopped in Miami some three hours later and then proceeded on to Chicago, arriving there about 9:00 p.m. He booked the flight and showed the schedule to Vivian.

"You're only booking one way?" she questioned, again sounding concerned.

"Well, I don't know if it will take three days, or four or five."

"But you're sure it's only going to take a few days, right?" she said again. "Otherwise I'm coming with you."

"Yes, only a few days," he said. "I promise."

Later in the evening, after watching TV, they went to bed. Vivian kissed him, and he kissed her back. Then she whispered in his ear and softly reached down beneath the covers, leaving no doubt in his mind what the "something" was that she had alluded to earlier. He smiled and kissed her more. And among the many kisses that followed, he thought how much he loved her and how much he hated leaving her. And with every kiss and squeeze and movement of her body, he realized how much *she* loved him and hated to see him go.

Afterward, as they lay side by side, holding hands, he thought more about the necessity of continually hiding things from her—this self-made subterfuge he found himself held hostage to. One of these days, he would tell her the truth and quit this damned job. But not now. Not yet. He couldn't—at least not until he followed this Petersen thing through to its conclusion. And he still wanted to somehow find Elaine's killers.

Then, he thought, he could quit. And then he would want to.

"I'll take you to the airport tomorrow," she said.

"And I'll call you just as soon as I get to Chicago. I promise."

CHAPTER THIRTY

The following morning, after breakfast, Morgan drove to his place to pack. He took his fishing gear from the backseat of the Jeep, and once inside he stowed it away in an otherwise empty closet. He thought how relatively little he and Vivian had actually used the house since he had leased it. While they had spent some evenings there, most nights had been at her condo. Still, it was good to have his own place. For one thing he didn't have to worry about her accidentally stumbling across his badge or gun when they weren't with him in the Jeep.

He showered and shaved, then packed everything he thought he would need for the trip—including the .45, both clips, and the extra ammunition. He removed the first clip from the gun, checked to make sure there wasn't a round in the chamber and then put everything, including his badge wallet, in the metal box and locked it. He put the box into his suitcase; and before calling Vivian to come pick him up, he called Cavanaugh in Miami.

"Hey, Tom," Cavanaugh said. "What's up?"

"I was wondering if you'd heard—Trumbull got our boat checked out while it was in San Juan yesterday, and, sure enough, the submersibles are still on it. They'll be on their way to Miami tomorrow."

"Yeah, that's what we heard. What're you planning to do now?"

"Well, I'm flying to Miami this afternoon, arriving around 5:30, and I was wondering if one of you guys— or maybe all of you—might be able to pick me up at the airport."

"Sure," he said. "What airline?"

"American...flight 1720."

"OK. I'll be there for sure," Cavanaugh said. "Maybe the others will be able to make it too."

"I hope so," Morgan said. "Remember, I promised to take you all out for some drinks, and I'll buy dinner too."

"All right, I'll tell 'em," Cavanaugh said. "Anything else?"

"Yeah, a couple of things. I'd like all of us to have a meeting with Trumbull sometime tomorrow—hopefully in the morning. I figure he's already on top of this thing. But I want to meet him and thank him for all the help you guys have provided. I'd also like to be involved in the planning for tomorrow night when our boat arrives."

"Well, I don't know his schedule," Cavanaugh said, "but I'm sure I can get something arranged. He's a hell of a good guy. You'll like him. What else?"

"I need to book a hotel room in Miami, and I want to be as close to the port as possible. I figured you could recommend the best place."

"Sure can," Cavanaugh said. "I'd try the Marriott first. It's on Biscayne Boulevard, and it looks right out at the port, which is on an island there in the bay. If no rooms there, I'd try the Hyatt.

"OK, thanks," Morgan said. "I'll see you this evening."

They hung up, and before he called Vivian he called the Marriott. They had rooms available, and he requested something high-up, with a view of the port if possible. When he hung up, he thought about what he'd do when he arrived. Cavanaugh—and hopefully the others too—would pick him up; they'd have some drinks and dinner; and afterward he'd call Vivian. But he'd have to fix it in his mind *not* to call her until five hours after his arrival in Miami—which would be about 9:30 Chicago time—to let her know he had finally arrived in "Chicago". He was now more interested than ever to see where this shipment of coke was headed—whether it was destined to stay in Miami or go on elsewhere.

Hopefully they'd be able to track it no matter where it went, and they'd be able to put everybody in this pipeline in prison—including Petersen. He closed his suitcase and called Vivian. She'd be at the bungalow to pick him up in ten minutes.

As he sat waiting, he thought back through the previous weeks: how they had met that first day; how they had met again at the Harborview when he was with Petersen; their days of sailing and snorkeling and diving; her reaction to the necklace when he gave it to her; how excited she had been when he rented the bungalow; their sail to St. Croix; their night together at the Great House; and all their nights together since. He hoped she knew how much he hated to be away from her, even for a few days. But the fact was, he hated the drugs more—and those who dealt in them. Over and over he'd seen the evil that drugs do; how they ruin lives and take lives—like his friends from high school, and like Elaine. That's why he had to put these sons-of-bitches like Petersen, and everybody associated with him, behind bars.

Furthermore, the Agency and Blackburn had always been the absolute best to him. So he would repay the debt, no matter what. He was going to get every one of the bastards in this pipeline and either put them away or kill them. He just hoped he wouldn't get shot in the process, or worse. He wanted to live, now more than ever. Still, he was going to do what he was trained to do and what he knew he had to do. And that was that.

It was nearly 11:30 when Vivian arrived. He locked the front door behind them, put his suitcase in the trunk of the Mercedes, and slid in beside her. He looked at her earnestly.

"Has anybody told you yet today how wonderful you are?" He smiled at her, and leaned toward her and kissed her—twice. "Let's go get some lunch and relax a little before I have to leave."

She smiled, put the car in gear, drove them down through the twists and turns of Symington to the main part of town, and then headed west on Waterfront. After a few blocks, she pulled into the parking lot of a small restaurant called Ocean's Bounty, and they walked inside. The air-conditioning felt cool, and good. White paper tablecloths covered all the tables, and on the walls were mounted examples of Swordfish, Tuna, Grouper, Dolphin, Lobster, and more. Music played softly through the ceiling speakers, and there was a hum of conversation from customers who were already seated. He didn't have to be at the airport until 1:30, so they had plenty of time for lunch. The hostess picked up two menus and seated them at one of the tables for two.

"Your waiter will be right with you," she said pleasantly. Then she returned to her position near the front door.

When the waiter arrived, he took their order and disappeared toward the kitchen. Vivian reached across the table with both hands, and Morgan extended his as well, touching and holding on to hers. She leaned forward.

"Do you have any idea how much I'm going to miss you?" she said softly, shaking her head just slightly for emphasis.

"I think I do," he said. "But no matter how much that is," he continued, "I know I'll miss you more." He smiled.

"And you're coming back to me, right? This is just for a few days, like you said?"

"Yes, just for a few days. And nothing is going to make me stay up there longer than that. I promise. My life is here now, with you. But I do have to tidy up a few things up there first."

"And you're going to call me every day?"

"Every day," he said.

They continued holding hands until their meal arrived. They had each ordered fish, and after the waiter placed their plates in front of them and departed, Vivian looked at him.

"Why don't you ever bring any fish home? You go every day."

Morgan paused. "I guess I'm just a lousy fisherman." He smiled whimsically and then added, "Actually, I do catch one once in a while. But they're usually too small and not worth keeping, so I toss them back. Some are even scrawny!" He smiled again, and she laughed almost audibly.

They continued with their meal, and when they finally finished, she drove them west on Waterfront toward the airport. When she pulled into the area for departures, Morgan got out, retrieved his suitcase from the trunk, and set it on the curb behind him. He leaned back into the car and kissed her.

"I'm really going to miss you," he said. Then he kissed her a final time.

She smiled. "Be sure to call me as soon as you get there."

"I will," he said. He smiled reassuringly as he closed the car door and picked up his suitcase. Then he watched her drive away on the airport road.

Inside the terminal he approached a female ticket agent and placed his bag on the scale.

"Hello," she said. "How may I help you?"

Morgan gave her his name and handed her his passport, explaining that he was booked on flight 1720, through Miami to Chicago.

"But my plans have changed," he said. "I'll be getting off in Miami, and obviously I'd like my bag to go only to Miami as well."

"Oh, that's fine," she said. "We can make that happen." She typed into her computer for a moment. "Anything else?"

"Yes, one other thing," he said. "I have my handgun in the suitcase, but it's packed in a locked box, according to TSA regulations. I assume there won't be a problem."

"No, not at all. As long as you've packed it as you say, it should be no problem whatsoever. I'll code the bag's ticket accordingly." She returned his passport and handed him his boarding pass to Miami, as well as his baggage-claim ticket. "Anything else?"

"No, I think that's it. Thank you."

"Well then, have a nice flight," she said.

He left the ticket counter and walked the short distance to customs, where he completed the required paperwork, indicating he had nothing to declare—except his weapon. He showed his passport to the agent and then walked to his gate to await his flight. It was approaching two o'clock and almost time for boarding. In a little more than three hours he would be in Miami.

CHAPTER THIRTY-ONE

When flight 1720 landed at Miami International and the plane pulled up to its gate and stopped, Morgan reached for his phone and called Cavanaugh.

"Hey, I just arrived," he said. "I'll be getting off the plane in a few minutes. Where are you?"

"We're just pulling onto the airport grounds as we speak," Cavanaugh answered. "All three of us."

"Hey, terrific!" Morgan said. "Glad you could all make it. I'll see you in baggage claim."

As the passengers ahead of him slowly exited their seats, he got up as well and walked toward the front of the plane, then into the jetway and the terminal. When he arrived in baggage claim, Cavanaugh and the others were already there. They shook hands, but there were also hugs all around. It was as if they were old friends who had not seen each other for years and were now happy to be reunited.

"How the hell are you guys?" he said. "Great to see you!"

"Good, good," they all responded. "Good to see you too!"

Eventually Morgan's bag appeared on the conveyor, and they departed for the car.

"Were you able to get a room at the Marriott?" Cavanaugh asked.

"Yeah, I was," Morgan said from the front passenger seat. "Thanks for the help."

As they left the airport grounds and headed east on the expressway, it was still rush hour, and traffic was fairly heavy. Nevertheless, Cavanaugh said the drive shouldn't take more than fifteen to twenty minutes. They used the time to reminisce about St. Thomas; and as they drove, Morgan noticed not only the occasional commercial buildings and homes, but the scores and scores of palm trees, and especially how broad and flat the landscape appeared compared to the hills of St. Thomas. As they approached downtown Miami with its high-rise offices, hotels, and other commercial buildings, they exited the freeway and headed south on Biscayne Boulevard. It was still quite light outside, and after a few blocks Brady gestured to their left, pointing out the causeway that led to the island port and its cruise ships—all clearly visible not more than a quarter mile away. Cavanaugh pulled up to the Marriott's valet parking, and they stepped out. Morgan retrieved his bag from the trunk, and they entered the hotel. As the others took seats on some couches in the center of the lobby, Morgan approached the front desk, introduced himself to one of the clerks—a young Hispanic man— and presented his credit card.

"When I booked the room," he said, "I requested something at least fairly high-up, overlooking the port. I hope you've still got something like that available."

The clerk looked down at his computer screen and typed. "I see your reservation is for a week," he said.

"Yeah, that's right," Morgan responded, "unless business demands otherwise."

"All right. I can put you in room 1137, on the front of the hotel, which overlooks the port."

"Great," Morgan said. "Thank you."

The young man handed him two plastic room keys and returned his credit card.

"By the way," Morgan said, "where's a good restaurant here in the hotel where my friends and I can have dinner?"

The clerk pointed across the lobby. "The Port O' Call, right over there," he said. "It has great food, and it's comfortable."

Morgan turned and walked over to the others. "OK, I'm all set." He pointed across the lobby. "The desk clerk says the Port O' Call over there is a great restaurant. I'll take my bag up to my room and meet you guys there in just a couple of minutes."

In his room, Morgan laid his bag on the bed. It was only a little past 6:30, and he walked immediately to the window. Yes. He had a good view of the island and the port. He studied the layout for a moment. He could see not only where the ships docked, but the surrounding bay and where he and the others might position themselves to await the *Princess*. He returned to the bed, opened his suitcase, and placed the metal box in the safe in the back of the closet. Then he set the combination lock and left the room.

At the Port O' Call, he found Cavanaugh and the others sitting in a large, semicircular, well-cushioned booth.

"All right," he said as he sat down, "you guys thirsty?"

"Yeah," they all answered.

"And hungry too!" Alvarez added.

"Then let's get something to drink—and eat!"

He motioned to a waitress, who immediately came over to them.

"We'd like to order some drinks, and some dinner too if we could."

"All right," she said. "What would you all like to drink?"

One by one they each gave their order, and when it was Morgan's turn he ordered his usual rum and Diet Coke with a wedge of lime. In a few minutes she returned,

leaving menus as well their drinks, and Cavanaugh offered a toast to all of them working together again. They
raised their glasses and drank. Then they continued
drinking and talking about all that had happened back
on St. Thomas. After a time the waitress returned.

"Can I get you all another drink, or would you like to
order dinner now?"

"Yes!" Morgan said enthusiastically, which made
them all laugh.

They ordered another round of drinks, and each
gave her their dinner order as well. When she returned
with the fresh drinks, Morgan handed her his phone
and asked if she'd take their picture, which she did,
snapping two or three photos of them, smiling, with
their glasses raised toward her. Morgan passed the
phone around to show the others.

"I'll text you guys a copy," he said as they returned
the phone to him, and he took a moment to do so. As
he finished the text, he continued. "I have to tell you all
again what a great job you did last week. And under some
really tough circumstances too. You were really terrific!"
He raised his glass in another toast, and they joined him,
all clinking their glasses together this time, causing him
to think again of Elaine. It seemed he just couldn't en-
gage in a toast like that without thinking of her—and the
unknown sons-of-bitches who had killed her.

"You know," he said, "starting tomorrow night we're
going to have our work cut out for us again, and we'll

have to be ready." He looked at Cavanaugh. "I assume you got our meeting set up for tomorrow."

"Sure did," he said. "Trumbull's office at 10:00 a.m."

"Then let's all enjoy ourselves tonight. Tomorrow will come soon enough." They agreed, raised their glasses once more, and drank heartily.

After the waitress brought their dinner, they continued their conversation, and after they finished their meal Morgan signed the check. They agreed that after their meeting with Trumbull, they would drive over to the port, get a firsthand look at the place, and decide on their specific movements later that night.

They left the restaurant and walked through the lobby to the hotel's entrance, where they shook hands and said good night. It was now nearly 9:00 p.m.—8:00 p.m. in Chicago. Morgan returned to his room and watched some TV. In a little more than an hour, it would be time to call Vivian and let her know he had arrived safely—in "Chicago".

CHAPTER THIRTY-TWO

At 9:45 the next morning, Morgan took his badge wallet from the metal box in the safe, relocked it, and went downstairs to take a cab the few blocks to Miami's DEA headquarters. The sky was a perfect, cloudless blue, and even at this relatively early hour he sensed that the heat and humidity here were already somewhat greater than what he had left on St. Thomas.

When he arrived at the DEA office, just as in Chicago, he showed his ID to the guards in the lobby. They provided a temporary, plastic elevator key and directed him to the fourth floor, where he was directed further by the receptionist to Jim Trumbull's office. With windowed, perimeter offices to his left and numerous cubicles to his right, the layout reminded him very much of his own headquarters in Chicago. When he reached Trumbull's office, Cavanaugh, Brady, and Alvarez were already there.

"Good morning, gentlemen," Morgan said as he stepped in.

The others all stood, and Cavanaugh performed the introductions.

"Tom," this is Jim. Jim, Tom Morgan." Morgan shook Trumbull's hand across his desk, nodded, and smiled. Like Blackburn, Trumbull appeared to be in his mid-fifties, and, though balding, he was very fit. He wore a white shirt and tie and a wide, yellow-gold wedding band, which, because of its width, stood out prominently.

"Have a seat, Tom," Trumbull offered, "and let's talk about what's going on."

Morgan sat down. "Well, before we get started with the business at hand, Jim, I'd like to express my appreciation to the Miami office—and to you personally—for your response to George Blackburn's requests for help, initially and then again a couple of days ago in San Juan. You couldn't have sent a better, more cooperative or dedicated groups of guys than these to help me in St. Thomas. And I don't know what they may have told you since they've been back, but they did one hell of a good job down there, staying on that boat around the clock, day after day. We wouldn't be where we are in this thing without them and what they did."

"Well, thank you, Tom, for the kind words. That's most generous of you. But I like to think we're all just doing our job. You know. We all want to get the bad guys."

"Yeah, we sure do," Morgan said. "So. How're we going to meet the *Caribbean Princess* and her cargo of coke tonight?"

"We've started planning for that," Trumbull said. "Glad you're here to participate."

They sat and talked for the next couple of hours about the details of the incoming shipment, what had been planned so far, and how they would meet and hopefully track the shipment successfully to its destination. At the end of the discussion, Trumbull reviewed who would be involved and how everything would be handled.

Number one: Cavanaugh, Brady, and Alvarez, and now Morgan too, would be assigned an unmarked speedboat and would set up a position at the port in order to view the arrival of the *Princess* as well as the removal and initial movement of the coke from the ship to its next location.

Number two: The coast guard would *not* be notified or involved. There was no need for any jurisdictional dispute or questions about who was in charge and who was responsible.

Number three: A dozen other DEA agents would be assigned, in six automobiles, to provide backup—but only if it was requested. Their primary function would be to follow the coke, if and when it was transported onto land.

Number four: There would be no arrests unless absolutely necessary. The primary mission for everyone involved was to monitor events, observe the drugs being detached from the ship, and then follow them to whatever their destination might be—on water or land, locally or elsewhere—in order to ultimately arrest and convict as many individuals as possible in the distribution chain.

Number five: Finally, checking with the cruise line, they had already established that the *Princess* was expected to arrive at the port at approximately 4:00 a.m. tomorrow. Thus, all agents would be in position well ahead of that time, in the event the ship arrived early. In addition, since meteorological reports indicated tomorrow's sunrise was expected to occur at 6:29, and assuming the drugs would be retrieved under cover of night—which was almost certainly the case—there would be a window of only two-and-one-half hours, maximum, for the drugs to be removed from the ship. Again, thereafter they would be followed to wherever they might be destined.

"Any other input, questions, or concerns?" Trumbull asked.

When they had none, he suggested they all go have lunch, and afterward Morgan and the others could go to the port and figure out where they would position themselves to meet the ship.

When they walked outside, the sun was still shining, just as it had been earlier. But at mid-day in the middle of June, to Morgan it felt both hotter and more humid than the islands. With the height of the buildings, the massive amounts of concrete, and little discernable breeze, he thought it was perhaps ten to fifteen degrees warmer than St. Thomas—probably at least in the mid-nineties; and, as they walked the block or so to the restaurant, he perspired considerably, even though he wore only an open-collared, short-sleeved shirt and light-weight slacks. The others seemed relatively less affected by the heat, but to him, the air-conditioning in the restaurant was entirely welcome. When they were seated, he used his napkin to wipe the perspiration from his forehead, and when the waitress brought ice water for them, he enjoyed the cool, damp feel of the glass as he picked it up and drank from it. The water felt cold and refreshing as it went down, and he drank one more full glass during their meal.

After lunch they walked back to the DEA building, said good-bye to Trumbull, and grabbed Cavanaugh's car from the parking garage for their drive to the port. Here again, the air-conditioning in the automobile felt welcome, and after driving the few blocks to the port and traveling across the causeway, they pulled into the parking lot near the ships. When they got out, the black-top almost steamed in the early-afternoon heat; and Morgan began to sweat once again as they walked the relatively short distance to the docks.

As they surveyed the area, they noted there were currently two ships at the docks. But it was obvious that there was room for at least a couple more, and fortunately, regardless of the number, Morgan was sure they could all be viewed from a single location out on the water. Thus, the four of them would need only the one unmarked speedboat, as already planned. However, because of the possibility of the ship arriving early—and potentially as much as an hour or two early—they agreed that they, and the other agents too, should be in position not later than 2:00 a.m. Morgan would come from the hotel and join the others with the boat somewhere along the docks around 1:45. The only question was, where exactly? Even though it would be dark, they wanted to be as inconspicuous as possible, so they walked until they located a place down toward the end of the port that would not be particularly well lit and where there were some palms and shrubbery that would provide at least some cover. They agreed that was where they would meet—again, at 1:45.

With those details settled, they left the port, headed back across the causeway, and dropped Morgan at his hotel. It was now a few minutes before 3:00 p.m. If the *Princess* was on time, it would be only a little more than twelve hours before she arrived. Meantime, he needed to get some sleep if he could. He also needed to call Vivian in a few hours, when he would supposedly be off work and back at his condo in Chicago. Meanwhile, he would call Blackburn to let him know the details of the Miami plan.

He went to his room, talked with Blackburn and then left a wake-up call for 7:00 p.m.—which would be 6:00 in Chicago. He also set the alarm on his cell phone, and then settled back on the bed. Gradually, he was able to close his eyes and go to sleep; and when he was awakened by the wake-up call, he turned off the alarm on his phone and called Vivian.

"Hi!" she said excitedly when she answered. "How was your day?"

"Oh, OK I guess. I'm slugging through it."

"You sound tired. Any idea yet how long all this is going to take?"

"No, I'm not sure yet," he said. "But I don't think it will take a whole week."

"Well, that's good news! You know I miss you."

"Yes, I miss you too," he said. "And I love you, more than I can say."

When their conversation ended, he continued sitting on the edge of the bed. He hated these ongoing lies about where he was and what he was doing. Hopefully one day soon this whole thing would be over, and he could begin some kind of normal life—hopefully with her. But he couldn't tell her the truth, at least not yet. She probably wouldn't understand everything he'd been through. And she might even hate him for pursuing her brother.

For now, though, he needed to get something to eat and try to get a few more hours' sleep, if he could, before meeting Cavanaugh and the others. He called room service, and then walked to the window and looked again at the cruise ships docked in the distance. There was a great deal at stake in this operation. If their estimate of a thousand pounds or more of cocaine in this shipment was correct, its value at wholesale would be in the range of $20 million—or more. And though this represented only a very small percentage of the total amount of coke arriving in the U.S. each year, it had the potential of exposing at least some portion of the drug trafficking network—and that would be invaluable. So there was no room for error in this. None.

CHAPTER THIRTY-THREE

M organ slept uneasily until 1:00 a.m., when his wake-up call from the hotel and his cell alarm rang almost simultaneously. He turned on the TV to watch and listen—at least intermittently—while he got ready. Since he'd probably be spending several hours on the boat, he dressed in a pair of cargo shorts, a polo shirt, and his boat shoes. He brushed his teeth. It was nearly 1:30 when he took the metal box from the safe and put it on the bed. He decided to call Cavanaugh, who said they were just on their way to get the boat. They'd be at the dock in fifteen minutes or so, as planned.

Morgan hung up, continued to watch TV for a few minutes, and then picked up the box. His first thought was simply to strap on the .45; but then he decided that, dressed as he was, he'd be less conspicuous going through the lobby—and probably less worrisome to some cab driver—if he kept everything in the box, at least for the time being. He double checked to make sure he had both the key to open it and his room key, and then he left.

Outside, he got into the first cab waiting in the queue. When the driver dropped him at the port, he walked to the far end of the docks where he had agreed to meet Cavanaugh and the others, and he saw them already waiting in the boat. He waved as he approached, then hopped aboard.

"Well, I guess this is game day," he said, "or rather game night." The others wore black, bulletproof vests with bright, gold-colored DEA lettering. "You guys look ready."

"We are," Cavanaugh said self-assuredly. "Here," he added as he handed a vest to Morgan. "We brought one for you too."

Morgan took the vest and put it on. Brady pushed them away from the dock. Alvarez started the engine, and they motored slowly out into the bay. Within a few minutes, they stopped and settled on a position a hundred yards or so away from the docks, where they could see not only all the ships but any boats that might approach them. Brady dropped the anchor. Alvarez cut the engine and turned off the running lights, leaving on only the single, white anchor light. Cavanaugh and Brady called the other agents in the cars, to make sure everybody was in position. They could do nothing now but wait.

It was a warm night. Downtown Miami loomed large and beautiful in the near distance, and its lights partially illuminated the water of the port. Nevertheless, Morgan calculated that at this distance from the docks, even with the city lights, they should be relatively inconspicuous. In addition, they would all keep the lowest possible profile behind the gunnels of the boat, so as not to attract attention by their movements on deck.

Morgan unlocked the metal box and removed the .45. He slid one of the clips into the receiver, shoved the weapon back into its holster, and threaded it onto his belt. The extra clip, along with his badge wallet, went into his right rear pocket for easy access, and he stuffed the extra ammunition into the side pockets of the vest.

"OK, I guess I'm ready," he said.

They continued to sit, mostly without moving, and when they spoke it was in soft tones, knowing that voices and other sounds travel easily over open water, especially at night when things are relatively calm and quiet. Occasionally, Morgan could hear traffic moving intermittently on nearby streets, or he would see and hear a boat somewhere in the distance. One of the cruise ships left the dock, presumably to head for its next port of call. Everything he observed seemed normal.

Cavanaugh had brought two pairs of night-vision binoculars onboard, plus a couple of night-vision cameras.

Morgan picked up one pair of binoculars and peered over the boat's starboard gunnel, scanning the hull of the two ships remaining at the dock. He was satisfied that, even at this distance, they would be able to see any activity around or near the ships. He eased himself back into his seat, took a deep breath, and slowly exhaled. They continued to watch, and wait.

When almost two hours had passed, Morgan noticed Alvarez fumbling nervously with the key fob at the controls. It was now nearly 4:00 a.m., and there was still no sign of the *Princess*, even at a distance. Clearly they were all growing anxious. Then, suddenly, Brady said he saw a ship approaching—almost certainly a cruise ship—perhaps a mile away but headed in their general direction. They all turned to look, and agreed that, indeed, it appeared to be a cruise ship. They watched; and as it drew closer, Morgan and Cavanaugh each picked up a pair of the binoculars to begin viewing it in greater detail. Within only another few minutes, its name became visible, and now there was no question. It was the *Caribbean Princess*—a few minutes late, perhaps, but essentially on time. They lowered the binoculars, smiled, and nodded to the others that it was their ship.

Slowly but surely the huge vessel continued forward, and then, very gradually, decreased its speed to near zero. Ultimately it eased alongside the dock, and ever so briefly the engines reversed, causing water to churn up at the ship's stern. Then it stopped. There was near silence. Morgan continued to watch through the binoculars for several minutes, and nothing of consequence occurred. He could still hear some traffic out on the streets, and an occasional boat moved somewhere off in the distance, just as before, but nothing else.

Then, almost out of nowhere, a boat twenty-five to thirty feet in length, with a dark-blue or black hull, slipped quietly into Morgan's field of vision. While not a speedboat, it had a low profile. No fishing tower. Not even a T-top. This was almost certainly the boat sent to retrieve the coke. He and Cavanaugh lowered their binoculars, pointed the boat out to Brady and Alvarez, then resumed their vigil. In a matter of minutes, two divers appeared on deck and slipped over the boat's transom onto the dive platform and into the water. This was it. No doubt about it. Brady pulled a night-vision camera from a bag and began taking photographs.

Several more minutes passed, and Cavanaugh and Morgan continued to watch through the binoculars. Two men remained on the other boat, and from time to time they moved about the deck, but no sign of the divers. Then, as quickly as they had disappeared, the divers reappeared at the stern of the boat. The other two lowered ropes to them and hoisted the first of the submersibles onboard. Brady, and then Alvarez too, took photos. For a moment, Morgan thought he could hear voices, undistinguishable in the distance; then the two divers disappeared again. He and the others continued to watch; and in another ten minutes the divers reappeared for a second time, bringing to the surface a second submersible. Morgan and Cavanaugh continued to watch through the binoculars, and Brady and Alvarez took still more pictures, until gradually a total of six submersibles were retrieved and brought onboard. Then, the divers—first one and then the other—mounted the transom ladder and were assisted onboard. In just over an hour, the entire operation of removing the submersibles from the ship had been completed, and everything had been photographed. Then the boat, with its four passengers and six submersibles, motored smoothly off.

Alvarez waited until the boat was well ahead—and in fact nearly out of sight. Then he started the engine; and, with running lights still off, they followed. They remained at a considerable distance behind the lead boat and continued to follow for perhaps two or three miles, talking from time to time with the agents in the cars, advising them of their progress and approximate position, so they too could follow. Then, very gradually, the lead boat began to turn toward shore, in the direction of what appeared to be a large warehouse. Alvarez cut the engine, allowing them to drift to a stop, and Morgan and Cavanaugh watched through the binoculars as the lead boat seemed to virtually disappear. It looked to Morgan as though it had somehow slipped right through the walls of the building, as if by magic.

Alvarez restarted their boat and headed toward shore, but to a position a hundred yards or so north of where the lead boat had disappeared. When they saw a pier jutting out into the water, they motored slowly to it, tied up, and Alvarez again shut off the engine. Morgan, Cavanaugh, and Brady stepped out and rechecked their weapons. They decided that—at least for the present— Alvarez would remain with the boat, but he should call the other agents on land, update them on this location, and have them move into the area to await developments. Meanwhile, Morgan and the others would walk south to the warehouse. If they needed Alvarez, or any of the other agents for any reason, they would call.

When the three of them arrived at the warehouse, they saw how the lead boat, in a canal of sorts, had maneuvered directly into the building at the level of its foundation, without a door having to be opened. They drew their weapons and moved cautiously through a side door. Inside, to Morgan's surprise, were scores of other boats—fishing and diving boats, speedboats, cruisers, and others—stacked row after row in dry dock. They could hear voices in the distance; and, after carefully scanning their surroundings, they made their way, crouching and dodging between the rows of boats, to a position where they could again see the lead boat, still in the water with the top of its gunnels nearly level with the floor of the warehouse. The four men from the boat, now aided by two others, were in the process of unloading the submersibles and placing them on metal racks, where they joined a number of others already in position. Morgan could hardly believe it. It looked as if there were perhaps two dozen or more of the submersibles in total, already on the racks, like so many torpedoes waiting to be launched.

After completing the unloading, the six men stood for a few minutes, talking and joking. Two of them smoked cigarettes, which they stubbed out on the concrete floor as they finished. Two others disappeared briefly, and when they returned, they were directing a flatbed truck loaded with a single automobile. The truck backed through a large overhead door into the warehouse and stopped near the submersibles. The driver exited the truck and handed some keys to one of the men, who jumped up onto the truck bed and unlocked the car's trunk. Another of them opened the metal doors on the side of one, and then another, of the submersibles and began retrieving duffel bags from them and tossing them up onto the truck bed. Morgan and the others watched as, one by one, the man on the truck placed the duffels into the car's trunk. As the two men worked, Cavanaugh, Brady, and Morgan took pictures with their cell phones and also entered the license numbers of both vehicles and the color, make, and model of the car into their phones as well. Cavanaugh told Brady to go outside, call the field agents on the ground—who were hopefully now in the immediate area—and have them establish visual contact and follow the truck, but *not* to overtake or apprehend.

Brady went outside to make the call, and within another minute, the man jumped down from the bed of the truck and handed the keys back to the driver, who produced a clipboard with papers. He and both of the loaders signed the document, and one of the loaders was provided a copy of the paperwork, which he took into the one-room office in the center of the warehouse. Another man reopened the overhead door, and the truck disappeared out into the early-morning twilight.

Before the door closed behind the first truck, however, a second flatbed, also carrying a single car, backed into the warehouse and stopped near the submersibles—after which the entire process was repeated, with several duffels of cocaine from the submersibles loaded into this automobile's trunk. Cavanaugh, Brady, and Morgan again took photographs of the activity and entered information on these vehicles into their phones. Before the truck departed, Brady was again dispatched to call the other agents on the ground with the same instructions as before. Then, yet a third truck with an automobile was guided in and loaded. Cavanaugh, Brady, and Morgan again took photos and entered the information, just as before; and Brady was again sent out to call the other agents with instructions. Morgan was amazed at not only the efficiency of the loading operation, but the business-like manner in which everything was carried out.

At the same time, he was now concerned. As each of the trucks left the warehouse, he could only hope the other agents on the ground were able to identify each of them and follow. If not, he wasn't sure how they would determine each truck's destination. The way events had unfolded, they could not have anticipated what they would encounter in the warehouse. If the other agents were for some reason unable to identify and follow the trucks, the best hope for tracing them was to somehow get a look at the paperwork now filed somewhere in this warehouse office. Perhaps that would contain information that would help. They watched and waited. Morgan could tell from the light now beginning to penetrate the few warehouse windows that it was past daybreak. He looked at his watch and was amazed to see that it was nearly 7:00 a.m.

In a matter of minutes, the man who had taken the papers into the office turned off the office lights, and he and the others departed the area. When it appeared to Morgan that they were no longer anywhere nearby—and hopefully not soon coming back—he asked Brady to go back to the boat, provide Alvarez an update on all that had happened, and remain there. Cavanaugh would stay with him and provide cover, while he went into the warehouse office and tried to locate the paperwork.

Morgan then cautiously made his way toward the center of the warehouse, darting between the rows of boats from one of the building's support columns to another until he arrived at the small office. He opened the door and went inside. There was now enough daylight throughout the warehouse that he did not need to turn on any lights—or even use the light from his cell phone. His eyes darted quickly from desktop to file cabinets and back to desktop, which, with stapler, tape dispenser, and a few ballpoint pens, was devoid of any kind of paperwork. Then he opened the center drawer and saw three sheets of yellow paper, which appeared to be duplicates of the paperwork they had seen being signed by the driver and the others. Morgan examined them carefully. Each appeared to be a kind of shipping order or manifest, listing not only the make, model, and license number of the particular automobile, but also the current mileage and the address to which it was to be delivered. One was destined for Pittsburgh, another for St. Louis, and the third for his own city of Chicago! The automobiles were, from all appearances, being transported for their owners, quite legitimately, to these cities; but, unknown to the owners themselves, while in transit the trunk of each contained a substantial amount of cocaine, which would no doubt be dropped off at an alternate address before final delivery of the automobile. It appeared to Morgan that if for any reason any of the trucks should be stopped along the way by the highway patrol, a local sheriff, or the police, the driver could produce his paperwork demonstrating the legitimacy of the car he was transporting. And if the cocaine in the trunk of any of the autos should somehow be discovered, the driver could profess absolutely no knowledge of what was sequestered there. The entire operation was absolutely ingenious!

Morgan quickly laid the documents down on the desktop, and one by one he took pictures with his phone. He also noticed that behind him was a copy machine, and he quickly made a photocopy of each of the documents as well, in case something happened to his cell. Then he returned the originals to the center desk drawer and, looking around, exited the office as quietly as he had come. He retraced his steps through the maze of boats to Cavanaugh, and together they left the warehouse and returned to Brady and Alvarez.

He wanted to contact Blackburn and tell him what had transpired, but it was still only a little after six o'clock in Chicago. He'd wait another hour or so until he and the others were back in the Miami office; then they'd call and fill him in on everything that had happened. Hopefully the agents now following the trucks wouldn't lose track of any of them.

CHAPTER THIRTY-FOUR

When the four of them finally arrived back at the Miami office, they advised Trumbull what had transpired during the recent few hours, and then called Blackburn and his counterparts in each of the two other cities, advising them of the shipments headed their way and currently being followed by Miami agents. They also transmitted a copy of the appropriate shipping document to each, and advised that Trumbull would continue to follow up with each of them in the interstate pursuit of all the trucks.

Meanwhile, Morgan was exhausted, which he imagined Cavanaugh and the others were as well. Outside Trumbull's office they said their good-byes. They would make a point of meeting up in the future—perhaps in St. Thomas, or maybe in Miami when Morgan was again passing through. Either way, they would definitely stay in touch. They shook hands, and Morgan left to catch a cab to the Marriott.

In his room, he settled back on the bed and got on-line with his phone to book a flight to Chicago. He knew almost certainly it would take the Chicago-bound truck the rest of the day and probably most of tomorrow to get there, and he definitely wanted to be there to meet it. He found a nonstop flight departing Miami that afternoon at 2:20—barely four hours from now. And though there would be no time for sleeping just yet, the flight time was perfect. He could probably get at least a couple hours' sleep on the plane. It would arrive in Chicago at 4:35. By the time he got through baggage claim at O'Hare, caught a cab, and fought his way through rush-hour traffic to his condo, he knew it would probably be 6:00 p.m. and time to call Vivian. But this time, he would call her from the real Chicago.

Meantime, he had not eaten since the evening before. He ordered breakfast from room service, showered, and dressed. After breakfast, he shaved and packed—taking care to unload the .45 and then place it and the other items back into the metal box, which he locked before stowing it in his suitcase. It was not yet noon, but he still had to check out and get to the airport. He would arrive there a bit earlier than necessary perhaps, but he absolutely did not want to miss this flight. He wanted to get to Chicago and call Vivian. He also wanted to see Weber and Sullivan, and he wanted to meet with Blackburn. He hadn't seen any of them in nearly six weeks. And he wanted—no, needed—to be part of everything that would happen after he arrived.

He closed his suitcase and paused for a moment, slowly moving his hand over the leather surface of the bag, which now bore multiple scars from periodic travels and careless baggage handlers. He remembered the day his parents had given it to him and how happy he had been back then. He also thought of Elaine, lying beside them in Oakwood Cemetery. He hoped he might yet—somehow, some way—bring her some justice. Maybe what he really wanted was revenge. But he didn't care. He wanted to get the sons-of-bitches who had killed her. He needed to. And maybe—just maybe—the drugs that were now on their way to Chicago would find their way to the bastards responsible for her death. At least he could hope.

CHAPTER THIRTY-FIVE

When Morgan opened the door of his condo and walked in, it was a few minutes past 6:00 p.m.—almost exactly the time he had predicted. He went to his bedroom, laid his suitcase on the bed, and reached for his cell phone. He was anxious to talk to Vivian; it seemed almost incomprehensible that he had not spoken with her in almost twenty-four hours. Her phone rang once, twice, a third time, and then she answered.

"Hello," she said. "I was just thinking about you. How was your day?"

"Pretty busy," he said. "I got up really early this morning, and I'm tired." He realized as he spoke the words that he had in fact been up most of the night, and except for the couple of hours on the plane, he hadn't had much sleep. "How was yours?"

She described a day that was not at all out of the ordinary, except to say that Petersen's fiancée, Allison, had stopped by. Charlie had flown once again to St. Croix; he was again staying overnight, and Allison was bored. So she had spent the night in Vivian's condo.

"I know it's only been a couple of days," she said, "but I really miss you. Do you miss me?"

"Of course I do! I can't wait to get back to you."

"Are you still on track to finish up in another few days?"

"Yes. Actually I'm hoping I can get everything wrapped up in another couple of days or so." He didn't want to be too specific, since he did not know how soon the cocaine might emerge once it arrived.

"What do you have to do yet?" she asked.

He took a deep breath, and made some general statements about modifications that were still being made to some of the programs he was responsible for, and he had become involved very deeply in how and when the changes were going to be implemented. He still had to work out some of the remaining details. Fortunately, the generalizations seemed to satisfy her.

"Well, I'll be glad when you get back," she said.

"Me too," he added, and he meant it. He wanted his old life, in Chicago, with the DEA, to be over. And he was more than anxious to resume the new life he was creating with her. "You know, I've missed having someone like you in my life," he went on. "And now that I've finally found you, it's really tough not to be with you every minute."

"Oh, I feel the same, Tom. I really, really do. Will you call me again tomorrow?"

"I will," he said. "I'll text you too. I miss you every hour of every day."

"I love you so much."

"I love you too," he said, and again he added, "more than I can say."

They ended the conversation. He was tired and hungry, but more tired than anything. He lay down on the bed, and without any effort at all he went to sleep.

CHAPTER THIRTY-SIX

The following morning Morgan arrived early at his office and met first thing with Blackburn, who told him what had transpired the previous day. Sometime after they had called from Trumbull's office, the Miami agents lost track of the Chicago-bound truck, so Blackburn had immediately contacted the highway patrol in each of the states the truck would travel through on its way north. Each state then put out an all-points bulletin in order to locate the vehicle—and it was ultimately discovered somewhere just south of Chattanooga, where the driver had stopped for the night. At that point local authorities managed to place a tracking device on the truck.

"We're now monitoring its progress," Blackburn said, "and when it gets up here, we'll be tracking it minute by minute. We'll know exactly when it stops, and where, and we'll be there." He added that he had already lined up enough people in the department to bust whoever was involved on this end. In addition, he believed Miami and the other field offices had been similarly successful in locating the other trucks and were now tracking them as well. As a result, he had big accolades for Morgan.

"Tom, because of the work you've done, we can now trace this stuff all the way from St. Thomas. And when we arrest Petersen and his buddies down there, I think we'll have a chance at finding out who's involved all the way back to Colombia—or wherever the hell the coke's coming from. You've done a really outstanding job; and the Agency, and I personally, congratulate you."

"Well, thanks, George. But remember, you're the one who suggested I should go down there in the first place."

"Yeah, but you're the one who did the work."

"And I couldn't have done it without the guys from Miami—or without your help in getting them for me."

The old man laughed. "Well, I guess there can be kudos all around, huh? But we better not congratulate ourselves too heartily. We've still got to arrest these fuckers. And they're pretty damn sure to put up a fight."

"Yeah, and I'm glad to be here for it," Morgan said. "Remember, I've got a personal stake in this."

"Yeah, Tom, I know," Blackburn said. "Look, why don't you go on out and talk with some of the guys. I'll let you know as soon as anything develops."

Morgan left Blackburn's office and went to his old cubicle. He put the metal box containing the .45 on his desk, looked again at the array of photographs still standing there—especially those of himself and Elaine—and then began walking around saying hello to everybody, starting with old buddies Weber and Sullivan, who were not reluctant to offer some ribbing.

"Hey, nice tan, Buddy!" Weber said. "Must be pretty nice duty down there in the Virgin Islands."

"Yeah, and leaving the rest of us up here to do all the work!" Sullivan added.

They laughed, and others began gathering around.

"All kidding aside," Sullivan said, "we all know what a great job you've done uncovering this pipeline. We gather there's probably going to be a sizeable bust here pretty soon."

"Well, tell you what," Morgan said. "If we can get these bastards and throw their asses in prison, I'll be a whole lot happier." They all clapped, and a couple of them whistled.

At noon, Weber and Sullivan and a few others who had been closest to Morgan took him to lunch, and when they returned, he peeked into the old man's office.

"Anything else happen yet, George?"

"Yeah. Just heard a few minutes ago that our truck has now passed through Indianapolis. Hell, at the rate this guy's going, he'll be up here in another three hours!"

Morgan walked out into the area of the cubicles and began updating some of the others. Immediately a kind of tension began to permeate the air—as it always did when something big was about to happen.

He returned to his own cubicle, unlocked the metal box, and loaded the first clip into the handle of the .45. Then he shoved it back into the holster and laid it on his desktop, along with the extra ammo. He put his badge wallet and extra clip into his right, rear pocket. He was going to need a vest, so he went downstairs to the property department to get one. When he returned to his cubicle, he loaded its side pockets with the extra ammunition. He was now ready.

He sat in his cubicle for almost an hour...drumming his fingers on the top of his desk and jumping his foot up and down...thinking about how the afternoon could end. It was nearly 3:00 p.m., and though he usually didn't call Vivian until later, when she would think it was the end of his workday, he nevertheless thought he should call her now and tell her how much he loved her. He dialed, and waited.

"Hello!" she said, sounding excited to hear from him, especially since it was earlier than usual.

"Hello!" he said in return. "How you doing?" He wanted to sound in a good mood.

"I'm fine," she said, pausing slightly. "You're calling a bit early today."

"Yeah, well, I was thinking about you—like always—and I wanted you to know it."

"OK," she said, pausing slightly again. "Is everything all right?"

"Oh, yeah, but you know how I always tell you I love you more than I can say? Well, I've figured out how to tell you how much." He paused. "I'd give my life for you, Vivian—and I wouldn't have to think twice about it."

"Oh, Tom," she said. "I hope you wouldn't ever think you had to do something like that. Are you sure you're OK?"

"Sure, I'm fine," he said, trying to sound as unconcerned as possible and lighten the conversation. "I'll call you again in a few hours. I just wanted you to know."

They ended the conversation, and as soon as he hung up, it was like the old man had sounded some kind of alarm. People were scurrying around, almost as if they had no destination. He went to Blackburn's office.

"What's going on, George?"

"The truck's now on I-94, west of Gary," he said. "It'll probably be in our southern suburbs in less than an hour, and I'm guessing it won't take them long to dump that coke. We've got to move—now!"

Morgan hurried back to his cubicle, grabbed his .45 and vest, and returned to Blackburn. Together, they and Weber and Sullivan, and a dozen others from the department, headed for the parking garage and drove south in several unmarked cars.

CHAPTER THIRTY-SEVEN

Blackburn drove, and Morgan rode shotgun in the lead car, with the others close behind. Blackburn used the radio to stay in contact with the office as they continued to monitor the location of the truck. He also spoke with a contingent of assault agents, all heavily armed with rifles, helmets, and body armor, and gave them the truck's position as it continued west. It was now on Illinois I-80, and he directed them to move into that area and head west as quickly as possible in order to join the caravan of pursuers.

Morgan, Blackburn, and the others in the unmarked cars gradually began to close in on the truck, and after a time the armored agents in two Hummers joined the caravan as well. After some twenty minutes, the office reported the truck had exited off of I-80 west and was now traveling in a northwesterly direction on 294. Then, after only ten to twelve minutes more, it was reported exiting 294 and heading due north, through stop-and-go traffic on Cicero Avenue.

After leaving the office and traveling more than forty-five minutes on freeways, Morgan, Blackburn, and those behind them had done little more than make a huge loop to the south and west, and then turn again north, only to wind up now in slow-moving traffic. Nevertheless they had managed to close in on the truck, and they estimated that they were now perhaps only a mile or so behind it—or, if they were lucky, perhaps less. Blackburn pushed their automobile forward as much as possible, dodging in and out of traffic, hoping those behind would keep up through the changing lights. It was unusually hot outside, especially for mid-June, and the sun beat down on the buildings and the pavement, causing the heat to rise upward. Suddenly, up ahead of them, only a little more than a block away, Morgan spotted an orange automobile carried on the bed of a truck.

"Hey, that's it!" he exclaimed. "Right up there, George! See it?" He pointed.

"Sure do!" Blackburn replied as he maneuvered their car quickly through more traffic, weaving in and out, trying not to get stuck at a red light and at the same time keep the train of other cars and Hummers in view behind them.

They followed the truck north for another block and a half, and then it suddenly turned left and entered an area of older, mostly brick, one-story warehouses.

Blackburn cautiously followed, and when they too entered among the warehouses, it was obvious that many of the buildings—some with broken windows and others with grass and weeds growing through cracks in the surrounding blacktop—were at least partially abandoned. He stopped for a few seconds, allowing the truck to disappear around the corner of one of the buildings. Then he eased the car forward, past one warehouse, just far enough to see the truck, now well ahead, drive into another of the buildings and disappear. An overhead door promptly closed behind it.

Blackburn backed the car up a few feet. He and Morgan got out and motioned to the others behind them—including those in the two Hummers—to drive forward close to them. Then Blackburn gathered everyone together and quickly laid out a plan. He directed that they take the Hummers and a few of the other cars and form a solid roadblock across the broad driveway immediately ahead. He wanted them to be absolutely certain to stop any vehicles that might try to exit the area. Next, he pointed to an adjacent building beyond the driveway, where he wanted everyone to assemble after creating the roadblock and remain there, out of sight of the target warehouse, until he could give them further instructions.

As soon as they had formed the roadblock and gathered in the shade of the adjacent building, Blackburn said they would proceed in single file toward the target warehouse, with the assault agents in the lead, himself and Morgan next, and the remainder of them following. Once they arrived at the target warehouse, the assault agents should surround the building and remain in place, guarding all exits. The remainder of them would gain access however they could, and at that point all radio contact would cease. At the appropriate time, he and those inside would initiate the bust. Now, it was time to *move!*

As they all approached the warehouse, the assault agents began surrounding the building as planned, with the remainder of the agents looking for an unlocked entrance. After searching the perimeter, they determined that none of the doors was unlocked. However Weber, with his smaller, wiry frame, volunteered to be hoisted up through an open window, and after he was inside he unlocked a nearby door. Blackburn, Morgan, Sullivan, and the others cautiously moved into the building as well; and, as Blackburn had directed, at that point all radio contact ceased. Morgan checked his watch. It was now almost 4:30. It had taken them only a little more than an hour since leaving the office to locate the truck, follow it to this destination, and gain access to the warehouse, which appeared to be full of an unlimited number of cardboard boxes with uncertain contents, stacked floor to ceiling on steel racks. Morgan could hear voices in the distance, and at Blackburn's direction he and the others began moving forward quietly toward locations that placed them in positions surrounding the area from where the voices came.

Blackburn, Morgan, and four other agents—including Weber and Sullivan—moved in close to the area of the overhead door where the truck had entered. It was still there, not more than twenty or thirty feet inside, with two automobiles nearby—one a Lincoln and the other a Cadillac, both black and highly polished. Half a dozen men stood near the truck, and Morgan immediately recognized two of them: the driver of the truck, whom he had seen in the warehouse in Miami, and the one dressed in a dark suit, with an open-collared white shirt and shined shoes. Morgan had seen him on more than one occasion in the company of Carlos Monterra. He had never been introduced to the man, but he was damn sure he was one of those present when he had been tied up and beaten in that basement. Now he was the one doing most of the talking. Clearly he was in charge.

After a minute or two of conversation, the truck driver bounded up onto the bed of the vehicle, opened the trunk of the orange automobile, and began handing to some of the others the first of several bags of coke. Some of the agents took pictures of the activity. Then Blackburn whispered to Morgan.

"OK, this is your bust," he said. "You've earned it. Go for it!"

Morgan did not hesitate. His .45 was already in his hand and raised just above his shoulder. He stood and took half a step to his right, partially exposing himself from behind the steel racks and dusty, palletized boxes that had provided his cover. He took aim at the man in the suit. "OK, this is the DEA, assholes! Put your hands up! You're all under arrest!"

In an instant the man in the suit grabbed a pistol from his belt and fired off a shot in Morgan's direction, causing the bullet to ricochet off the metal racks just above Morgan's head. He ducked and immediately returned fire in the man's direction, as did the other agents from their positions nearby.

While the man on the truck bed ducked behind the orange car, two others jumped into the Lincoln and sped forward, tires screaming and screeching as they crashed through the closed overhead door and roared out of sight. At the same time, two others opened the back doors of the Cadillac. Each produced an automatic rifle and began spraying bullets randomly at agents elsewhere in the area. Morgan fired off numerous more shots—at them and the man in the suit—as did Blackburn, Weber, and Sullivan.

In the exchange of gunfire, sparks flew as hunks of lead hit bricks and beams and the body of the Cadillac. For what seemed to Morgan perhaps two or three minutes, the exchange heated the air fire hot and spread the acrid smell of spent gunpowder throughout the area. Morgan exhausted the bullets in his first clip, and immediately replaced it with the second.

Several more shots from him and other agents tore into the head and chest of the man in the suit, and he collapsed face down onto the cement floor. Likewise, his two companions with the automatic rifles were hit by the returned gunfire, and they too fell, bleeding and dying if not already dead. Finally there was no sound at all. Blue-gray smoke hung, barely moving, in the still air. Morgan waited. Then he slowly stood once again.

"You want to come out from behind that car…with your hands up?" he yelled to the man still crouching on the truck bed behind the orange automobile. The man raised his hands, stood up hesitatingly, and then stepped around the back of the vehicle toward the edge of the truck bed. "Now put your hands behind your head and drop to your knees," Morgan commanded.

As he did so, Morgan and the others, their weapons still drawn, closed in on the area. Some of the agents checked to see if any of the three on the floor had a pulse, but they found none. Others assisted the man on the truck to jump down, and then placed him under arrest and in handcuffs. Two of the armored agents from outside emerged through the broken, overhead door, their rifles lowered but still ready to be fired. They walked toward Morgan and Blackburn.

"What's going on outside?" Blackburn quickly asked.

"Nothing now, sir," one of the agents said. "We stopped them at the roadblock. One's dead. One's still breathing—a little."

Morgan felt no sympathy for any of them. They had brought about their own destruction, and he was not unhappy to see them dead, or dying. He put his .45 back into its holster. They called a hospital for an ambulance, as well as forensics and the Chicago police—the latter to take the truck driver into custody. They also called the morgue. Morgan looked at his watch. It was nearly five o'clock. After the picture taking and cleanup, many of them—Blackburn, Weber, Sullivan, and himself included—would no doubt go out somewhere and have a few drinks to celebrate. Somewhere along the way, he would call Vivian again; and tomorrow they would return to the office and file their inevitable paperwork, reporting the details of the shootout and apprehension of the coke. He felt good about the afternoon's work. They had gotten at least one more of the sons-of-bitches who had participated in his beating—and maybe even some of those who'd been part of Elaine's murder. He was curious about the automatic refiles now lying on the warehouse floor, but he'd have to wait and see what was reported from ballistics to know for sure.

CHAPTER THIRTY-EIGHT

The following morning Morgan arrived at the office, met briefly with Blackburn, and then went to his cubicle to do his part of the paperwork. He worked for nearly two hours and then joined a few of the others who were standing together and drinking coffee in a mid-morning break. After talking with them for a few minutes and reviewing some of the events of the previous afternoon, his cell phone rang. He pulled it from his pocket and saw that it was Vivian.

"Hello," he said, sounding both surprised and pleased as he began walking in the direction of his cubicle.

"Oh, Tom," she said, sobbing, "I've got the most horrible news." She paused for a moment. "Charlie's gone!" She sobbed again.

"Gone?"

"Yes! I got a call from Allison a few minutes ago, and she said she'd just been contacted by some aviation people. His plane crashed out at West End somewhere, and he and his pilot were both killed! They *burned up,* Tom! *They burned up!*" She was sobbing and crying uncontrollably.

"Oh my, Viv," he said. He paused slightly. "I'm so sorry. So sorry." In truth, he was sorry, for her, and he was sure he sounded sympathetic. But at the same time, he did not feel any real sorrow for Petersen. While he might have preferred to see him arrested and forced to spend some serious time in prison, he still did not greatly regret his death. He was a mean-spirited, guilty son-of-a-bitch and Morgan could not feel sad about his fate.

"Can you please come back, Tom? Please?"

"Sure, Honey," he said, "I'll get there just as soon as I can. I'll try to catch a flight this afternoon."

"Call me and let me know, will you? I need you here."

Morgan hung up and immediately went online to check available flights. There was a plane with a few seats still available, scheduled to leave Chicago at 1:30. It stopped in Miami, but it would get him to St. Thomas by 9:45. It was already 10:30. He could make the flight, but he had no time to waste. He had to get back to his condo, pack, and get to the airport in the next couple of hours. He booked the flight, and then walked to Blackburn's office.

"George, I'm afraid I'm going to have to head back to St. Thomas."

"Already?" he said. "What's going on?"

Morgan described the desperate call he had just received from Vivian, telling him about her brother.

"He's apparently got himself killed in a plane crash down there, the son-of-a-bitch. She's understandably upset, and I've got to go to her. You can dock me for the time if you want."

"No, I understand," Blackburn said. "When do you think you'll be back?"

"I don't know, George. I've been thinking about it. I've really started to love this woman. I may not be able to come back."

"Well, let me hear from you after you get down there," he said. "We can talk about it. If you still need a little more time, it shouldn't be a problem. It still hasn't been a full two months."

They shook hands. He left Blackburn's office and swung by Weber's and Sullivan's cubicles. He told them he was heading back—and why. They hugged, and, with promises to see each other again soon, they patted him on the back.

"Take care, Buddy," Weber said.

"Give us a call after you get down there," Sullivan added.

Morgan picked up his metal box and left the building. At the curb, he caught a cab to his condo and packed. He also called Vivian, telling her he was about ready to leave for the airport and gave her his flight information. He'd be on St. Thomas a few minutes after 9:30.

"I'm sorry; that's the best I could do," he said.

"All right," she said. "Just get here, please. I'll be waiting for you at the airport."

He closed his bag, and at the front door he paused for a moment and looked back in. He had lived for the past seven years in that condo, and he had many memories of his time there, with friends, with Elaine, and with others. But it had all ended badly, and he didn't know how he could ever return to it. It represented part of his old life; and now, more than ever, he felt ready to move on to a new life—with Vivian. He closed the door, and left.

CHAPTER THIRTY-NINE

When Morgan stepped off the plane in St. Thomas, it was well past dark; and, as he walked across the tarmac toward the terminal, he thought briefly about the day of his first arrival, with the sun shining brilliantly on the soft green of the hillsides. So much had happened since then. But now, Vivian would be here, waiting for him; and when he stepped inside the building, in the lights and amid the stream of other passengers, she ran to him and into his arms. At first there were no words—only tears as she threw her arms around him and buried her face in his chest. He felt her desperation, and he held her close, swaying her tenderly and whispering in her ear that he loved her. When he finally looked at her again, he saw the tears still welled up in her eyes.

"I've missed you so much," she said. "And now this."

He pulled her close once again and held her. "I've missed you too," he whispered softly, and then he repeated it. "I've missed you too. But I'm here. I'm here."

After a few minutes he took her hand, and they walked together to baggage claim. He picked up his suitcase, and they continued on to her car and to Charlotte Amalie. The lights of the city shone brightly and reflected out onto the water of the harbor, just as they had in all those nights before he left. And in the distance, he could see the cruise ships with their lights, just as before. To the casual observer, it would appear that nothing had changed during these past few days. Yet, for him and for her, the only thing that had not changed was the love he had for her and that she had for him. She pulled the car up to her condo, and they went inside.

"Would you like a glass of wine?" she asked.

"Yes, I would," he said, "but you have a seat. I'll get it." He walked to the kitchen, selected a bottle of red from the refrigerator, uncorked it, and, with two glasses, returned to the living room and sat with her on the couch. He poured the wine and handed one of the glasses to her. Then they both settled back, with his arm around her. He held her close.

"This has been a really, really rough day," she said, looking down at her glass. "I spent most of it with Allison. She's as devastated as I am. But at least she has some family. I don't know what I would have done if I didn't have you coming back to me."

"And I'm so glad to be back," he said. After a long pause, he added, "Do you know what we have to do tomorrow?"

"Allison said they told her that both Charlie and his pilot had been burned beyond recognition. So I guess there's nothing to do but go ahead with plans for his funeral. We decided to have him buried beside Mom and Dad. I think he would have wanted that." Her eyes filled with tears once again, and her lips and chin quivered uncontrollably. She looked down at her glass and then took a sip of the wine.

Morgan could not help but think again of the similarity of their experiences. He had lost both of his parents, as she had. And now she had lost her only brother, as he had lost his only sister. He would help her to get through this, just as she had helped him. He pulled her still closer and kissed her on the forehead. He hoped she knew how much he loved her. He would do anything for her. At the same time, there was one thing he knew he could not do. He could not tell her the truth about her brother—at least not yet.

CHAPTER FORTY

P etersen's funeral was held not far from downtown
Charlotte Amalie, in one of the largest and best funeral homes. Flowers were everywhere, and among those
present—besides Vivian, Allison, and Morgan, who
stood in front of Petersen's closed casket—were members of Allison's family; a number of employees from the
mill, the plantation, and the hotel; and the two Petersen
associates in the drug business. Even dressed in shirts
and ties, Morgan easily recognized them. They stood together only a few steps away, and he decided to use this
opportunity to try to learn their last names. Cavanaugh
and the others had said they got a good look at them
under the lights of the pier and felt confident they could
identify them in court. But who in the hell were they
exactly? There was little prospect of dragging them into

court if they remained unknown. He approached them and reached out his hand.

"Hey, guys," he said, speaking softly and smiling faintly. "I'm Tom. Tom Morgan. We met at Charlie's house a few weeks back—remember?" He didn't know what Petersen might have told them about him, if anything, but he wanted to sound open and friendly.

"Oh, yeah," said the heavier one with the crew cut and the scar on his jaw. "I'm Jim."

The other one, with the big nose and the tattoos, said, "And I'm Mike."

They each shook Morgan's hand. They did not exactly smile, but from their other gestures, he thought they seemed friendly enough.

"Too bad about Charlie," Morgan offered.

"Yeah, he was one hell of a guy," the first one said.

"You can say that again," the other one added.

Morgan knew he was not going to get their last names—at least not now. Regardless, there were other ways of getting them—certainly from Allison if from no one else. Perhaps they'd also signed the Registry when they came in. In any case his main concern now was Vivian. He shook hands with them once again and returned to her, still standing in front of Petersen's casket.

As he resumed his place with her, and others approached to express their condolences, he scanned the room for more familiar faces. Then he saw his favorite bartender, Jerry, in the distance. Jerry approached them and spoke first with Allison, then Vivian, and then Morgan.

"Hey, Mr. Morgan," he said quietly and smiling slightly. "Long time since we see you. Too bad it under tese circumstances."

"Yes, too bad," he said. "But good to see you nevertheless." He engaged Jerry briefly in some pleasantries, and then shook his hand before he departed.

After most of those present—who apparently did not know Petersen as Morgan did—had expressed their condolences, the funeral director invited everyone to take their seats. He made his comments and introduced the minister, one Reverend Robert Stevens, who stepped to the podium near Petersen's casket. He cleared his throat and began.

"Charles Petersen's death is a true tragedy," he said. "For you, Vivian and Allison—and for all the rest of you, his many friends—his loss is no doubt like being left terribly alone in the dark, when late at night the power suddenly goes off. But you should have no doubt that, in your pain and grief, God is with you. The Bible tells us that God, even while He is in heaven, is close to those who suffer. Blessed are those who mourn. They shall be comforted."

Morgan thought on what the minister was saying, and he found himself wondering again, as he had for so long, about God and heaven and whether either might actually exist. He also wondered if Petersen had a soul—if indeed anyone had such a thing. Likewise, he wondered if, despite his drug dealings, the man might have somehow found his way to this heaven the minister had referred to—again if there was such a place somewhere in the universe. He knew Elaine, her goodness and her desire to always make the world a better place. She may not have been perfect, but if anyone deserved to be in heaven, she did. Could this Petersen, and those like him, with the death and destruction they brought to the world, also somehow find their way there? If Petersen had perhaps recanted and asked for forgiveness seconds before his plane crashed, might God have forgiven him? After all, God was supposed to be loving and forgiving, wasn't He? Might He somehow have permitted Petersen entrance into His heaven, to reside alongside good and decent people like Elaine? Again, that was if God and heaven even existed. Morgan wished he could know the truth of it, but it was a conundrum to which he had no answer, and he seriously doubted he ever would.

When the minister completed his remarks, a few of those who had worked most closely with Petersen carried his casket outside to the hearse. Like most days since Morgan's first arrival on the island, the sun again shone brilliantly in an almost-cloudless sky. He and Vivian and Allison and her parents entered the limousine immediately behind the hearse; and, with a number of other cars behind them, they followed the hearse to a cemetery on the outskirts of Charlotte Amalie, where Petersen's casket was placed on top of a crypt, alongside the crypts of his parents. At first, Vivian wept openly, then quietly. Morgan put his arm around her and pulled her close. She patted her eyes with a handkerchief. Allison cried as well, and clung to her mother and father.

Finally, the minister stepped forward and addressed the assembly again, but briefly this time. After his remarks, he invited them all to join him in the twenty-third Psalm, followed by the Lord's Prayer.

When the graveside service was complete, those in attendance walked back over the dry, brittle grass of the cemetery and departed. Later, some of them, including Petersen's two associates, arrived at his home on the hill and spoke encouragingly to Vivian, and to Allison. Morgan stood close to both of them in the kitchen and offered what comfort he could. Later still, after Allison left with her parents and the others had departed, he and Vivian left as well. She locked the door behind them; and when they returned to her condo, she drank several glasses of wine. Morgan knew she wanted to escape her pain, and sleep. He understood completely. He went to the bedroom with her and held her close.

CHAPTER FORTY-ONE

During the next week, Morgan all but abandoned the bungalow and was Vivian's almost-constant companion, doing what he could to help her overcome her grief. Initially she took him back to his place to get the Jeep and retrieve a few items of clothing; and while he would occasionally return for something else, he was otherwise with her day and night. He made breakfast each morning and most other meals as well—although she often seemed to have little appetite. He plumped the pillow beneath her head when she only wanted to lie on the couch and watch TV, or sleep. He made the bed every day. He did the laundry when necessary, and always, *always* he kissed her tenderly on the forehead or cheek as he looked after her needs.

For several days she was reluctant to go outside or down into town. And when she did finally go to the gallery for an hour or so, he accompanied her. Sometimes he would remain with her the entire time, looking through the art and sculpture. If he left the gallery at all, he did so only to browse briefly in one of the nearby shops and then return to her.

One day, when he was in one of the shops, he noticed a stack of fliers advertising boats for sale; and as he scanned the ads, he saw that some were for sloops not unlike the *Bon Voyage*. He took one of the fliers with him, and later, after they returned to the condo, he showed it to her, pointing out a few of the boats he thought might interest her.

"I thought if you wanted to, we might make some calls and maybe even go see one or two of them. What do you think?"

At first she seemed reluctant, but then she mentioned that, during the days he had been away, she had received a check from the insurance company. The salvage firm was also airfreighting the items retrieved from the boat—their dive gear, their bags, her purse— and she was expecting them almost any day.

"Maybe we could go and take a look," she said, sounding mildly interested but still somewhat weak.

Together they reviewed the ads and discovered that one of the boats, very similar to the *Bon Voyage*, was docked in the basin at Red Hook. They called, and afterward they left in Vivian's Mercedes to go see it. Morgan drove, steering them through all the twists and turns of Route 30, which now seemed more than routine. But when they finally arrived at the yacht basin and were shown the boat, off to one side Vivian confided that she could not decide what to do. Should she make an offer on it? If she did, and the offer was accepted, did Morgan think she would be happy or satisfied with it? And what about the name? Should she keep the name already given to it, or rename it? Perhaps *Bon Voyage II*? Or something else? Or maybe she should just wait, and perhaps buy a new boat. Again, what should she do?

Morgan had never seen her like this—so indecisive, seemingly unable to make any decisions. She also confided that she had other concerns, about the plantation, the mill, the hotel, *everything*! She was clearly overwhelmed; and as they stood beside her car, she clung to him. He looked into her eyes, red with tears, and pulled her close, wrapping his arms firmly around her.

"Hey," he said softly but reassuringly, "don't feel that you have to make any of these decisions now. They can wait until you're ready. You don't have to get another boat—especially not yet, if you don't want to. And remember, there are people with jobs still in place at the hotel and the mill and the plantation. They'll continue to keep things going, just as they have been. And if questions come up, I'll help you answer them, or help you find the answers. OK?"

"I just haven't known what to do," she said, "about anything."

"It's all right. I understand. I'm here," he said. "I'll help you."

She looked up at him with her arms still around him, and then hugged him tightly, with her face against his chest. "I don't know what I would do without you, Tom," she said in a whisper. "I just don't know what I would do."

CHAPTER FORTY-TWO

As more days passed and Morgan continued attending to Vivian's needs, he began to see a gradual improvement in her state of mind. She began returning to the gallery for at least a little while most days, and he continued to accompany her. She also contacted some of the key people at the plantation, the mill, and the hotel, saying they should feel free to call her, or Morgan, with any questions or concerns. He heard her explain that he was taking a big load off her shoulders, especially now, and that they should feel comfortable in going directly to him, with anything.

And calls did begin coming his way. When they did, he provided answers if he felt comfortable and confident in doing so. If not, he waited until the end of the day and discussed them with Vivian over dinner, before providing a response.

The hotel's Director of Marketing called, wanting a decision on what to do regarding the upcoming season's rates. In the prior year, the hotel had had 100 percent occupancy during that period, and the Director was recommending a five percent bump in room rates. What did Vivian want him to do? The mill's Operations Manager had called as well. The mill was producing at capacity, and they were on schedule with shipments to distilleries and other customers. At the same time, even with overflow to the Great House, they were running out of room to accommodate production. Should he rent some additional warehouse space? He had identified a reasonably-priced building of an appropriate size nearby. He needed approval to proceed.

As he and Vivian discussed these and other matters, Morgan was learning something about each of the businesses; and he was at the same time helping her to reach appropriate conclusions. It occurred to him that they were once again working together as a team, just as they had before, on the boat; and he was pleased to be able to help her. He tried in every way he could to lift her spirits. Gradually they resumed their former routine of going out to lunch each day; and he made certain these times were as enjoyable as possible, in restaurants that were lively or otherwise entertaining. If they stayed at home in the evening, and after dinner watched a movie, he made certain it was a comedy or something light-hearted. He did everything he could think of to ease her burden, and very gradually he began to see her former self reemerge.

One day after they'd had lunch and Morgan had dropped her at the gallery, he left for a meeting with executives at the hotel, and on the way, he received a call from Blackburn.

"Tom, I've got some news I think you'll be interested in." Morgan pulled the Jeep over to the side of the road and stopped. "You know those automatic rifles we recovered from the shooters in the warehouse? Well, the police ran them through ballistics, and you'll never guess what they found out. One of them was the gun that killed your sister, Tom. I thought you'd want to know."

Morgan paused. He could hardly believe what he heard. His eyes filled with tears. Now, finally, it looked like at least one of the sons-of-a-bitches who had killed Elaine was dead himself; and maybe the others with him had been involved too. Thank God, he thought. Maybe there was some justice in the world after all.

"Thanks, George, for letting me know. I really appreciate it."

"Oh, and one other thing," Blackburn said. "Turns out at least two of these guys working for Petersen had prior records. Cavanaugh and the others identified their file photos, and Trumbull had local authorities down there arrest them last night on charges of suspected drug trafficking. They're being flown to Miami today, where they'll be arraigned in federal court. Before we're done, I think we just might get information from them about the others involved, and who's been flying the drugs into the islands."

"That's great news, George. I don't know how to thank you."

"No thanks needed," Blackburn said in his typical style. "Just part of the job. I'm glad the fuckers are going to prison." He paused briefly, then added, "By the way, have you made up your mind yet what you want to do about your job? We're growing kind of short on time."

"Yes, I know," he said. "Can I have just a couple more days?"

"OK, but I'm going to need to hear from you soon."

As their conversation ended, Morgan put the Jeep back into gear and resumed his drive to the hotel. After his meeting, he picked Vivian up at the gallery, and later, when they had returned to her condo and had dinner, he brought their wine from the table and sat with her on the couch to watch TV. He punched up the evening news, hoping to see coverage of the arrest of Petersen's friends, and at first there was nothing. But after a few minutes, the newscaster began the story of two local men who had been arrested on drug charges, and the accompanying video showed them in handcuffs, in police custody, being escorted into jail.

"Oh my God!" Vivian exclaimed. "Do you see that?"

Morgan eyed the screen. The men had their heads slightly bowed as they were led away by the officers, but there was no mistaking their identity. "Yeah, I see," he said, as the news anchor went on to report that, after their arrest, the two had been flown to Miami, where they were to be arraigned on federal drug charges. "Serves the sons-of-bitches right," Morgan said.

"Do you suppose Charlie knew about them?" Vivian asked.

Morgan paused. He had previously not known how or when he might find it possible to tell her about her brother. Yet, with this information on the news, and her direct question, it now seemed time to tell her the truth. Maybe even the whole truth.

"Oh, he knew about them all right, Viv. He knew."

"What do you mean 'he knew'?" she said. "How can you say that with such certainty?"

"He was in it with them, Viv. Or, rather, they were in it with him."

"Tom, how could you know a thing like that?"

"Let's just say I know. OK?"

"No, it's not OK," she answered with obvious anger. "My brother is dead now. He was no angel. But he's not here to defend himself; and you're accusing him of being involved in drugs? I thought I knew you better than that!"

"Vivian." He paused. "I'm sorry. I haven't been completely honest with you—at least not about everything."

"Well, I've been honest with you about everything. What haven't you been honest with me about?"

Again he paused. "Do you remember that night in the hotel when Charlie reintroduced us, and I told you that I worked for the DOA? Well, that wasn't exactly the truth. I work for the DEA."

"The DEA? The Drug Enforcement Administration?"

"Right," he said, nodding his head.

"Well, why did you have to lie about it? Why didn't you just tell us the truth?"

"Viv. It's just not the kind of thing you tell people—especially those you don't know well, or those you've just met."

"And you've been lying about it all this time?"

"That wasn't my original intention," he said. "But later, when we went to St. Croix—and spent the night at the Great House—I..." He paused again. "I discovered several bags of coke hidden under the floor there. And the next day, when we got back here to St. Thomas, I followed the yellow plane, Viv. It was Charlie in the plane. Charlie and his pilot, Hamilton. I followed them, and I followed Charlie in his car down to the pier next to the hotel; and his two buddies—the same two we just saw on the news—took the cocaine from Charlie's Mercedes and put it aboard his boat, *Charlie's Change*. Later, we got pictures, Viv. Pictures!"

"How could you do all that and keep it from me, Tom? How *could* you?"

"My job, Viv. My job." He looked down at his wine glass and ran his index finger slowly around its rim. "My stinking, fucking job. I love you, Viv. But Charlie was dirty. He was."

"And what about the trip to Chicago, or wherever the hell you were? What was that all about? I suppose that was a lie too!"

"No, I went to Chicago. I did. We were tracking the drugs at the time, all over the eastern half of the country. That's why I was gone for nearly a week."

"I don't know, Tom. I don't know. How can I ever trust you again? You've lied to me about all of this? About everything?"

"Not about everything, Viv. I never lied about loving you—ever."

She looked down at her own wine glass. She held it by its stem and slowly turned it between her thumb and fingers. She took a breath and exhaled.

"Like I said, Tom, I don't know. I just don't know. I'm going to bed."

She got up and, without looking at him, walked into her bedroom and closed the door.

CHAPTER FORTY-THREE

Morgan spent the night on the couch. He propped his head up with a couple of throw pillows, but he slept uneasily—when he actually managed to sleep. Maybe he had really messed up by telling her about her brother. Maybe he should have just kept his mouth shut. On the other hand, one day soon the Agency would show up to go through all of Petersen's financial records, and with that and everything else that was sure to follow, she would unquestionably learn about her brother—and likely about himself as well. And, if she was going to learn the truth, better she learn it from him. Hopefully, after she'd thought about it some, she wouldn't wind up hating him. But if she did, there was nothing he could do about it. He had done his best. His absolute best. If she wanted nothing more to do with him, he'd just have to pack up and go home—as painful as that would be. Either way, until he talked more with her—or she showed him to the door—he wouldn't know what to tell Blackburn. She'd had the night to sleep on it. Maybe she wouldn't still be pissed at him. Hopefully she still loved him.

It was just breaking daylight when he walked into the kitchen and fixed a pot of coffee. Then he returned to the living room and sat on the couch, cup in hand, waiting for her to come out of the bedroom. It was another hour before she emerged, sleepy-eyed and wearing one of his polo shirts. She walked into the living room and sat down, bare-legged, on the end of the couch opposite him.

"Want some coffee?" he asked.

She took a deep breath and exhaled. "Yes, I suppose."

Morgan got up, went into the kitchen, and returned with a cup for her—black, just as she liked it. When she took it from him, her fingers touched his own slightly. He smiled a faint smile, and then sat down again on the couch, but still on the end opposite her.

"What am I going to do with you, Tom Morgan?" she said as she looked at him across the few feet that separated them. She looked down at the cup of coffee, and then up at him once again. "You're a liar...and a son-of-a-bitch." She said it in a way that he knew she meant it. She sat her coffee down on the coffee table and then looked at him once more. "But I still love you. I do." Her eyes filled with tears.

"Tell me what you want me to do, Viv, and I'll do it. Anything. I want with all my heart to be here with you— to stay here with you and never leave. But it's up to you."

After a minute passed, she scooted slowly across the couch and looked again at him, but this time directly into his eyes. "I want you to promise me you'll never lie to me again, about anything— ever."

"It's only that one thing that I lied about, Viv. But I promise. I'll never lie to you again, about anything—ever."

She studied his face for what seemed to him a long while, and then she leaned toward him and kissed him, tenderly. "And don't you ever leave me either," she said, "ever." She kissed him again. And he kissed her back, softly, lovingly. It was the first time they had really kissed since he had come back from Chicago.

CHAPTER FORTY-FOUR

Later that same morning, Morgan drove to the bungalow one last time, to collect the remainder of his things. Before leaving, he sat in the living room and called Blackburn.

"Hey, Tom, I was just thinking about you. Have you made up your mind what you're going to do?"

"Yes, I guess I have," he said, with some resolution in his voice. "My life is here now, George. Vivian is here, and I have no choice but to stay."

"Well, I hate to hear that," he said, "but I understand." He paused briefly. "You've been the best, Tom. I've never known an agent more dedicated than you. By the way, some other things you might be interested to know. A few days after you flew back to St. Thomas, Trumbull called and told me that he and his people in

Miami had not only arrested the warehouse workers there—and confiscated all the submersibles and the coke—but they arrested a number of distributors in the Miami market as well. I also learned from St. Louis and Pittsburgh that agents there were able to arrest or kill gang members in those cities too—and seize the coke, of course. That was one hell of an operation you put together. The Agency is really going to miss you. Hell, *I'm* going to miss you!"

"I'm going to miss you, too, George. I really am."

"Well, I'll get the paperwork started, and I'll see to it that you get paid through today," Blackburn said finally. "But you be sure to get your ass over here to see me anytime you come back to Chicago, you hear?"

"I will, George. You know I will."

They hung up, and before he left the bungalow, he thought he should also call Weber and Sullivan. This time he called Sullivan's cell.

"Hey, Tom," Sullivan said when he answered. "Good to hear from you. Have you heard the latest about the arrests in Miami and everywhere?"

"Yeah, I just talked with George. He filled me in."

"Well, the Agency has sure scored some big hits because of what you started down there. So, when you comin' back?"

"Well, that's the thing, Scotty. I guess I'm not coming back—at least not for some time. I just told the old man that I'm quitting, as of today."

"It's that woman down there, isn't it?"

Morgan paused. "Yeah, you might say that."

"So what are we gonna have to do? Come down there to see you?"

"Why not? You might find you like it. It's like a whole new world down here."

"Well, maybe this winter," Sullivan said. "Maybe Dan and his wife would like a little vacation too, that time of year."

"Well, it'll be great to see you whenever you can get away. It'll be just like old times."

"I'll be sure to tell Dan," Sullivan said.

When their conversation ended, Morgan put his suitcase and his fishing gear in the Jeep and locked the front door. It was Friday. His lease on the bungalow was just about up. He'd return the keys to the real estate company on Monday, and he'd take the Jeep back to the rental agency as soon as he could get another car. Maybe he'd get another Jeep. Or maybe the rental agency would sell him this one. He'd actually become kind of attached to it.

By the time he returned to Vivian's, she had showered and dressed and was wearing red shorts, a white, collared blouse rolled up and tied at the midriff, and matching red lipstick. She was still barefoot.

"I've quit the Agency," he said as soon as he walked in and saw her. He dropped his suitcase and closed the door. "Guess I'll return the keys to the bungalow next week, and take the Jeep back too. Or maybe they'll let me buy it."

"Well, don't worry. You can use my car until we can get you another one."

"Which reminds me," he said. "You know the DEA is going be here in a matter of days, swarming all over the place and looking into everything."

"What do you mean?"

"Well, they're going to be looking at all of Charlie's financial records, personal and otherwise. They're going to confiscate his bank accounts, any investment accounts, and all of his personal property—his car, the boat, and anything else titled in his name."

"They're not going to try to take the hotel, or the mill, or the plantation, are they? And not the house either, I hope. I grew up in that house."

"I can't imagine they'd try to do that," Morgan said. "But it depends on how they're titled."

"Well, Charlie and I inherited those properties years ago, when Daddy died. We've both held title to them since then."

"What about Charlie's income? How was that handled?"

"He was always paid a salary for each of his roles, managing the hotel, and overseeing the plantation, and the mill. Then, at the end of each year, we split the net profit from each operation—fifty-fifty."

"Well, since you inherited the properties jointly and that was several years ago—presumably before Charlie got involved with drugs—it's unlikely they would try to seize any of those things. But like I said, they will be snooping around for a while, and they'll damn sure confiscate anything and everything he held personally or purchased on his own since your inheritance."

"About the house…" she said. "You know, I'd actually like for us to move into it. It's always been home to me. And now that Charlie's gone, I'd like us to live there. What do you think?"

"It's up to you," he said. "I don't care where we live. As long as I'm with you, I'm happy."

"Well, I've talked with Allison, and I think she might want to buy my condo."

"You don't suppose she might also be interested in buying mine in Chicago, do you?"

Vivian smiled slightly. It was the first time he'd seen her smile since he'd been back.

"Oh, you know what else?" she said. "While you were at the bungalow, our things arrived from the salvage company. Everything is still a bit damp, so I put it all out on the patio to finish drying out."

Morgan walked to the sliding doors and looked out at the bags—hers and his. His leather carry-on looked stiff and stained from saltwater. But bad as it looked, he knew he wouldn't toss it. He couldn't. In a few days, when it was dry, he'd buy some leather restorer. Hopefully he could bring it back to life.

CHAPTER FORTY-FIVE

The following day was Saturday. It was another beautiful day. He wanted to continue getting Vivian out of the condo as much as possible, and he suggested that they go to the beach somewhere. She agreed and wanted to try Magens Bay.

"It's just a short drive north," she said. "It has probably the most beautiful beach on the island—and maybe anywhere in the world." Morgan realized when she said it that, while he had been there himself a few days after his arrival, they had not been there together.

"Sounds good," he said. It would be nice to enjoy the beauty of the place, especially now, with her.

After lunch they put on their bathing suits and left in the Jeep, heading north out of town on Route 35. Morgan easily remembered the dense foliage as they followed the twists and turns of the road through the Central Highlands, and when they arrived at the bay, he stopped the Jeep beneath the same group of sea grape and coconut trees he had parked under his first time there. They got out and walked across the expanse of sand to a spot near the water, put their towels down, and kicked off their flip-flops. Vivian took off her cover-up. She was again wearing the bright-yellow bikini that contrasted so beautifully with her tan, and she looked alive again. Maybe she wasn't fully recovered, but at least she was on her way. He smiled at her, and she smiled back, that same wonderful smile he had known before.

"Come on," he said. "Let's go for a walk." He took her hand, and after they reached the water's edge they turned and strolled slowly in the shallows. He brought her hand up to his chest, and for a moment he held it there, close to his heart, which made her smile again. He was pleased to see her like this, and as they walked, he thought about Elaine, just as he had his first time there. He also thought again about his best friend, Adam Wells, and others he'd lost in Iraq; about his mom and dad; his high school friends he'd lost to drugs—and even Charles Petersen. Drugs, disease, war, accidents, natural disasters, and all the rest. He'd seen it all. He knew there was no place safe—not even here. But he still didn't know if there was a God or a heaven, although for the sake of those he had loved, and still loved, he hoped there was.

He also didn't know why he had chosen to come to these Virgin Islands. True, Blackburn had suggested it to him, but only among several possibilities. Maybe it was just a lucky choice on his part. On the other hand, maybe, somehow, he was destined to be here. He would never have met Vivian if he had not come to this place. And chances were pretty good he would not have found his way to Elaine's killers if he had not come here.

They continued to walk for a time and then stopped. He put his arm around Vivian's shoulders, and together they looked off toward the horizon, between the two expanses of land that formed the bay. No, he still didn't know if there was a God or a heaven, and he doubted he would ever know the truth of the matter. But if there was a heaven, he hoped it would be something like this— and somewhere warm. Maybe it'd be safe there.

Made in the USA
Middletown, DE
06 December 2015